THE
KILLING
JAR

THE
KILLING JAR

JENNIFER BOSWORTH

FARRAR STRAUS GIROUX · NEW YORK

For the women who raised me—Kathleen Knott,
Amy Jespersen, Borgny Erickson, and Gertrude Knott

Farrar Straus Giroux Books for Young Readers
175 Fifth Avenue, New York 10010

Copyright © 2016 by Jennifer Bosworth
All rights reserved
Printed in the United States of America by
R. R. Donnelley & Sons Company, Harrisonburg, Virginia
Designed by Elizabeth H. Clark
First edition, 2016
1 3 5 7 9 10 8 6 4 2

fiercereads.com

Library of Congress Cataloging-in-Publication Data

Bosworth, Jennifer, author.
    The killing jar / Jennifer Bosworth. — First edition.
        pages cm
    Summary: When she was ten years old Kenna discovered that she had the ability
to drain the life from another human being, and ever since she has been afraid to
touch anyone—but when she uses that power to save her mother and twin sister
from an attacker, her mother finally reveals the secret origin of her power, and
she is forced to choose between the Kalyptra and a human life.
    ISBN 978-0-374-34137-4 (hardcover)
    ISBN 978-0-374-34138-1 (e-book)
    1. Paranormal fiction.   2. Mothers and daughters—Juvenile fiction.
3. Twins—Juvenile fiction.   4. Sisters—Juvenile fiction.   5. Secrecy—Juvenile
fiction.   6. Horror tales.   [1. Supernatural—Fiction.   2. Mothers and daughters—
Fiction.   3. Twins—Fiction.   4. Sisters—Fiction.   5. Secrets—Fiction.
6. Horror stories.   7. Horror fiction.]   I. Title.

PZ7.B6532Ki 2016
[Fic]—dc23   2015004146

Our books may be purchased in bulk for promotional, educational,
or business use. Please contact your local bookseller or the Macmillan Corporate
and Premium Sales Department at (800) 221-7945 ext. 5442 or by e-mail
at MacmillanSpecialMarkets@macmillan.com.

All that lives must die,
Passing through nature to eternity.

—Shakespeare, *Hamlet*, Act 1

PROLOGUE
THE KILLING

I TRY NOT TO THINK ABOUT IT, THAT TIME I KILLED A BOY. But the problem with trying not to think about something is you'll think about it even more.

So that's what I do. I think about it. I dream about it. I obsess.

But I never, ever talk about *him*, the boy whose life I took. I didn't want to kill him. At least . . . I don't think I did. Or maybe that's just what I tell myself so I can live with what I am. What I did. How I did it.

I was ten years old, and so was he.

His name was Jason Dunn, and on the outside he appeared as normal as his name. His family lived next door to mine on the outskirts of town. My bedroom window gave me a direct view of the path to the river. I watched Jason take that path every day after school. He always came back smiling to himself in a way that made me feel cold and queasy, like I'd eaten something bad. So I followed him, and I found out why he smiled like that.

Jason liked to kill.

Insignificant things mostly. Small murders that would go unnoticed. He chopped up worms into wriggling segments and fried them with a magnifying glass. He pulled the wings from moths, or misted trails of ants with hairspray and set them on fire. Miniature tortures that parents tend to write off as boys being boys. Cruelty as a phase, like puberty.

Jason's preferred method of torment was to put butterflies in his killing jar, the kind entomologists use to kill insects quickly without damaging their specimens. There was a swab of poison in the bottom, a fast-acting toxin. Although Jason had a corkboard where he pinned dead butterflies and moths, beetles and spiders—he brought his collection to school every time we had show-and-tell—he wasn't in it for the scientific observation. He just liked to watch things die.

But then he went too far.

My twin sister, Erin, is allergic to everything with fur, so our mom wouldn't let her have pets. Still, she secretly adopted a stray orange cat with a missing ear and a scar over one eye that liked to hang around our house, especially after she started leaving food out for it. She named it Clint Eastwood because its squinty eye reminded her of the classic Eastwood glare, and Erin was going through a spaghetti western phase. It turned out the cat was a female, though. She had a litter of kittens in the shed behind our house. Erin and I visited the mother and brought her clean towels and bowls of tuna fish.

We watched her kittens jitter and worm about, figuring out how to use their weak limbs, mewling in tolerant protest as Clint licked them clean. Their mother purred like an engine while her brood fed.

One day the kittens' eyes were sealed tightly shut. The next they were open and black, and fuzz covered their bodies.

But when we came back to see them the next day, the kittens were gone, and so was their mother. Erin was distraught. She begged me to search the woods for her cat and the kittens. She just wanted to know they were all right. Erin couldn't be a part of the search because of her "condition," which was what we called it for lack of a name that ran the gamut of my twin's maladies. Defective heart. Weak bones. Anemia. Asthma. Severe allergies. Autoimmune disorders.

It was better that Erin didn't come with me to search for her pet anyway. Better she never had the image of what I found trapped in her head.

I knew as soon as I found Clint Eastwood's mangled body by the river, surrounded by her drowned litter, that this was Jason's work. But if I needed further proof, I got it when I saw him at school the next day, his hands covered in raw, red scratches. Clint Eastwood put up a fight. Good for her.

I told Erin I couldn't find Clint Eastwood and the kittens, but in truth I buried them in the woods and marked their grave with a pile of river stones. While I dug the grave with my bare hands, I thought about how I was going to make Jason pay for what he'd done.

I could have told my mom what Jason was up to, but I

doubted she would believe me. Jason was an expert at hiding the monster inside him. He was unfailingly polite to adults. He never got into trouble at school. He was quiet but not too quiet. He played sports, but he wasn't too aggressive, never pouted when his team lost. He was everyone's idea of the perfect kid, and I had no evidence to prove otherwise.

If someone was going to teach Jason a lesson, it had to be me. I *wanted* it to be me. Because even though Erin and I didn't have the kind of uncanny twin connection that allowed me to read her mind, I felt it when she was in pain. She was a part of me and Jason had taken from her one of the few things that made her happy.

So I was going to take something from Jason, because I could. Because I had recently come to understand that I wasn't like other people.

"You have a gift that very few people in this world possess," my mom had told me in confidence. "But you must never use it. Promise me you'll never use it, Kenna, because you're too young to control it, and if you start I don't know if you'll be able to stop."

So I promised, but my promise was a lie. If someone tells you that you're special, that you can do something extraordinary, you have to try it at least once.

Three days after I buried Clint Eastwood, I trailed Jason into the woods, observing him, stalking him the way I imagined he stalked his doomed victims. He caught a monarch butterfly in his net and let out a whoop of triumph before inserting it into his killing jar.

"Can I see?" I asked, stepping from the trees and walking slowly toward him, my arms hanging loose and casual at my sides. I didn't want to seem like a threat. Not until it was too late.

He clutched the jar to his chest, like I might try to take it from him. "Why?" he asked, his eyes empty, not the eyes he showed to adults. These were his real eyes. His vacant crow's eyes.

I didn't answer his question. I lowered my gaze to the jar and the butterfly trapped inside, its crisp wings the color of Halloween, velvet black and flame orange. The butterfly beat against the walls of its glass prison until it lost the will to fight and drooped against the bottom like wilted lettuce.

Jason's empty eyes beamed with excitement then, and fury uncoiled in me like a rising cobra.

He never saw it coming. I grabbed Jason by the wrist and felt something unfurl from my skin, connecting me to him like a shared vein. His mouth opened in a distended O, but he couldn't scream. I didn't give him the chance. His life, his essence, a sensation like rising and expanding, like I'd swallowed a sunrise, flooded my body. At the same time, Jason's color waned from pale to waxy gray. His skin shriveled into a dehydrated shell. The hair fell from his head in hunks. His eyes turned black as underground tunnels and his cheekbones protruded in chalky, white wings.

When he fell, his killing jar hit a rock and glass exploded like brittle fireworks.

I've never told anyone about the hurricane of raucous, feral energy that poured from Jason into me, so heady and rapturous that it almost lifted me off the ground. It told me I could do anything. Run a thousand miles. Swim an ocean. Live forever. Raise the dead. Anything. It was all within my grasp.

It told me I was a god.

I knelt beside the shattered killing jar and cupped the limp butterfly in my palms. I touched its wing with the tip of my finger, and watched as a hair-thin strand of white light emerged and attached briefly to the insect's thorax. The wings stiffened and twitched. A moment later the monarch juddered into the sky and vanished from sight.

Then I ran. Not because I'd killed Jason Dunn, but because it was the only thing I could think to do with the energy boiling through me like rocket fuel. I raced through the woods, across the river where Jason had drowned the kittens, and into the mountains.

When I finally returned home two days later, the euphoria that had filled me after I killed Jason was gone, and I needed it back. I was certain I would die without it, or that I was already dead, because that was what it felt like to lose the light I'd taken from inside Jason. Who knew there could be such light inside someone whose soul—if he had one— was so dark?

I could tell as soon as my mom opened the door that she knew what I had done. And what I *wanted* to do. To take again, and take and take. To drive away the dead hollowness inside and replace it with perfect euphoria.

A fever took hold of my body and pushed acid sweat from

my pores. My stomach seized and cramped and I doubled over, retching up searing bile. My organs ached like they were shutting down. My blood thickened and decelerated to an oily crawl in my veins, and my heartbeat slowed and then revved, slowed and then revved. A sensation like I was covered with biting insects tortured my skin until I scratched it raw.

"You were right," I told Mom, sweating and holding myself and raking my arms bloody. "You have to take me away and lock me up or I'll do something terrible."

Mom said nothing, only nodded and gave me some of Erin's pills to knock me out, and when I woke up I was in an empty room alone. A room with a locked door and no windows. I wasn't sure how long she kept me there. Five days? Ten? Thirty? I lost track of time as the fever melted my skin and invisible pincers snapped at my insides. Imaginary army ants chewed on my flesh and my stomach heaved and heaved, even when there was nothing inside it. My throat tore and I coughed blood until I passed out. I tried to forget why I was locked in the room. I tried not to hear my mom crying when she brought me food I couldn't keep down, telling me she was sorry . . . sorry for what I was.

When she finally let me out, I was string thin and wasted and unwashed, but I was under control.

Mom studied me a long time before responding.

"What you did to that boy . . . you can never do that again."

"I know," I told her.

"We can never talk about this," she said. "Not ever. We have to pretend it never happened."

11

"Okay." I began to cry. Both of us did.

"You have to be normal. Be just like everyone else."

"I'll be normal. I will."

Mom and I never talked about my dangerous secret again, or about my confinement, or about Jason Dunn. Sometimes it feels like we haven't really spoken since the day she let me out of the locked room. We move our mouths and sounds come out, but we never actually say anything.

Aside from my mom, no one knows the truth about me, and I hope they never will. What happened with Jason can't happen again. I won't let it, though every time I touch another person, I feel the life contained within them like a bottle waiting to be uncorked. So I never touch people if I can avoid it, just like I never tell anyone what really happened to Jason Dunn. I keep distance between me and everyone else because the temptation is too much. Often I wake in a desperate, greedy fever, remembering how taking Jason's life felt like drinking sunlight and eternity, and I want more. So much more.

I want life. Not my own, but theirs. Every life but my own.

But I try not to think about that either, because thinking leads to wanting and wanting always, inevitably, leads to taking.

GRAY GIRL

SOMETIMES YOU FORGET YOU'RE ALIVE UNTIL YOU'RE scared to death. As I took in the massing herd of festival attendees, I felt more alive than I had in years. Alive and sick, my stomach churning like a cyclone. I should have skipped dinner, and probably lunch, and breakfast, too, because I was likely about to lose them all in front of hundreds of people.

"Nervous?" Blake asked, eyeing me from the driver's seat. The endless line of cars we'd been trapped behind began to move, and a parking attendant wearing a tie-dyed T-shirt waved us forward.

"Nope," I said, my voice trembling. "Not a bit."

"Seriously?"

He looked so hopeful I hated to disappoint him. "You know how people always say they have butterflies in their stomach when they're nervous? I have ostriches. A stampeding army of ostriches. I envy the people who have butterflies. They don't know how lucky they are."

"A.," he said, "you have nothing to be nervous about because you're going to kick ass. B. I'm stealing your ostriches. Think of it: an army of savage, alien ostriches living on a squishy pink planet that resembles the lining of a stomach."

"Sounds homey," I said. In a week, Blake would have drawn a whole new comic inspired by my anxiety and posted it to his blog. "You better at least dedicate the story to me."

"To my reluctant muse, Kenna, and her stomach full of ostriches." Blake grinned at me, but seeing my expression his amusement curdled to a sheepish cringe. "Are you really freaking out?"

"You said this was a small festival," I reminded him. "I was not prepared for this." I gestured toward the stage, and the sea of festivalgoers.

"Well . . . I've never been to a music festival. I didn't have anything to compare it to."

A female parking attendant wearing tube socks and cutoff Daisy Duke shorts directed Blake toward a space that looked barely big enough to accommodate a motorcycle. By some miracle, he managed to wedge his rattling 4Runner into the space, and the short-shorts-wearing attendant gave him a double thumbs-up and a dizzy grin. Blake smiled back at her, and a pang of jealousy gonged in my chest.

He's not your boyfriend, I reminded myself. He can check out whomever he wants.

Still, I couldn't help glaring at Short Shorts through the passenger window. She sneered at me and turned away, but not before I read the words printed on her tie-dyed festival shirt:

Folk Yeah! Fest 2016
Folk You!
Folk Me!
Folk Everybody!

"Either way, it's too late to back out now," Blake said. "Someone's already blocked us in."

The parking was tandem, and we were jammed in front and back. There would be no leaving until the festival was over. Until my song was over.

My heart began to pound so hard I could feel it in my kneecaps. "Can we sit here a little longer?" I asked.

"We need to get you signed in."

"Please? One minute. That's all I need." That was not all I needed, but it was all I was going to get.

The engine idled. An old-fashioned string band called Long Way Home played through the speakers. I'd introduced Blake to them as part of his musical reprogramming. When I'd first met Blake at the beginning of our junior year—after his family moved into the house next door that used to belong to the Dunns—his iPod playlists had been in a sad state, filled with such no-brainer, Top 40 hit makers as Miley Cyrus, John Mayer, Maroon 5, and, God help me, Ke$ha.

"Ah, you're a music snob," he'd deduced after I told him

15

every twelve-year-old girl in America called and said she wanted her taste in music back.

Blake had good-naturedly shrugged off my teasing. "So I'm not a music person."

"That's because you're listening to the wrong music."

"Then teach me, Wise One," he'd challenged, and I accepted. Three months later, Blake was not only listening to Tom Waits and Father John Misty and a few dozen other respectable musicians, but I'd started giving him guitar lessons. I suspected he still listened to his Top 40 staples when I wasn't around, but even a music snob like me couldn't turn my nose up at a song solely because it was popular. I just tended to like things old school, before voice modulation software and glorified karaoke competitions that churned out universally acceptable talent.

But then two weeks ago Blake threw down a gauntlet of his own—a gauntlet that came in the form of a flyer announcing a music festival called Folk Yeah! Fest. And one of the features of the festival was a competition for emerging artists. Participants would play one original song in front of the Folk Yeah! audience. The audience members would vote, and the winner would have a song professionally produced and included on the Folk Yeah! compilation album.

Blake had signed me up without telling me, claiming it was better to ask forgiveness than permission. I tried to decline, but it was too late. Blake had told Erin about the competition and she demanded I go through with it.

"It's my dying wish," she proclaimed, making me wince. I would never get used to Erin's cavalier attitude toward the likely chance of her own premature death.

"You play that dying-wish card once a week," I said, but Erin propped her garden hose arms on her bony hips and narrowed her eyes at me behind her thick glasses.

"If you don't play at this festival, I'll never forgive you," she amended.

I sighed and said yes, as if I'd ever had a choice. It was impossible to say no to Erin when I didn't know how much longer she'd be around.

"Your minute is up," Blake said, and killed the engine. Long Way Home's hectic but harmonious guitar/banjo duet went silent, and the muffled strains of live music coming from the stage replaced it. My heart started beating in kick-drum bursts. The passages between my throat and lungs narrowed, signaling an oncoming asthma attack. I fished in my bag and found my emergency inhaler.

"Are you okay?" Blake's eyes widened in alarm. I tried never to use my inhaler in front of him or anyone else. It made people nervous, I'd observed, and I already had a tendency to make people nervous.

"Yeah. Fine." I sprayed my lungs with an acrid fog of medicine, and the tension in my chest eased.

Blake stuffed his keys into his jacket pocket, but made no move to open the car door. "Kenna, if you really want to withdraw—"

"No. I promised Erin."

But my promise wasn't the only reason I needed to finish what I—or technically, Blake—had started. I was about to start my last year of high school, and I had no desire to follow graduation with any of the things that sounded responsible, going to college and majoring in something practical in the hopes of someday getting a normal job and securing a normal life as if I were some normal girl.

Normal lives were for normal people, and I was not one of them.

I reached for the door handle. "Let's go. The longer I sit here, the more likely I am to chicken out."

We went around to the back of the 4Runner and Blake popped the trunk. I reached for my guitar in its scuffed, black hard case, covered in scraps of my favorite lyrics scrawled with silver pen. Blake beat me to the handle and picked up the guitar. "I'll carry it for you."

"Oh. Um. Thanks." I would rather have carried it myself. My guitar was like an extension of me, a Horcrux containing a piece of my soul. It was a gift from my mom, given to me shortly after the Jason Dunn incident. After I stopped touching other people or letting them touch me. She didn't encourage me to change my new rule. Instead, she brought me something I *could* touch without worrying whether I would hurt it. She taught me my first few cowboy chords, and then I was off to the races, teaching myself to play using video tutorials and songbooks I ordered online.

But I let Blake be the chivalrous guy he wanted to be and

carry my guitar because it made him happy. He was always doing stuff like that. Opening doors for me. Offering to let me try whatever he was eating. Laughing at my jokes even when they weren't funny. I wanted to tell him to stop trying so hard to win me over. I was already won. He had me from the moment he'd knocked on our door to introduce himself and offered oatmeal raisin cookies he'd made himself. I hated raisins, but apparently I was a sucker for "boy next door" types like Blake, who looked like a shy, English prep school student with his pale, freckled skin and his thick, brown hair parted on the side. He was the kind of guy who belonged in a school uniform with a striped tie and a blazer, whose cheeks turned bright pink in the wind. His innate sweetness was, to a lost ship like me, a beacon in a black night.

But I couldn't admit that to Blake, because if I did he would want us to change our relationship status from "just friends" to "something more complicated," and that was where things got tricky. It wouldn't work, and I'd end up losing my best friend. Unacceptable. Besides, what guy wanted a girlfriend who wouldn't let him touch her?

We headed for the wide-open field, where a stage jutted from the landscape, and were ingested in the flow of people heading in the same direction. The festival had been going since noon. Blake and I could have arrived earlier and seen some of my favorite indie folk bands play, but I'd needed the extra hours to rehearse my song. I'd probably practiced too long. The tips of my fingers were sore, and my throat felt raw as a scraped knee.

The crowd pressed in around us, and I felt my back stiffen. I tried to make myself smaller so I could avoid touching anyone around me, but it didn't work. Some stoned guy wearing a slouchy beanie cap stepped on the back of my heel. A college-age girl taking a selfie elbowed me in the arm. Suddenly Blake's shoulder was pressed right up against mine, the back of his hand against my hand.

I felt the life under his skin, warm and bright and ebullient.

I jerked away, my heart rattling like machine-gun fire.

"Sorry." Blake looked startled. "I'd give you space if there was any."

"Don't worry about it," I said, trying to sound casual even though I was the one who'd drilled it into Blake's mind that he *should* worry about it. I'd never figured out the right explanation to give Blake about my "no touching" rule. If there was anyone I did want to touch it was him, especially when he looked the way he did tonight, trying so hard to fit in that he'd made himself even more conspicuous: clean-cut, East Coast preppy masquerading as a scuzzy hipster. Still, he blended better than I did. With my blond hair bleached and tinted the color of a gloomy sky, wearing my signature shades-of-gray ensemble, I looked like a watered-down goth, Girl with the Dragon Tattoo–Light. The rest of the festival attendees were a sprawling patchwork of color and texture. Flower prints and neon and plaid. Leather and lace and suede fringe. Denim and dreads. Hair dyed lavender, cotton-candy pink and blue, mermaid green, sunset shades of orange and magenta. People dressed as decades, ranging from the Gatsby era to the stonewashed eighties.

Compared to the rest of the festivalgoers I was as drab as smog. But I didn't really care. Gray was how I felt, so I wore my spirit color openly. It was the one true aspect of myself I showed to the world.

Except I didn't feel gray around Blake. That was the best and worst thing about him. I was used to gray. I wasn't prepared to deal with the rest of the spectrum he brought out in me.

Blake did the talking at the sign-in table, where a man and woman who looked like they'd time traveled to the festival from the dust bowl era—the man wearing a porkpie hat and suspenders, the woman in an unflattering, vintage sack dress with a Peter Pan collar and buttons down the front—handed me a document to sign and a square of paper with the number 7 printed on it.

"Kenna Marsden, you are lucky number seven, our last performer for the competition. I was worried you weren't going to show up." She beamed at me. "I loved your entry song. Is that the one you'll be singing?"

I nodded, feeling dazed as I stared at the number in my hand. "There were only seven entries?"

"Oh, no, we had hundreds, but we winnowed it down to our favorites."

She gave me more instructions, but I felt like I was listening through a wall. Luckily, Blake was attentive enough for both of us.

"Good luck!" the sign-in girl called as we headed toward the stage.

"See?" Blake said. "Hundreds of entries and you were one of seven chosen! That has to make you feel good."

It was impossible to explain to Blake why I rarely felt "good" about anything. Blake's family bought the house that had formerly belonged to the Dunns, but as far as I knew he was ignorant of the tragic fate of the Dunn family. After losing their only child, Jason's parents got divorced, his dad lost his job, and shortly after that lost his mind. He was remanded to a psychiatric hospital in Portland, where, rumor had it, he raved about how his son's soul had been sucked out of his body by a demon girl. That would be me, the one who'd been with Jason when he died. Who had run from the scene and vanished into the mountains. Fortunately, Mr. Dunn was the only person who had jumped to the right conclusion.

Blake stepped in front of me, forcing me to stop. His expression was adorably stern, like a little boy pretending to be a drill sergeant. "Come on, Kenna. You spend all this time making me listen to other people's music, when your stuff is just as good, and you hoard it away like it's some shameful secret. No matter what else happens tonight, just be proud of yourself for two seconds."

I gritted my teeth to keep the truth contained. I would never be like him. Blake drew his quirky, deranged comics and posted them on his blog without a second thought. The comments people left ranged from fanatical praise to troll scum vitriol, but when I asked him if the belligerent comments bothered him, he just shrugged. "It's not personal."

But the songs I wrote, the lyrics, the mournful, funereal, guilt-drenched melodies . . . those told the truth I guarded so carefully. The truth I could never admit, or I might see the answering candor in the eyes of someone I cared about.

Condemnation. Disgust. Revulsion.

He doesn't understand, I thought, *because he doesn't know his best friend is a murderer. He doesn't realize that if you do something bad enough, it follows you for the rest of your life.*

I didn't get a chance to answer his question. We were interrupted by Erin's voice shouting my name.

"Kenna! There you are!"

I turned, and saw my bespectacled twin waving, our mom at her elbow. I gasped as Erin darted into the crowd, weaving past a grouplet of hipsters and hippies.

I sped to Erin's side and snarled at the few jolly festivalgoers who didn't get out of her way quickly enough.

"Are you okay?" I asked, looking her over as though she'd been in a car accident. Anyone who didn't know Erin was my twin would never have believed we were even the same age, much less two halves of the same egg. Erin was so small and scrawny she could have passed for a malnourished, little-girl version of Keith Richards. There was no official name for the condition that forbade Erin from thriving in the body with which she'd been born. Whatever it was, it kept my mom and me in a constant state of alarm. Erin's bones were so brittle she could trip on a crack in the sidewalk and fracture her ankle, and her blood so thin she was liable to pass out if she had to stand too long. She had a bad heart along with asthmatic tendencies, but where my asthma seemed to manifest only during moments of stress, hers was exacerbated by pollution, exercise, dust, and a hundred other things I could list from memory.

"When do you go on?" Erin asked, pushing up her comically thick glasses, which had slid to the tip of her nose. "Are you freaking out? I'm freaking out! Did you know Lorde was only seventeen when she won a Grammy? That could be you!"

"If I ever win a Grammy, it will be because of you," I told her.

Erin was the only person I never turned away when I was working on a song. I let her sit in the basement and listen to me play as long as she wanted. She may have had a broken body, but her mind was sharp and analytical. If my entry for Folk Yeah! had impressed anyone, it was partly thanks to Erin's critical ear.

Our mom wrestled her way through the crowd to reach us. She must have come straight from her bakery, Knead. Flour powdered her jeans and her shoulder-length, blond hair, which she always cut at home with a pair of scissors that needed sharpening. I had a vague childhood memory—my first memory—of my mom's hair long as a horse's tail, of sitting on her lap and wrapping myself in it like hiding inside a curtain. I would have thought I was imagining this version of my mom, but for the huge, intricate tattoo of a moth on her back, stretching across both her shoulders like a shawl. Whoever Mom had been before she had Erin and me, she must have been a lot more interesting than she was now. There was also the matter of our father—or lack thereof—and how Mom told us she didn't know his name. But Erin and I had done the math, and we knew our mom had been only eighteen when she gave birth to us. Much of her passion for life must have been lost to the stress of having one daughter who'd been knocking on death's door since she was born, and another who had *sent* someone through that door.

Mom took Erin's chin in her hand and tipped her head up to face her. "I told you to stay right next to me," she said as though she were speaking to a five-year-old who'd wandered away in the grocery store.

Erin rolled her eyes, but redness crept into her pale cheeks. She was used to our mom treating her like a baby in front of me, but in front of Blake it was another story.

"Give her a break, Mom," I said.

"A break is what she'll get if she falls or gets knocked down out here."

"Can you guys please not talk about me like I'm not here?" Erin said, her voice small and barely audible over the buzz of the crowd.

Mom and I shared an anxious glance, and I knew we were both thinking the same thing: if Erin's doctors were to be believed, Erin *wouldn't* be here much longer.

My twin was dying, and she had been all her life, ever since she was born blue and cold and with a hole in her heart. Our mom, too, had nearly died during childbirth right along with her. Afterward, she told us in a rare moment of openness, she went through a period of postpartum depression so vicious that she'd considered suicide. She probably would have gone through with it if it weren't for the fact that we would have become orphans without her. But Mom's postpartum depression had never really ended, and I thought I might have inherited my own depression issues from her. Then again, we both had plenty of practical reasons to be depressed, the first of which was the constant threat of losing the person we loved most.

When she was a baby, Erin's doctors said she probably wouldn't make it to her fifth birthday, but she had. Then they told us she wouldn't make it to her tenth birthday, but she had. Then they said she wouldn't make it to fifteen, and here she was, seventeen and still alive. But the thing I didn't tell Mom—that I hardly dared admit to myself—was that I had begun to sense a change in Erin. I couldn't explain it, but when I was near her, I felt her diminishing fast, the life hissing out of her like she'd sprung a leak.

But Erin didn't live like she was dying. She hadn't attended school since an accident on the playground in fifth grade, but Mom had homeschooled her and Erin had already gotten her GED and was taking online college courses. One would think she'd prefer to spend her time enjoying herself, but her nightstand and desk were stacked with books that made my brain hurt just to look at them. Historical biographies, Victorian novels, anything by Carl Sagan, Stephen Hawking, or Neil Degrasse Tyson. I was in awe of her. If I'd been the one in her situation, I probably would have spent the majority of my time locked in my room crying and cursing God or whoever for dealing me such a crappy hand.

Most of the time I tried not to think about Erin's condition, but with the stress of my first live performance bearing down on me, and Erin and Blake looking at me with such hopeful expectations, it was all too much. Tears burned the backs of my eyes, and my mind whirled like a top about to spin off a table.

"I can't do this," I muttered, but no one heard me because I couldn't get enough air into my lungs to make myself heard. How was I supposed to sing when I couldn't breathe?

Then someone in a Folk Yeah! T-shirt was calling out my number, beckoning me toward the side entrance to the stage. Blake pushed my guitar case into my hands and whispered, "You're going to be great." Erin clapped and squealed with excitement.

My mom shocked me by reaching out and brushing a lock of gray hair back behind my ear. I couldn't remember the last time my mom had touched me, and I sucked in a breath as I felt the promise of energy restrained beneath her skin. My immediate impulse was to reach for it, to pull that energy into me, but I set my teeth and refused to comply. Mom withdrew her hand quickly.

"Go on," she said, her smile sad and anxious and twitching a little at the corners. "Show them what you can do."

I swallowed a fist-sized lump in my throat and nodded.

It happened fast and achingly slow at the same time. A festival liaison briefed me, then a sound technician miked my acoustic guitar, and before I knew it I was walking up a short flight of steps and onto a stage, looking out at hundreds of faces.

I searched for Blake and my family, but didn't see them. My eyes stopped on a middle-aged man with gray at his temples. He looked out of place with his brown hunting jacket and his dead, black stare. He reminded me of someone, but I couldn't decide who. And was it my imagination, the hatred and rage he projected toward me from those cold eyes of his?

My heartbeat thundered. I began to tremble and panic and reached automatically for my emergency inhaler, thinking, *One person in the audience already hates me, and I'm supposed to sing?* But my bag was gone, and I had a vague memory of handing it to the festival liaison to hold until I was finished. Could I subtly hint for her to bring it to me? Leave the stage for a second to retrieve it?

I tore my gaze from the man in the hunting jacket and my eyes finally landed on Blake, right in the front row, just off to the side so I hadn't been able to spot him right away. He stood with my mom and Erin. Erin was smiling so wide her jaw would probably be sore tomorrow. She had never in her life been allowed to attend an event like this, and she probably never would again.

My twin met my eyes, reading the distress on my face, and mouthed one word.

Breathe.

I did.

Everything after that was a blur.

WHEN THE MUSIC'S OVER

I RESTED MY FOREHEAD AGAINST THE CHILLY GLASS OF THE passenger-side window and watched the road slide by beneath Blake's 4Runner, a fast-moving conveyor belt carrying us home.

But I didn't want to go home, because then this night would be over.

"Can we keep driving?" I asked. To my bass-numbed ears, my voice sounded like it came from the bottom of a lake. My mom and Erin had left the festival shortly after I played, but Blake and I had stayed to hear the rest of the bands. For hours we'd lost ourselves in music and voices, in black night and white stars. I forgot to care if I won the contest. I'd played and that was all that really mattered. Erin was the happiest I'd seen her in years, and my mom had hugged me. Actually *hugged* me. It was a brief embrace, over almost the instant it began—before I could even acknowledge the hunger that raised its voice at contact with another person—but it was enough to tell me that something had changed between us tonight. Maybe the apprehension she'd held toward me since Jason Dunn's death was finally starting to fade.

And then there was Blake, who kept staring at me when he thought I wasn't aware, smiling like he was reliving a happy memory, who'd told me a hundred times already how great I'd been, how the audience had loved me, how they'd gone still and silent the moment I started playing and hadn't seemed to breathe until I was finished.

Blake, who made me feel good about myself, made me feel like I deserved to feel good.

He stretched his fingers on the steering wheel, like a race-car driver about to jam the pedal to the floor. "Any particular destination in mind?"

"No destination. Let's just keep moving forward." I leaned back in my seat and let my head loll toward Blake. The glow of the dashboard gauges created a rim light that traced his profile. "This is probably going to sound dramatic, but everything seems different now."

"Maybe it is." His smile faded and he looked at me for a moment, nodding seriously.

Heat crept into my cheeks and gathered in my stomach. My will to resist Blake was weakening, and I wasn't sure I cared anymore.

Ahead, I saw the turnoff to the long drive that cut through

several hundred yards of forest before reaching my house. An unfamiliar brown Bronco was parked on the side of the road next to our mailbox.

"Whose truck is this?" Blake asked, slowing into a turn and then pulling up next to the SUV.

Both of us peered into the cab, but saw no one inside.

I shrugged. "Maybe the driver broke down and didn't have a cell phone to call a tow truck."

"Who doesn't have a cell phone?" Blake asked. He'd moved to the midsize Oregon town of Rushing from a pristine Connecticut suburb, where I imagined no one ever abandoned a broken-down SUV next to his mailbox, or if they did it would be promptly hauled away.

Blake accelerated slowly and continued down the gravel driveway to my house.

"What happened to driving all night?" I asked, trying not to sound disappointed.

Blake glanced over at me. "You were serious about that?"

"Nah," I lied, and forced a laugh. "You know me. Spontaneity is my mortal enemy. Pull over here, okay? I don't want my mom to hear your car and wake up." I was supposed to be home by midnight. It was almost two.

Frowning, Blake slowed and steered onto the shoulder, under a canopy of trees. He was probably counting the number of points he'd lose with my mom for keeping me out past curfew, respectable young man that he was.

"Relax," I told him. "I'll sneak in through the basement

window so she won't hear the front door. I have a whole system."

"You do this often?" he asked, raising an eyebrow.

"Well, I probably shouldn't tell you this because my order has a code and everything, but I'm a vampire slayer, which involves a lot of late-night outings."

I was relieved when he chuckled and let the subject drop. I didn't want to tell him what I really did at night when I couldn't sleep. Didn't want to admit how often I snuck out and went to the place where I'd buried Clint Eastwood and her kittens. I brought my guitar, sat with my back against a nearby tree, and I played to the pile of smooth stones and sang so softly I was almost silent. I did it because sometimes it was too much temptation to be in a house at night with two helpless, sleeping people—two people who could provide the same thing Jason Dunn had provided, a way to be free from myself for a little while.

So I played music instead, because it was the only thing that kept me grounded. Kept me under control.

"You went away," Blake said.

I blinked and focused on him, realizing I'd been staring out the window in silence for a long moment. "Yeah, I guess I did."

He smiled in that shy way he had, that made me feel like I was the bold one. "I'm going to remember tonight for the rest of my life," he said, and then laughed and lowered his eyes. "Now *that* sounds dramatic."

"Then I guess I like dramatic." I found myself leaning toward Blake across the console. I heard the knocking of my own heartbeat. Or maybe it was Blake's I was hearing. Or both, beating perfectly in sync.

He looked at me, his eyes the color of newly minted pennies. The cedar and honey smell of his cologne in my lungs made me feel off-kilter, half-dreaming, like I'd inhaled some kind of intoxicating hallucinogen.

Blake began to lean toward me, too, but I froze as the rational voice in my head spoke up, reminding me about my rule, which was for his own good as much as mine. Blake was the best friend I'd ever had, and taking things to the next level meant I would risk losing him. But could I really exist in this state of limbo with him forever, both of us wanting more and me always saying no? Wouldn't that end the friendship just as surely?

"I better go." I took a deep breath and opened the car door.

The grumble of the engine died. I glanced back at Blake.

"I'll walk you," he said.

"You don't have to," I told him, but I didn't mean it. Part of not wanting the night to end was not wanting to say goodnight to Blake, even though he technically lived next door to me. In our neck of the woods, which mostly consisted of actual woods, "next door" meant our houses were separated by a couple hundred yards of forest. Not that I minded living so many miles from town proper. Surrounded by trees, with a river running through our backyard and the mountains looming, I felt isolated from civilization, and I figured I was better off that way. Easier to stay away from people when you lived like a witch in the woods.

"There's no way I'm going to let you wander off in the dark, especially with that mystery truck parked by your mailbox," Blake said.

"Then who's going to walk you back to your car?"

He thumped his fist against his chest. "I am man. I walk the world alone without fear."

I turned my face away so Blake wouldn't see me smile. Blake was almost as skinny as I was, despite his addiction to any and all kinds of cookies. His favorite joke was to buy a box of cookies and then check the ingredient list and say, "Hmm. Interesting. These cookies contain one hundred percent of my daily requirement for cookies." When he found out my mom owned a bakery, I thought he might do a backflip.

"What about my guitar?" I asked, gesturing toward the trunk.

"I'll bring it to you tomorrow," he said. "Good excuse for me to show up at your house unannounced."

I hesitated. I hadn't spent a night without my guitar since my mom gave it to me. But if I trusted anyone with it, it was Blake.

"When have you ever needed an excuse before?" I asked, batting my eyelashes at him.

He feigned shock. "Careful or I'll revoke your oatmeal raisin surprise cookie privileges."

"You never told me what the surprise was."

"The raisins," he said, as though this should have been obvious.

"You refer to them as oatmeal *raisin* cookies. That kind of ruins the surprise."

"The surprise is that most people hate raisins in oatmeal cookies, but in these you actually like them."

"You're so weird."

"But you like weird."

"That's right. I do."

I smiled.

He smiled.

I swallowed.

He cleared his throat. "Well, I guess that's enough witty banter for now."

We both laughed, breaking the tension, and started up the road, our shoes crunching on the gravel. Mom had been meaning to get the drive paved for as long as we'd lived in our house, just like she'd always meant to finish the basement, but she'd never quite gotten around to either task. Erin's medical bills exceeded what her insurance covered, so there was rarely much extra money lying around at the end of every month. Not that any of the treatments or medications or studies had helped Erin, nor had they answered any of the questions we had about her condition, but Mom couldn't sit back and do nothing.

A breeze moved through the trees and caught my hair, lifting it and chilling the skin of my neck. The moon overhead appeared to have been sliced cleanly in half. The cool air was sharp with the scent of pine trees, a smell that reminded most people of Christmas, but not me. I'd heard a person's sense of smell was closely linked with memory, and the tang of pine trees often sent me back to my time lost in the forest after killing Jason, bombarding me with fractured snippets of recollection. Of charging through trees, my blood surging with rapturous, sparkling, effervescent energy; the forest bending and warping around me, trunks twisting and bowing over me, and the sunlight pouring down through the cracks like a waterfall of liquid light. Of night, when the stars began to fall like snow and the moon was close enough to touch like a reflection in a pond. Even now I woke from surreal, kaleidoscopic dreams that felt like dreams within dreams, memories of what it had felt like to be lost in the woods and lost to myself; and I wanted it again, so badly I could hardly draw breath and had to take a dozen hits on my asthma inhaler to make my lungs open up for plain old air.

For two days I had lived that intoxicating dream while search parties scoured the woods, looking for me. They had even tried to search Eclipse, the bohemian commune situated in an isolated valley nestled on the other side of the Cross Pine Mountains. The people at Eclipse lived in seclusion, only driving into town when they had to buy supplies they couldn't grow or make themselves. The search party had nearly come to blows with the Eclipse people, who'd refused to let them in. But before a warrant could be acquired, I had woken from my dream and returned home to the terrible reality of what I had done.

I lied to everyone but my mom, told them I'd seen Jason drop dead, and I'd been so scared I ran away. Ran and ran until I was lost.

And everyone believed me, with the exception of Thomas Dunn, Jason's dad. He told anyone who would listen that I was a demon who had drained the life right out of his son. He ranted and raved about the evil child next door until they locked him up. I wondered sometimes if it would help Mr. Dunn to know that his precious Jason wasn't the golden boy he remembered. That he was as much a monster as I was.

Blake was unusually quiet as we walked. Normally he never shut up. Blake was a chatterer, the kind of person who always broke an awkward silence, even if it was with the most random statement that popped into his head. *Did you know mosquitoes are completely unnecessary to the ecological balance of nature? Did you know that about seven babies are born every second? Did you know the lead guitar player for Queen has a PhD in astrophysics?*

I glanced over at him as we walked, wondering how much he'd heard about Jason Dunn's death. He had to know something. People still talked about it. How could they not? Rushing had a population of only twenty thousand people. Jason's death was the most interesting thing that had ever happened here.

We reached the place where the woods met my front lawn, and I turned to Blake, feeling as though I were standing under a spotlight. His brows were drawn together and tilted in an expression of worried concentration. There were things I wanted to say, but they scattered like a pile of fall leaves kicked by a sharp wind, and all that was left was what I wanted to do.

Before I could stop myself, I stepped toward Blake, putting my mouth so near to his that I was breathing him in. We weren't touching, weren't kissing. We paused in "before," balanced on a tightrope between what we were and what we would become if either of us moved.

"Kenna . . ." he said, sounding excited, and worried. Whatever concerns he had, I didn't give him a chance to speak them, because then my own concerns would rear their ugly heads.

I brushed my lips against his, feeling the energy buzzing beneath his skin, but I was careful not to want it. Not to open myself to it. After a brief moment of hesitation, his mouth sighed open and overlapped mine. He tasted like brown sugar and cinnamon.

His kiss was just like him: considerate, gentlemanly, sweet. It frustrated the hell out of me. After so much time spent keeping him—keeping all guys, all *people*—at a safe distance, I was finally ready to let one of them in. I wanted more than a polite kiss.

I made my lips softer but kissed him harder. He responded, arms wrapping me, fingers burrowing into my hair. A sublime sense of vertigo, a magnetic gravity overcame me. I was falling and standing at the same time. Our kiss became less considerate, more impatient and eager, and there it was: the ferocity under the sweetness. The rogue under the clean-cut boy next door. Blake's teeth nipped at my bottom lip. His tongue skimmed mine. A low groan purred in his throat. My temperature rose until it felt like a fever, a delicious sickness, the kind that could wipe out an entire population. My fingertips, calloused and always slightly numb from infinite hours spent playing guitar, dug into his back. But I was careful. I kept a grip on the old, greedy need that lived inside me.

Distantly I heard a noise like a cry, but I ignored it. Kept kissing him. Desperate now. Starved for this. Starved for him as much as I'd been starved for the light I'd taken from Jason Dunn.

The cry came again, and Blake pulled back so suddenly he left me reeling, swaying on my feet.

"What was that?" he said.

I heard it again, though I still wasn't sure what *it* was. My skin prickled in primal warning. It sounded like someone, a person, crying out in despair or pain. But there were birds that made that sort of sound—birds and other creatures, like mountain lions with their furious shrieks. This close to the forest, plenty of animals confused our property with theirs, some of them more dangerous than others.

"Let's get you inside," Blake said decisively.

Blake walked me to the basement window, which was on the opposite end of the house from my mom's bedroom. Reading the disappointment on my face, he cupped my cheek with one hand in a gesture I'd only seen men use in movies. My skin thrilled and yearned for more. I felt the glowing life inside him, but what I craved at that moment was him. Just

Blake. His mouth and his arms and his touch and his warmth. I didn't want to take anything from inside of him. I only wanted to stay next to him, to bask in the closeness of him.

"Nothing changes," he said.

"Or everything does," I pointed out.

"For someone who wears as much gray as you do, you have a tendency to only think in black and white."

I started to deny this, but his lips shut me up and his soft, summer-warm mouth made me forget all about the cry until it came again.

"Good night," he whispered. "Get your ass inside where it's safe."

"My ass would be safer with you. Just come in with me and sneak out when it's light."

He considered this for a moment before shaking his head. "I'm out past curfew, too, remember? And I can't exactly call my parents at two in the morning and tell them I'm spending the night at your house. They're cool, but not that cool."

He kissed me one more time, and started jogging back in the direction from which we'd come.

Feeling unmoored, I slid the basement window open and lowered myself inside, then stood there a moment in the dark, leaning against the cold wall. The unfinished basement consisted of concrete floors and framed-in rooms, but only one had drywall and doors.

My stomach was giddy, lodged somewhere between my lungs.

Me and Blake. Blake and me. It was amazing how life could change on a dime if you made a choice. If you let yourself have what you wanted.

The cry came again. It clawed through my thoughts, reeled me back to reality.

It was louder now. Much louder.

It was coming from inside the house.

SO MUCH BLOOD

FOR AN INSTANT I STOOD PARALYZED. THAT SOUND HAD not come from a bird, or any other animal. It came from somewhere in the basement. But all the bedrooms were on the first floor. Why would my mom or Erin be in the basement at this time of night?

A more important question: Why would either of them make that sound? That desperate, wordless plea of suffering. Someone in terrible pain. Someone who needed help.

I heard something else then, and it made my heart beat so hard I thought it might crack my ribs. Heavy footfalls from above. Clomping. Stomping. Neither my mom nor Erin could make that much noise walking around if they tried. That meant there was someone else in the house. Someone big. Someone who wasn't supposed to be here.

The mystery truck parked at the end of the drive.

Cell phone.

Police.

My brain merged these three elements and a plan was born. Call the freaking cops. Don't wait to find out if it's all a misunderstanding. Do it now.

I forced my joints to bend and reached into my bag, fumbling for my phone. My fingers found my inhaler and moved on. My lungs were tight, my airways cinching closed, but this was no time for an asthma attack.

Upstairs someone stomped around the kitchen, making no effort to be quiet. What did that mean? Oh God, what did that mean? My mom . . . Erin . . . one of them had made the sound. The cry.

A sob welled in my throat, and I smothered it with one hand while the other, shaking uncontrollably, dialed 9-1-1.

Keep it together, I commanded myself as I waited for the ringing to begin. *Stay calm, make sense, be coherent for the operator.*

My eyes were hot and tight with the pressure of tears, and every sound made my nerves snap.

"9-1-1, what's your emergency?" a woman's voice answered. She sounded brusque. Alert.

I opened my mouth and heard a thin wheeze of a response, "There's someone in my house. I think he—" *Say it.* "I think he might have done something to my family. I think he . . . hurt them."

Saying the words aloud made me shake even harder, but

the operator was all business. "I'm going to send officers out to you right away, miss. Tell me your address."

For a moment my mind went blank. What was my address? *What the hell was my address!*

The answer landed in my head and I blurted it out, too loud. I went still. Listened. No movement upstairs.

A creak from above. A cupboard door opening. He was looking through our kitchen cupboards.

"Miss?" the operator was saying. "Miss, officers are en route. Are you in a safe place?"

"He—he doesn't know I'm here," I said.

"Okay, that's good. Stay where you are."

The cry came again, and this time I pinpointed its origin: the north end of the basement, where the only semifinished room was located. Mom used the room for storage. It was the only one with walls and a door.

The cry came again, weaker now, and more desperate at the same time. I recognized the voice.

Erin.

I couldn't wait for the cops. I had to get to her.

"Miss?" the operator said. "Miss, what's happening now?"

More sounds from above. Wooden chair legs scraping across tile. He was sitting down at the kitchen table, making himself comfortable. What was he eating? Mom had made lasagna yesterday. There were plenty of leftovers. He had probably helped himself.

Rage churned inside me. It battled with my terror until the

two joined and filled me with a chaos of emotions that made it impossible to think straight.

"Miss? Are you there? What's happening?"

"I have to go," I said, and hung up. I silenced the cell in case the operator tried to call back, and shoved it into my pocket. Then I was moving.

There was no light. I walked softly, but every step I took nearly gave me a heart attack. I was sweating ice water and shivering, and I couldn't see a thing. I bolted silently across the remaining distance, but slipped and fell when I was almost there. I touched the ground and felt sticky wetness.

Please don't be blood, I thought. *Please don't be blood.*

Then my fingers found something else. I picked up the fragile object. A quick exploration with my fingers told me what it was: a pair of eyeglasses, the lenses shattered.

Bile rose in my throat. I wiped my hands on my jeans and pushed to my feet.

The sounds from upstairs had stopped, but I imagined I could hear the man chewing. In my head the sound was as loud as his stomping footsteps—the gooey, wet smacking and gnashing of teeth.

I stole the rest of the way to the north end of the basement. The door to the storage room was closed and there was light coming from beneath. I leaned with my ear close to the crack, straining to hear through the wood.

A girl's shuddering whimper penetrated the barrier.

I opened the door.

The bare bulb glaring above cast a mean, relentless light

over everything. Over the lake of blood that swamped the concrete floor. My mom was propped against the wall like a forgotten doll on a shelf, her head lolling forward, her white nightgown drenched red with blood. I couldn't tell if she was breathing.

"K-Kenna."

The voice was barely a voice. It was a wheeze. A thready gasp.

Erin lay crumpled in the corner of the room. I skirted around the blood and dropped painfully to my knees beside her.

Suffocated sobs tore at my throat. Erin's face was a disfigured purple landscape, one of her eyes a swollen mound sealed with a crust of blood. Her pajamas, too, were soaked in blood. My hands hovered over her, wanting to help, unsure what to do, or if there was anything I could do. She needed medical attention, and fast. She was so small, so delicate, it was a miracle she was still alive. How long until the police came? How long did my sister have? Minutes? Seconds?

Erin opened her mouth and tried to speak again. Blood gurgled in her throat.

"Shhh. Don't talk," I said, my chest so tight I could barely produce the words. "Help is coming. I called the police."

But we lived so far from town. It took Blake and me twenty minutes to drive to school every morning. How much time had passed since I'd called 911? Five minutes? Three? I should call again, tell them to send an ambulance. I reached for my phone.

Erin's eye rolled toward me. "Get . . . out," she managed. "He wants . . . he wants . . . you."

The man upstairs started moving again, and this time his footsteps were tromping down the stairs.

Erin's one eye went wide and she started breathing fast. But her lungs couldn't handle the air, and she started choking until blood speckled her lips.

He was coming. There was no way for me to get back to my hiding place, to get anywhere, before he blocked me in.

I rushed to the door, closed it, and locked it. I spun around, searching for something to prop against the door. I went for a chest of drawers painted butter yellow, which had been mine when I was a kid. As I shoved it in front of the door it made a shrieking sound across the concrete.

The footsteps halted for one deafeningly silent moment, then thundered as he ran.

I got the chest of drawers in front of the door just as the man twisted the knob. When it refused to turn, he pounded the door.

I backed away, my heart thrashing. My vision darkened around the edges with every rapid thud. I retreated to where Erin lay and huddled beside her. Every time the man struck the door, my whole body jolted and my teeth ground together like I'd received an electric shock.

"He won't get in. The cops will be here soon. Don't worry. Don't worry." I wasn't sure if I was talking to Erin or to myself. I checked her face to see if she was even conscious and a moan escaped my throat.

Erin was limp. Lifeless.

A memory burned behind my eyes . . . a butterfly gone slack, sagging to the bottom of a glass jar.

My moan became a wail. A banshee shriek of grief. I pulled Erin into my arms and crushed her against me.

My sister. My broken twin self. My best friend.

Gone.

The pounding ceased, and then something worse followed.

The man on the other side of the door began to laugh.

LIGHTS OUT

MY WAIL AND THE MAN'S LAUGHTER COLLIDED, MAKING a horrible, discordant sound. I clamped my mouth shut, but my chest strained, filling up with unvoiced anguish. Something was sure to pop. To tear apart inside me. A lung. A heart.

The man finally stopped laughing. "It's about time you came home, Kenna. I thought you might keep me waiting all night."

I rocked my sister's body, holding her so tight I would have hurt her if she were alive. I tried to speak. I wanted to scream that the police were on their way, that he better get out while he could. But I opened my mouth and all that came out was a silent, hissing scream. My chest was on fire. My body, my skin and bones, tingled like a limb coming back to life.

"Are you wondering why?" the man said. "Why your house? Your family? I came for *you*, Kenna." His voice lowered, so I had to strain to hear him. "I've been watching you for a while now. I wanted to know who you were, to understand why . . . why you would kill an innocent little boy."

My breath stopped in my throat. I remembered the man in the crowd who'd stood there glaring at me with such hatred. There was only one person in the world who had a reason to look at me like that.

Thomas Dunn.

"My son. My perfect little boy." He pounded his fist against the door and a strangled sob wrenched from his throat. "You stole him from me!"

A scream loosed from my throat. "Get out of my house!"

A sizzling burn swept across my skin. I felt as though I were coming apart, like filaments of me were peeling away, threads of flesh reaching out from my body and waving in the air, the tips ending in raw, tender nerves.

"Open the door, Kenna. It's time you paid for what you took."

I shivered so hard my teeth made a sound in my head like helicopter blades cutting the air. I moaned and buried my face in my sister's hair. There was blood in it, already starting to coagulate, turning her thin strands into stiff, tacky dreadlocks.

It was my fault. All of this was my fault.

The image of the dying butterfly flashed behind my eyes again. The shattering glass of its prison. Jason Dunn's empty eyes sinking into their sockets. His face turning gray. His skin shrinking against his skull.

The butterfly's wings tensing, batting, lifting it into the sky. "Open the door, you murderer!"

He struck the door and a crack formed. I didn't know how much time had passed since the 911 operator told me the police were on their way, but I didn't think they were going to make it in time.

I gathered Erin in my arms and lifted her. She was so light she seemed to float into the air, resting weightlessly in the crooks of my elbows. The sound of the door splintering was far away now. Numbness filled my ears like cotton. My fingertips burned as though I'd been handling hot coals. My entire body felt like one prickling nerve ending, those strings of me that had unraveled continuing to quiver and dance above my skin. I felt like an electric sea creature. Lightning made flesh.

I laid Erin's body down over Mom's outstretched legs, and then I burrowed in against them, dipping myself into their cooling blood. I didn't feel revolted. The only thing I felt was all-consuming grief and the tingling extension of my skin. The room seemed brighter than it ought to be. The bare bulb overhead radiated an intense, white light, almost too dazzling to look at. It grew brighter and brighter and then began to flicker for a moment, and right before it popped, I thought once more of the butterfly careening drunkenly into the sky.

The lightbulb exploded, and shards of thin glass rained down from the ceiling. Everything shook.

But the room did not go dark.

The blinding white light remained, but a hundred new

hues had joined it. Swirling mists of green, blue, lavender, sparks of yellow, and flickers of red and orange in the air, like ghosts made of fire. A storm of light and color, bubbling and blossoming and fogging around me.

I saw them now. The strands of light stretched from my body, an expanding network of colored electricity, reaching through the door, the walls. A mushrooming matrix of luminous, hair-thin ribbons. Everything was quaking, and I was so hot and so cold, and my eyes ached from the light and vibrant color that condensed and billowed toward me like a gathering storm, a violent aurora borealis trapped in this tiny room. I tangled my arms with my mom's and Erin's limbs so I was touching them, no longer afraid to hurt them. Those veins of light extending off me seemed to pierce my family's skin and connect us, creating one organism.

Then something new. A vacuuming sensation at the tips of the strands, like they'd all become miniscule whirlpools, and I was filling up inside. Elation fluttered my heart. Joy. Madness. A ferocious euphoria, and it was so wrong, so wrong to feel this way right now. But I couldn't help it. Whatever was happening was beyond my control.

My emotions flashed from rage to hunger. From buzzing excitement to terror. From yearning to passion to feverish arousal to a predatory desire to hunt, kill, and taste blood in my mouth. To poison. To bite. The urges kept coming, shifting faster. The impulse to cower. To protect. To run. To fly.

It was too much . . . too much . . . I was drowning in impulse and color and light. So much light!

Then the room began to darken little by little, light and color washing from the air like night overtaking a sunset. I was so overwhelmed, so mesmerized by what was happening that I didn't realize the pounding on the door had stopped.

The mayhem inside me reached critical mass, and I felt like I would explode if I didn't release it. The vacuuming sensation reversed and all that joy and exultation and wildness rushed through the strands connecting me to my mom and Erin, strained by colored tubes as thin and strong as spider silk until every mad, euphoric sensation was gone.

I cried out as the colored strands vanished from sight. I'd lost the light again and I was empty. The light and color were gone. The maelstrom in my head and heart were gone. I felt as though I'd gone blind and deaf.

Then something stirred against my hand. The stirring became a spastic flutter of flesh.

In the dark, I screamed.

I struggled to my feet, caught in legs and limbs. I forgot about the blood. My feet skidded out from under me and for a moment I was midair, tilting upside down.

Then my skull hit the concrete floor, and the darkness got darker.

Before I blacked out, I saw a figure lurching through the darkness. Thomas Dunn was inside the room then.

So he would be the last thing I saw.

I supposed that was what I deserved.

IMPOSSIBLE

"WAKE UP. KENNA. WAKE UP!" A WOMAN'S FAMILIAR voice.

"Is she okay? Mom, is she okay?" This time the voice came from a girl.

"I don't know. She's breathing. I think she might have hit her head. Kenna? Kenna?"

My lids peeled open over my eyes and pain boomed in my skull, a sledgehammer blow that made firecrackers explode in my vision. Darkness and sparks . . . darkness and sparks. But this pain was nothing compared to the hollowness inside me, a vacant feeling like some vital organ had been removed.

"Mom? Erin?" I said in a tearful moan. Had I followed them into death? I'd never subscribed to any particular belief about the afterlife, but this was not my kind of heaven, not this dark place. I was cold and empty and wet, as though I was still in the basement, soaked in—

In blood.

I sat up fast, blinking out the shadows and the skull-splitting pyrotechnics. The pain in my head blossomed, but my vision began to clear and my eyes to adjust. A narrow bar of moonlight shone under the door, enough light for me to recognize I was in the storage room, and there were two people in the room with me. Two people who were kneeling on either side of me in their own blood, and neither of them was Thomas Dunn.

My mom and Erin.

Alive.

Impossible.

My memory reversed, and I saw the moments before I blacked out. A figure staggering through the darkness. The phantom lights that came from everywhere and nowhere, filling me to bursting and then vacuumed out of me, cracking me open as they left. The bulb overhead bursting, showering slivers of glass. Thomas Dunn hammering at the door, and then . . . silence. He'd stopped trying to get in, perhaps startled by the light in the room, if that had even been real.

Was he still out there, lying in wait to finish what he'd started? What *I'd* started when I took his son's life.

My eyes, adjusting to the darkness now, scoured my family. Despite my aversion to physical contact, I reached out with a trembling hand and touched my mom. She was warm. I sensed the force of her vitality like static electricity, and her eyes . . . her eyes were black, pupils expanded to the size of pennies. Why, I didn't know. But who cared? My mom was alive, and so was Erin. That was all that mattered.

I pulled Erin into a hug, tears burning my eyes, and released her just as quickly. Something about her was different. She *felt* different.

I held her back and studied her face. Both of her eyes were open and black, the same as my mom's, even though when I'd first seen her in the basement, one of her eyes had been a mound of swelling, the lid sealed shut with blood.

"How?" I asked.

Mom shook her head, touched the slash marks in her nightgown, as though she were remembering how she got them, who gave them to her. Her head turned toward the splintered door and her upper lip curled to show her teeth. "Where is he?"

"I—I don't know," I said. The door was barely a door anymore. If Thomas Dunn had wanted in, he would have been in.

Mom rose unsteadily to her feet, her movements disjointed, like those of a newly birthed foal trying to stand for the first time, gawky on unfamiliar legs. She crept in a herky-jerky style toward the door. She peered through the ragged hole he'd made, and then shoved aside the chest of drawers.

"Mom," I said sharply, but she turned the knob and

wrenched the door open, revealing an unmoving figure lying facedown on the floor outside. I saw that Thomas Dunn had a handgun tucked into the back of his pants.

Mom bent to grasp Dunn's wrist and checked his pulse. I braced myself for him to roar to life suddenly, pull out whatever knife he'd used to slay my family the first time around, and do it all over again. Or maybe this time he would use the gun.

There was a brittle, cracking sound, and then Mr. Dunn's arm broke off at the elbow like it was no more than a piece of old, charred wood. Erin screamed and clung to me. I would have screamed, too, but I couldn't find my voice.

Mom dropped Mr. Dunn's arm and it hit the concrete, shattering to dust.

When Erin's scream ended, I heard the sound of tires grinding to a halt on our gravel drive outside the house, followed by the upstairs door crashing open and footsteps pounding across the floor.

The cavalry had arrived, but I wasn't sure the old "better late than never" maxim applied this time. There were going to be questions, and, as had been the case when I ran from Jason Dunn's lifeless body, I didn't have any answers.

Boots thudded down the stairs and flashlight beams cut through the shadows.

"We're over here," Mom called to the cops. She raised her hands so they would see she was harmless, but she couldn't seem to hold them still. That herky-jerky, wind-up-toy jitter continued.

The flashlight beams located her and froze long enough for the responding officers to take in the sight of a crazed-looking woman drenched in blood before one of them barked, "Lie down on the ground!"

"This is my house," Mom said. "My daughters and I were attacked, but—"

"Down on the ground!" the same cop insisted. Mom did as she was told, lowering herself to her knees and then lying down flat. Erin and I did the same. I ended up next to Thomas Dunn's body, looking into his face, and I gasped, even though I knew what I would see. Thomas Dunn looked like he'd been dead for a month. Or a year. His skin was lizard gray and leathered, warping around the bones of his face and arms. His eyes, black and wrinkled like prunes, had sunk deep into their sockets. The fingers on his remaining arm were curled into raptor claws. Even as I watched, his hair continued to detach from his scalp and shed onto the floor around him.

He looked just like Jason had when I'd gotten through with him.

The police swarmed us, checking for weapons. When they were assured we were the victims, not the perpetrators, they refocused their attention on the dead man and his kill room.

I explained that I'd made the 911 call and that, despite the blood on my clothes, I was unhurt, and let myself be escorted upstairs. My mom and Erin remained in the basement. The police, assuming they were still injured, chose to restrict their movement. A part of me wanted to stay downstairs with them, to never let them out of my sight again . . . and at the same time, I wanted to distance myself from them. *Needed* to distance myself.

I was all too aware of a growing hunger inside me, a gnawing sensation, not in my stomach, but everywhere. In every cell. Every pore. In my blood and my brain. This cavernous craving was familiar. I'd felt it seven years ago when I'd emerged from the forest, the state of euphoria I'd lived in for two days having abandoned me, leaving me empty and ravenous.

Whatever I'd done to bring Erin and my mom back from the dead, it had also brought back my hunger.

Two cops guided me to the kitchen and requested I stay there. I spotted the plate Thomas Dunn had used, still sitting on the kitchen table. He had, indeed, helped himself to leftover lasagna. An impressionistic pattern of red sauce and cheese had dried onto the plate. How insane had he become over the years since his son's death that he could massacre a family and then eat comfort food? Maybe cruelty ran in his blood, and he'd passed it down to Jason.

Our kitchen had one of those greenhouse-style windows over the sink, all glass, with two shelves where my mom kept an array of houseplants and potted herbs. As I entered the kitchen, I saw that the plants my mom cared for so meticulously had turned the color of ash, and drooped in their pots. Some had crumbled like ancient paper.

"Did you place the 9-1-1 call?" a female officer asked me, striding into the kitchen. She might have been five two on her tiptoes, but she looked to be all muscle under her uniform. She had eyes like a boxer, squinty and darting. The kind of eyes that didn't miss a thing.

"I did," I said, still studying the plants.

She examined me, taking in my bloodstained clothes. "Are you hurt?"

"No," I told her, ignoring the throbbing pain in my head. If I said yes, someone would insist on examining me, and I couldn't have anyone touching me right then. I didn't know what I might do.

"Are you sure?"

"I'm fine," I snarled, my tone so vicious it made the officer take a step back.

"I'm sorry. I'm just . . . I need my inhaler," I wheezed, and bolted past the officer, tore open the kitchen junk drawer, and found the inhaler Mom always kept there. Erin and I used the same one. I didn't have a prescription because the doctor Mom took me to claimed I didn't have asthma, that it was all in my head.

I sucked in three inhalations of the bitter medicine and then stood with my hands propped on the counter, my head hanging as my airways relaxed.

I looked up to find the officer studying me with those sharp eyes of hers.

She took a step toward me. "Look, I've seen some weird things in my life, but never anything like what's out there. I have to ask . . . what in God's name happened here tonight?"

I stared at her, confused, and her eyebrows went up.

"You don't know?" she asked.

I was moving toward the front foyer before she could stop me.

The door stood wide open, allowing the cops and EMTs to come and go. I slipped out onto the front porch and had to grip the wrought-iron railing to hold myself upright as I took in the sight of the land surrounding the house. It was a clear night, the moon high and luminous, allowing me to see enough so I understood immediately what the female officer had meant when she said she'd never seen anything like what was "out there."

It was dead. The lawn. The bushes that used to stand like sentinels around the house. Mom's lush, unruly garden. The bullet-shaped evergreen trees. Everything that had been living within a hundred feet of our house appeared to have been scorched.

"Kenna!"

I heard my name shouted from across the barren land. A cop in uniform was busy cordoning off our yard with yellow police tape, but I spotted Blake and his parents on the other side of the perimeter, talking to another officer. Blake waved his arms at me.

I remembered kissing Blake and thinking I wanted to keep going until the sun came up. What if we'd ignored the cry in the night and just kept on kissing? My family would be dead, and Thomas Dunn would still be waiting for me to come home so he could get his revenge.

My feet found their way down the porch steps. The soles of my shoes crunched on the dead grass. It sounded as though I were walking on ice chips. Behind me, the female cop called my name, told me to come back to the house, but I ignored her command.

I began to run through the dead world. It looked like what was left after a nuclear bomb had been dropped, after everything burned and then went cold.

When I reached Blake, he climbed over the police tape, ignoring the cop who kept telling him not to. I threw myself into his arms, and he held me so tight I couldn't breathe.

The female cop caught up to me and insisted I come back inside, that she needed to collect my clothes as evidence. My clothes, covered in blood.

Evidence of what? I wondered. The perpetrator of this particular crime was dead and gone. There was no one to catch.

I ignored her and clung to Blake. Over his shoulder, on the barren side of the yellow tape, I caught sight of a scattering of tawny mounds that looked like piles of dirt in among the blackened trees. Fresh graves. It took me a moment to realize what they really were.

Deer. A herd of dead deer. There had to be twenty of them.

I squeezed my eyes shut and felt the energy contained under Blake's skin. I wanted to reach inside him and take a little, just enough to make my hunger go away.

I released him quickly and stepped back.

"What is it?" he said, his eyes wide with fear as he took in the blood soaking my clothes. "Are you hurt? Is your family . . . are they okay?"

"They're alive," I told him. "We're all . . . we're okay."

But that wasn't true. I, for one, was definitely not okay.

CIRCLE OF DEATH

"IT'S SIMPLY NOT POSSIBLE," DR. WONG, THE SENIOR EMERgency care physician, announced to me in his private office at the hospital.

It was six a.m. Four hours that felt like four years had passed since I'd kissed Blake in the woods . . . woods that were now dead, along with every shred of life they'd accommodated. Fallen squirrels and birds littered the ground around the trees, as though they'd made some kind of spontaneous suicide pact. Rabbits, foxes, deer, even a bobcat had been found within the circle of death, their bodies stiff and desiccated. If you looked closely, you could see a powdering of tiny, lifeless insects on every surface, and larger ones—crickets and grasshoppers, spiders and beetles, and thousands upon thousands of moths—mixed in among them.

Outside Dr. Wong's window, half a dozen news vans

lurked in the parking lot. I didn't plan on leaving the building anytime soon.

"I spoke with the police," Dr. Wong went on. "They estimate there was around ten liters of blood in your basement, which supposedly originated from your mom and sister."

I swallowed hard, but there was a knot in my throat that wouldn't go down, and a low, constant fluttering sound in my ears that was driving me insane. Worse was the empty, cavernous hunger inside me—not in my stomach, but in every fiber of my being. In my teeth. In my eyes. In my fingernails. Worse still was the sensation that I was dying as I sat here, that I was shriveling and shrinking as my body cried out for more . . . more of whatever I'd given to my mom and Erin to save their lives.

"The average adult has between three and five liters of blood in his body." Dr. Wong spread his hands and allowed me to do the math. "Your mom and sister were awake, aware, and walking around when the police arrived. With the amount of blood each of them supposedly lost, that isn't possible."

Supposedly. Dr. Wong liked that word.

My jaw was rigid. I could barely move it to make words. "So how do you explain it?"

"I don't," Dr. Wong said, raising an eyebrow. He was one of those people whose age was impossible to guess. His hair was a solid mass, thick and black, his skin unlined. But he had an adult's BS detector, and he wasn't buying mine. "There is also the matter of the wounds. In essence, there aren't any, which begs the question: Where did all that blood come from? And there is your family's behavior, their enlarged pupils, and their tremors. We tested them for drugs, chemicals of some kind, but they were clean." He took a breath and let it out. "And finally, there is your sister's condition. Your twin sister, is that right?"

"Yes." A wave of chills swam over me, making my teeth rattle. I had changed clothes before leaving our house—my bloody clothes had been bagged as evidence—but I barely remembered choosing what to wear. I wished I'd brought a sweater, but at the time I'd felt feverish. Now I was freezing, and my skin was starting to crawl. I fought the urge to rake it with my fingernails.

Dr. Wong consulted the chart in front of him. "I remember Erin. I treated her when your mom brought her in a few years ago. She'd fallen and broken several bones."

I winced as I recalled the incident in fifth grade, the last year Erin had attended school. Erin had disobeyed our mom's strict mandate never to use the playground equipment, but she'd gotten tired of sitting on the sidelines with her books, watching the other kids swing and run and have a good time. It was my job to watch her, make sure she never did anything dangerous, and usually I did. But that one day, I turned my back for a few minutes and Erin ended up with multiple fractures in both tibias after dropping only a foot from the monkey bars and landing normally. Erin's bones were not meant to withstand that kind of impact, and she'd spent the next few months in double casts and a wheelchair.

My mom had been furious with me for not taking better care of her.

She needs you, Kenna, my mom had told me while tears of guilt poured down my face. *You're the strong one. You have to protect her.*

I braced myself for bad news as I asked, "What about her condition?"

The doctor spread his hands in a gesture that implied helplessness, but a ghost of a smile lifted the corners of his mouth. "I don't understand what happened at your house last night, and maybe I never will. But as far as your sister's afflictions are concerned . . . she no longer seems to have them. She's perfectly healthy."

I swallowed and finally the lump in my throat went down. Tears stung the backs of my eyes and my breath hitched in my throat.

I stood, my knees trembling. "Can I see her now?"

My mom and Erin had been relegated to a suite on the third floor, where they would be kept for observation and testing until Dr. Wong had satisfied his curiosity. I exited the elevator and walked quickly to their suite, but froze outside when I heard my mom's voice. I cracked the door open slightly and peered inside. I caught sight of a broad-shouldered man in a suit, blocking the view of my mom. He held a pad of paper and was writing quickly. I guessed he was a detective.

I stood still and listened, realizing my mom was giving

a statement of what had happened last night. I needed to know what she said so I could repeat it.

"We went to bed later than usual," Mom said. "We'd been at a music festival near Portland, watching Kenna perform."

"Kenna is your other daughter?" the detective said. "The one who came home later?"

"That's right," my mom said. "She was out with her boyfriend."

"Name?" the detective asked.

"Blake Callahan."

"Are they talking about me?"

I whirled to find Blake standing behind me. He looked exhausted and wonderful and worried. I wanted to throw my arms around him and bury my face in his neck. Instead, I took a step back from him and put a finger to my lips to shush him. He nodded, and leaned in to listen.

"So," Mom continued, "it was after midnight when we went to bed. My guess is Dunn was already in the house waiting for us when we got home. I woke up about an hour later with a gun pressed to my head. He . . . he had Erin. He told me he wouldn't hurt her if I did what he wanted." A choked sob followed. Tears sprang to my eyes and I had to press both hands over my mouth to hold back a sob of my own.

"He lied," my mom said, her voice bitter and cold. "We cooperated with him because he said he wouldn't hurt us if we did. He marched us down to the storage room in the basement, probably because it was farthest from the front door. He didn't want Kenna to hear anything if she came home while he was"—she paused—"while he was in the middle of things."

"What did he do once he had you down there?" the detective asked.

"He was insane," Mom said, not really answering the question. "We knew him, you know. He was our neighbor a long time ago, but after his son died he lost his mind. We tried to reason with him, but he wouldn't listen. He started screaming at us about Kenna, saying she had killed his son, which is ridiculous. Obviously he needed someone to blame."

I had to hand it to my mom, she was a good liar. I almost believed what she was saying even though I knew it was bullshit.

"And then he . . . attacked you?" the detective asked, sounding cagey, like he wasn't sure how to broach this subject. "I mean, he must have attacked you. Your blood was all over that room."

"Yes," my mom and Erin said at the same time.

"And then?"

A pause, and then Mom said, "We don't remember."

"What do you mean, you don't remember?"

"That's all we can tell you. Thomas Dunn attacked us. He had a gun, but he didn't use it, probably didn't want to alert the neighbors. He used a knife instead, and while he was . . . while he was busy with me, I yelled for Erin to make a run for it. Sh-she—" Her voice cracked, and Erin cut in.

"He caught me before I could get out of the basement,"

she said in a tremulous whisper I could barely make out. "He hit me and broke my glasses and dragged me back to the room. I . . . I don't remember anything after that."

"You don't remember Kenna coming home?"

"No," Mom said.

"No," Erin said.

"And you don't know how Thomas Dunn died?"

"No," they repeated.

"Or what happened to the land around your house? No theories? Aliens? Astrological event? Divine intervention?"

"No," my mom said firmly. "We have no idea what happened. We don't know why we're still alive. All we can do is be thankful that we are. I'm sorry, there's nothing more we can tell you, Detective."

"Then I hope Kenna can fill in a few blanks. Thanks for your time."

The detective's footsteps moved toward the door. I motioned Blake into the room next door to my family's, which was thankfully empty. Blake and I hid behind the curtain, both of us breathing fast, until the footsteps faded.

Then Blake looked at me. "You're shivering." He took off his jacket and wrapped it around my shoulders. It smelled like him. Like brown sugar and cinnamon, honey and cedar. I wished I could press my face to his neck and breathe him in, let him put his arms around me. But I didn't dare let him touch me. The hunger was getting worse, a raw ache. A cavernous emptiness that begged to be filled. Withering cells crying to be sated. The papery fluttering in my ears continued, louder now, and my skin prickled like I was being jabbed by a thousand acid-laced stingers.

You've been through this before, I told myself. *You made it through that time. You can do it again.*

But that had been different. I had been locked in a cell alone, not surrounded by people.

"What are you going to tell that detective?" Blake asked. "You can't avoid him forever."

I shook my head. "I don't know," I said, but I understood what Blake was really asking.

What happened to you last night? What did you do? What are you hiding?

"I need to see my family," I said to change the subject. "Alone."

Blake nodded, doing his best to hide his disappointment that I wasn't ready to confide in him. "I'll wait in the hall."

I started to turn away, but Blake caught my hand and pulled me back, holding on tight when I tried to pull away. I gritted my teeth behind closed lips so he wouldn't know the torture it was to be so close to him, so close to what was inside of him.

Life. So much irresistible life.

"You can trust me," he said, holding my gaze. "No matter what you tell me, it stays between us, okay?"

"Okay. I know." I slid my hand from his and breathed again. But even when I'd left him behind, I could still feel the pulsing seduction of life inside him, and I wanted it.

Needed it. In an instant I went from shivering to sweating. My muscles cramped and my stomach roiled with nausea. It was all I could do to keep from doubling over and retching.

I paused at the door to take a few deep breaths, which helped a little. Then I stepped inside.

There were two beds in the suite. The curtains that would normally partition the patients had been pushed back, so the room with its peach-colored wallpaper and benign country art on the walls was wide open.

I looked from my mom to Erin. For several seconds all I could do was stare. Whatever had caused their spasmodic movements had calmed. Both of them shone with health and vitality, their skin porcelain smooth and radiant, which seemed doubly impossible because no one looked that good under fluorescent hospital lighting. My mom's and Erin's hair fell in melted-ice-cream waves over their shoulders. Erin's dishwater-blond hair had always been thin and brittle, but now it was the color of butter, and was so thick and satiny I had to wonder for a moment if she was wearing a wig.

I stood there for a moment, not sure what to do. I couldn't tear my eyes from my twin's, couldn't stop seeing the bruises that had blackened her face a few hours ago, the swollen lump of her eye and the blood soaking her pajamas. My sickly, frail twin who once broke both legs dropping a foot from the monkey bars, who was so tiny, so skeletal that Mom had to buy her clothes from the children's department . . . my sister was transformed as though she'd spent the night in a chrysalis and had been reborn into a new body. A healthy, strong, perfect body.

"Is it true?" I asked her. "You're . . . you're . . ."

She beamed at me, her eyes filling with tears, and nodded. "So much for not living to see my next birthday."

There was a chair next to Erin's bed. I dropped into it before my watery knees gave out. Erin had terrible eyesight. When she wasn't wearing her glasses, she tended to squint like a mole. But her glasses were gone, and her eyes were wide open.

"What do we do now?" I asked the room.

My mom and Erin shared a furtive glance.

"Plead ignorance," my mom said, keeping her voice low in case anyone was listening outside the door. "No matter what they ask, we don't remember anything, all right? Kenna, it's especially important that you remain vague."

I turned to Erin and saw her clear, bright eyes fill with tears and her chin begin to quiver.

"Do you remember?" I asked softly.

She licked her lips and swallowed. "You brought us back," she whispered. "I was outside my body, just sort of drifting. Then I felt this tug, like I was a balloon on a string, and you were the one holding the end." She smiled sadly and wiped her eyes as the tears dripped down her nose. "You saved us. You saved *me*."

I wanted to tell her no, she was mistaken. I hadn't saved them. I had damned them. I was the reason Thomas Dunn did what he did.

I was the reason they had died in the first place.

Then the door opened and the detective stepped inside. He was middle-aged, graying, twenty pounds overweight. His tired eyes pinned me down. "There you are," he said. "I'm the detective handling your family's case. I need to take your statement."

"Can we do it here?"

He shook his head. "Just you and me." He gestured impatiently for me to follow. "It won't take long. Come on, let's talk in the cafeteria, get some coffee. Your boyfriend can come, too," he added with a half smile, as though he were trying to be charming.

Reluctantly, I stood and followed him, my fever ramping up a few degrees. I wanted to take off Blake's jacket, but it felt like a layer of armor, a protective shell. I curled my hands inside the sleeves.

Blake waited in the hallway outside the room, pacing restlessly. When I emerged, he stopped pacing and moved to my side. He tried to take my hand, but I folded my arms and stuck my hands in my armpits.

"I'm Detective Speakman, by the way," the detective said. He held his hand out to me. I ignored it.

"What do you want to know?" I asked. "You already have your man and he's dead. What's left to investigate?" What was left that didn't call for an episode of *The X-Files*?

He raised his eyebrows at me, but lowered his hand, gazing at me with a blank expression. "I just need to get all the facts."

IT'S HAPPENING AGAIN

I SPENT THE NEXT HOUR SITTING AT A TABLE IN THE cafeteria, sipping and cringing at incredibly bad coffee and picking at a stale Danish as I told Detective Speakman the abridged version of my story. Blake backed me up on all the parts for which he'd been present. The rest was mine to alter, since there were no witnesses to contradict my account.

Finally, Detective Speakman closed his notebook and stashed it in the inside pocket of his suit coat. "So that's it. You came home. You found your mom and sister wounded, blood everywhere. Thomas Dunn trapped you, and then you fell and blacked out and you don't remember anything else."

"That's right." Out of the corner of my eye I could see Blake studying me, trying to decide if I was lying, just like Detective Speakman was doing openly.

The detective put his hands facedown on the table. "Well,

I suppose that's all then." He pulled a card from his wallet and passed it to me. "If you or your family miraculously remember anything, be sure to give me a call."

"We will," I said, and the detective rose to leave. He started walking away from the table and then paused. "One more thing. Thomas Dunn's son, Jason, the one who died seven years ago . . . you were the last person to see him alive?"

I nodded, trying to keep my expression neutral. Under the table, I clasped my hands together to keep them from shaking. Sweat gathered in my palms, making them slick.

"When they found him, his body was desiccated, looked like all the moisture had been drained out of the tissue, just like his father's after . . . well, after whatever you don't remember happened to him. I find that to be a strange coincidence. A very strange coincidence. In my line of work strange coincidences usually have a connection. I just haven't found it yet."

I tried to swallow but my throat had gone dry. "Maybe it runs in the family, like a genetic disorder."

"Maybe so," the detective said. "Whatever it is, I'm sure I'll figure it out."

When he was gone, I exhaled and wrapped my arms around myself, bowing over the table and resting my forehead on the surface.

"You don't look so good," Blake said.

Now I was both shivering and sweating, and my stomach felt like it was filled with broken shards of glass, jabbing and slicing at my insides.

"I'm fine," I said, but I wanted to shred my skin with my

fingernails. The crawling sensation came and went in waves, and I was currently surfing a bad one.

"No, you're not," he hissed, low and frustrated. "You need to see a doctor."

He stood and took me by the arm, trying to haul me out of my seat. I wrenched violently away. "I told you never to touch me!"

The cafeteria went silent, all eyes turned toward us. Blake glanced around nervously, licking his lips, eyes as wide as they would go.

"I'm only trying to help," he said. "Why won't you let me help you? What's going on?"

I couldn't meet his eyes. My control was slipping, and I was afraid, so afraid of what I might do to him if I lost control for even a second.

"What the detective said about that kid and his dad dying the same way . . ." He lowered his voice another octave. "Do you know how it happened? Did you . . . did you have something to do with it?"

"You need to leave now," I responded, my voice sounding flat and dead. "I can't explain anything. Please, Blake, just do what I ask this one time and leave me alone."

"But Kenna—"

I shoved my chair back and stood to face him. I dragged a breath down my throat. It was getting harder to breathe. My lungs were filling up with cement, hardening, and I was shivering so violently it felt like I would make the building shake.

"Just go! Leave me alone!" I ran from the cafeteria and didn't look back to see if he was following me. I hoped he wasn't, because a part of me hoped he was. That part wanted to get him alone and then let my aching, trembling, rebelling body have what it wanted. The rushing, throbbing, fluttering in my ears was so loud now, it was like standing next to an industrial fan as its blades whacked at the air. I needed to be alone. I needed to be locked away somewhere safe. I needed to get out of this hospital before I did something terrible.

But I couldn't think straight. The pain in my guts and the fever chills and the shuddering vibration in my ears drove away all rational thoughts. I wandered. I walked the halls. My vision blurred around the edges and turned gray in the center. The people I passed looked like ghosts, their faces chalky blurs. I kept my head down and tried not to see them because I knew that any of them could fix me. The life inside a single one of them could end my agony. These people were walking bottles of medicine, living, breathing panaceas for my unique affliction. But the medicine I needed came at too steep a cost.

I was trapped. Trapped in a body that had become hostile territory, a private war zone, and I was the enemy under attack by my own cells. How long before I had no choice but to surrender and give them what they wanted?

I didn't know where I was going. Everything moved past me in a rush, like I was on a high-speed train. Nothing seemed real. I couldn't even feel my feet touching the floor. There was only the clutter of knives in my stomach and the wings in my ears and the terrible, sucking emptiness that was every-where. Everything.

I blanked out for a while. I wasn't sure how long.

When I came back, I was standing next to Erin's bed.

My twin was sleeping, and when I glanced behind me I saw that my mom was too.

I shouldn't be in here, I thought. But I didn't move. I wanted to see my sister, remind myself that even though I was in hell, even though I was dying, she was alive and healthy for the first time in her life.

She was going to live a long, long time, and her life would be beautiful. My brilliant sister would do amazing things.

A year ago, Erin almost died. She got a bad cold, and that was all it took. Her body gave up, tried to shut down. Mom and I checked her into the hospital, where she remained for ten days. On day seven, we were alone, and she said, "I need you to do something for me, Kenna. I need you to say good-bye to me now."

I remembered how the blood drained, not only from my face, but from my entire body down into the floor, leaving me cold as a corpse.

"No," I had told her, shaking my head. "No."

"You have to," she insisted. She told me she was tired of fighting. She tried to convince me it was okay, that she was ready, that this was no life, being trapped in this body, that I should let her go. She asked me to make her a promise. She asked me to live for her after she was gone. To stop hiding from the world and let myself be happy. She tried to take my hand. She had tears pouring down her cheeks as she begged me to be happy. For her if not for me. But instead I broke down sobbing, and I ran from her, from her touch, from what she wanted from me, because it was impossible. Impossible.

I could not say goodbye. I never did.

Now it was time for me to ask of her what I couldn't give. I was dying, and I needed her to live for me.

I stood by her bed, holding myself because I felt like, at any moment, my skin might open up and pour my dying guts out onto the floor. I gazed down at her sleeping face. She looked like me now, almost identical. We'd never looked alike, not one day in our entire lives. She'd always been a shrunken, distorted version of me. A homunculus. But now we were the same. She was me, and I was her. But there was so much life in her now, more than she needed. I could feel the life radiating off of her like heat off of a sunburn. I had given her too much, I thought. I should have kept a little of that life for myself, because now I was the one dying. What if I could take just a little of what I'd given to keep us together?

I reached a hand toward her arm but didn't touch her, stopped within an inch of her. Still, I could sense the flow of energy trapped beneath her skin. The delicious medicine inside her, of which she now had an excess. My skin seemed to stretch toward her, strands of me unraveling as they had done in the basement. I looked down at my hand and saw searching threads of light emerge from my palm. I tried to will them to shrink back into me, but my stomach lurched and the invisible pincers snapping at my skin bit deeper, and I couldn't stop. The pain drove my rational mind into hiding, so all that was left was need and desperation.

Erin's eyelids began to flutter. She whimpered and I startled back from the bed, gasping, curling my hands into fists. The spell I'd been under was temporarily broken. The filaments of light that had emerged to connect me to my twin were gone, but I could feel them struggling to break free. I tightened my fists until my fingernails dug into my palms.

Erin's brow furrowed tightly, creating a row of wrinkles between her eyes. Her eyelids twitched rapidly. She whimpered again and muttered something under her breath. I leaned closer to hear.

"Don't hurt her," she cried softly. "Please stop it. Please don't hurt my mom! No, no, no, NO!"

Erin began to thrash wildly on the bed, arms flailing, fighting against some unseen enemy. But I knew the enemy's name.

Thomas Dunn.

Trapped in her dream, my sister screamed.

"Erin. Erin, it's okay. It's just a dream," I tried to tell her, but she was still caught between waking and dreaming.

Footsteps pounded toward the room. The door burst open, and a frantic nurse with her hair falling out of a ponytail charged inside.

"What's wrong?" my mom asked, awake and sitting up now, climbing out of bed.

"She's having a nightmare," I said quickly, guiltily. "It's okay. It's just a nightmare."

As though these words reached her through sleep, Erin's eyes flashed open, huge and alarmed. Unfocused and confused. And then they found me and her face crumpled. A howl of misery escaped from her throat.

"I want to forget. I want to forget all of it, Kenna." She choked on the words and began to cough and cry at the same time. She curled into the fetal position and hid her face in the pillow as her body was wracked with sobs, each one a tiny, desperate shriek.

I swallowed a taste like acid from my mouth.

The nurse administered a sedative through Erin's IV, and a moment later my sister's torment faded as she slipped back into unconsciousness. I hoped she wouldn't dream again. I hoped she'd find some way to forget, even though I knew that was impossible.

The nurse left with an admonition that I needed to let Erin rest, and I turned to face my mom. I felt exposed, a hunted animal that has run out of cover. Sweat beaded on my forehead, slicked my spine, but my teeth chattered and my skin shriveled against the air, like I'd stepped inside a freezer unit.

My eyes found my mom's, and I saw in them the knowledge of what I was about to say.

"It's happening again."

Her expression showed no surprise, only dismay. It was like she'd been waiting for me to say the words. Still, it shocked me when she ripped off the tape keeping her IV needle flat to her wrist and then carefully slid the needle from her arm.

"We need to get out of this hospital," she said. "Is Blake still here?"

I averted my eyes and shook my head. "I told him to leave. I was afraid I would—" I didn't finish. Didn't need to.

"Call him," she told me. "Tell him to come right away and pick us up. Not at the front entrance, though. We need to leave without being seen. There's an exit along the side of the hospital." She set the IV tubing aside and plucked at her hospital gown. "And ask him to bring me some of his mom's clothes."

The Road to Somewhere

I PEEKED MY HEAD OUT THE SIDE EXIT AND GLANCED LEFT to right in the alley where Blake had parked. There were some delivery guys at a loading dock farther toward the back of the building, but they weren't paying attention. Other than them, we were alone.

"Are you okay?" Blake asked, climbing out of his 4Runner, his brow so deeply furrowed I thought he might develop permanent worry lines by the time this was all over—if it were *ever* over. At least he seemed to have forgiven me for yelling at him in the cafeteria and sending him away.

"Not really," I admitted. I was past the point where lying would do me any good. I met his eyes. It wasn't easy. "Thanks for coming back," I said.

He nodded, and I held the door open for my mom, who still wore her hospital gown and a white bathrobe.

"Blake," she said in greeting.

"Hi, Anya," Blake said, an uncomfortable smile flickering on his lips. My mom insisted Blake call her by her first name, even though Blake was a staunch believer in calling all adults Mr. or Ms.

Blake looked past my mom. "Where's Erin?" he asked.

I hadn't had time to explain much to Blake over the phone.

"She's staying," my mom answered curtly, ending the inquiry. She'd left a note for Erin with a vague explanation that we'd gone out to "get a few things." Our sudden departure was sure to raise alarms among the police and hospital staff, but Mom assured me that it was imperative we leave as soon as possible, and I couldn't disagree with her.

"Where to?" Blake asked when Mom and I were huddled in the backseat beneath a blanket so the reporters wouldn't spot us as we drove away.

"Take the Alta Highway into the mountains," Mom said. "I'll tell you where to go once we reach the summit."

"Okay . . ." There was uncertainty in his voice, but he did as he was told.

When we were a mile away from the hospital, Mom threw back the blanket. I sat up and rubbed my temples. The sound in my ears had abated slightly now that we were out of the hospital. I wondered if it was the presence of so many people that made it worse. The fever chills and stabbing stomach cramps and prickling on my skin continued, but were also slightly less intense than they had been inside the building.

Blake handed my mom a paper grocery bag. "I brought

some of my mom's clothes. I'm not sure they'll fit, but it was the best I could do."

"Thank you." Mom opened the bag and pulled out a pair of sneakers with balled-up socks stuffed inside, yoga pants, a university T-shirt, and a gray hoodie. Blake kept his eyes trained carefully on the road as my mom changed. When she pulled her hospital gown over her head, exposing her naked back, I got the first good look at her tattoo I'd had in years. She kept it carefully covered, never wearing tank tops or bathing suits. Now I took the opportunity to examine the tattoo carefully while her back was to me. The inked drawing was intricate, obviously created by a gifted artist. I saw now that the wings on her shoulder blades were only a part of the tattoo, that there was an entire mural covering her skin. There was a depiction of a large house on her lower back, and forested mountains in the background. The phases of the moon stretched the length of her spine, transitioning into the moth's thorax and head. The moth itself had black eyes and perfect black circles in the centers of its wings. It seemed to tell a story, one that my mom had certainly never told to me.

She pulled the T-shirt over her head, ending my scrutiny. "That's better," she said, wadding up the hospital gown and shoving it into the paper bag. She turned her head toward the window and gazed out at the dwindling houses now being overtaken by forest as the highway wound into the foothills of the Cross Pine Mountains.

"Mom, where are we going?" I asked, and then, lowering

my voice, even though there was no way to keep Blake from hearing, "Are you taking me to the . . . the same place as last time?"

"What place?" Blake asked, glancing at me in the rearview mirror.

My mom drew in a long breath and released it. "No," she said, and looked at her hands in her lap. "I'm taking you where I should have taken you a long time ago. I made a mistake, Kenna." She rubbed her eyes and then stopped rubbing and left her hands there, covering her face. "I thought if you didn't know about them you would never become one of them. But I was wrong. I was wrong about so many things."

I stared at her, mouth parted, my heartbeat frantic. "I don't understand."

She took another deep breath, lowered her hands, and looked at me. "You will. Soon enough, you'll understand everything."

Blake's car crested the summit. At the top of the mountain, we had a view of the bucolic valley on the other side of the Cross Pine range, all verdant forest and rippling fields of tall grass, no cities or towns or even a gas station in sight. From this vantage point, the rest of the world might as well not exist.

The volume on Blake's stereo was turned down low, but I heard the faint strains of the band that had been playing last night when we arrived at the festival. Long Way Home.

As we started down the other side of the mountain, I had

the distinct feeling it would be a very long way home, and I had no idea who I would be when I returned.

"Pull over here," Mom said when we reached the base of the mountain.

Blake slowed and veered onto the shoulder of the highway. I was about to ask why we'd stopped when I saw the narrow, rutted dirt road—barely a road, more of a path—leading off through a field and then disappearing into another row of mountains.

My mom put her hand on Blake's shoulder. "Blake, I hate to ask but . . . would it be all right if you waited here while we took your car the rest of the way?"

"Mom!" I said, shocked that she would even consider such a thing. "You can't ask him to just sit on the side of the road until we get back!"

"The people I'm taking you to see are extremely private," she said, and opened the door as though the decision were already made.

For a moment, Blake and I were alone in the car. He sat facing forward, hands clenched on the steering wheel. He loved his 4Runner. He'd saved up and bought it himself, and he cared for it like it was a prized Bentley, washing it every weekend and using special cloths on the paint.

"I'll do it," he said. "I'll stay behind."

"Blake, no. Just no. You won't even let *me* drive your car."

"I don't care about the car," he said quietly. "I care about *you*. I want to help, and it seems like this is the only way I can." He twisted in his seat to face me, and for a moment we looked at each other and said nothing, but I could read the frustration in his eyes and in his furrowed brow. He looked older than he had yesterday. I guessed I probably did, too.

"I don't understand any of this," he said.

"That makes two of us."

"I hope your mom knows what she's doing." The protective edge to his voice told me he didn't trust my mom as much as he pretended to.

Still, when Mom knocked on Blake's window he opened the door and got out, leaving his keys in the ignition and the car running. Mom climbed into his seat, and I got out and dragged myself reluctantly to the passenger side and got in.

"I'll be back before nightfall," my mom told Blake.

I couldn't help but notice she said "I," not "we," but just then a lightning bolt of pain lanced through my guts and I decided not to question her.

Blake shoved his hands in his pockets. "No problem." He looked at the ground and kicked at a clump of grass with the toe of his sneaker. I wished I could kiss him goodbye, hug him, something. Anything.

Nothing changes, he had said last night after our kiss.

Or everything does. That had been my response, but I had no idea how possible that was.

Blake opened his mouth to say something more to me, but he never got the chance. My mom put the car in Drive and pulled onto the dirt road. In the rearview mirror, I watched Blake until he disappeared, my throat swollen with sadness. I managed not to cry, but only because the grinding pain in my guts and the ache in my bones was a handy distraction from my overwhelming emotions.

"He'll be okay," Mom said after we'd been bouncing and lurching down the overgrown dirt road for a few minutes in silence. She glanced over at me. "You really like him, huh?"

"Can we talk about something else, like where we're going? I assume you didn't want to tell me in front of Blake."

She was silent a moment before nodding. "It's better that no one knows." She took a breath and exhaled the answer: "I'm taking you to Eclipse."

"Eclipse," I repeated, assuming for a moment that I'd heard her wrong. Eclipse was a place everyone who'd grown up in Rushing was aware of, but no one I knew had ever actually been there. I had seen people from Eclipse in town before, but only a few times, when they made runs to the post office or the hardware store or the gas station. They rarely left their isolated commune tucked away in the mountains, and were, as far as I knew, almost entirely self-sufficient and off the grid, and had been for several decades.

"Why?" I asked after this announcement had sunk in. The last thing I needed was to be around people, and I doubted the residents of Eclipse wanted anything to do with me.

"Because . . ." Her grip on the wheel tightened. I could see the strain all the way up to her neck. "I think they can help you. I hope they can. Or will."

"Why would they be able to help me?"

My mom chewed her lip.

"Mom, *please*," I said sharply, holding myself to control a sudden bout of fever chills. "Don't make me beg for every answer."

"Okay, I'm sorry." She looked at me with her eyes swimming, and I knew she meant it. "It's hard to talk about after all these years. There's so much I never told you about where I came from. About the Kalyptra. That's what they call themselves, the people who live at Eclipse."

"Kalyptra?" I repeated. I was fairly certain I'd never heard the word before, but that wasn't surprising. Pretty much the only thing people in Rushing knew about those who lived at Eclipse was that they existed. "What does that mean?" I asked.

"Nothing. It's just a word."

I narrowed my eyes at her, trying to decide if she was lying to me, but I couldn't be sure either way.

We hit a pothole and both of us jolted forward in our seats.

"It's a good thing Blake has an SUV," Mom said. "I forgot how rough this road is."

"So you've been to Eclipse?" I had a thousand more questions, but before I could ask the next in line Mom began to slow the 4Runner. We had reached something man-made: a gated fence made of barbed wire and two-by-fours, closing off the narrow road wedged between two jutting hills.

I blinked in surprise when I caught sight of a man sitting on the other side of the fence, lounging against the trunk of a maple tree and picking lazily at the strings of a banjo. He wore a faded chambray shirt tucked into jeans, and his dark, tousled hair grew wild over his neck and ears.

As Mom rolled toward the gate, the man set his instrument aside, rose, and approached the fence, his air of relaxed indifference slipping away. The sleeves of his shirt were rolled up to his elbows, and as he folded his arms over his chest I saw his tan, muscled forearms flex. Even from yards away, I could gauge the intensity of his blue eyes, sapphires fringed by inky lashes.

Mom braked in front of the gate, which was closed and secured with a softball-sized padlock. Several large wooden signs were propped against the fence, making declarative statements like, "Absolutely NO trespassers allowed," and "Unwelcome visitors will be treated as such."

"Is he one of the Kalyptra?" I asked. He didn't look much older than me, probably in his early twenties.

"Yes. His name is Cyrus."

I glanced at her, wondering how often she came to Eclipse that she recognized this man on sight.

"He doesn't look very friendly," I observed.

"I told you, the Kalyptra don't like visitors," Mom said. "But don't worry. I'll handle him."

She was out the door before I could argue. I watched her approach the fence. When he saw who she was, his lips parted and for a moment he only stared at her. But he recovered quickly from whatever shock she'd delivered, shook his head, and pointed back up the road. I figured he had just told her to go back where she came from, or something of that nature. His expression was stony, unaffected, but then Mom said something that took him aback. His eyes widened, and he looked directly at me. My heart began to pound, and the back of my neck grew hot under his stare.

Then he reached into his shirt and pulled out a long, leather thong, on the end of which hung a key.

As he unlocked the padlock and opened the gate, Mom climbed back into the 4Runner. Her hands shook as she shifted into Drive.

"What did you tell him?" I asked.

"That I needed to see Rebekah."

"Who's Rebekah?"

My mom eased her foot down on the gas pedal and we proceeded through the open gate. I locked eyes with Cyrus for a moment as we passed him, and I felt my temperature rise again.

"Rebekah is the person who founded Eclipse," Mom said, glancing at me before adding, "She's also your grandmother."

&CLIPSE

I GAPED AT MY MOM, FORGETTING MOMENTARILY ABOUT the torment my body was in. Then the questions piled out of me, one after another. "I have a grandmother and you never told me? Does she know about Erin and me? Why hasn't she ever come to see us? What's she like?" I paused to catch my breath, and another realization hit me. "You're from Eclipse, aren't you? That's why you never talk about your past. You didn't want us to know."

She simply nodded, keeping her eyes trained on the road.

"But why?"

Her face pinched, as though she were recalling a painful memory. "Rebekah—my mother—and I are not on good terms. She never forgave me for choosing a normal life over life with the Kalyptra."

"But it's not like you went far. You're just on the other side of the mountain."

"To Rebekah, that might as well be the other side of the world. As far as she's concerned, I died the day I left."

"That's extreme."

"That's Rebekah." Her eyes flicked toward me, troubled. "You and she are a lot alike, you know?"

"No, I don't know. You'll have to actually tell me since I've never met her."

Mom sighed. "The way you take everything to extremes. The way you obsess. You can never do anything in moderation. It's all or nothing with both of you."

I sat back heavily in my seat. This was the most honest conversation I'd had with her in years, and I wasn't sure I liked it. Not that she was telling me anything I didn't already know, but it still bothered me to hear myself assessed this way.

"Well, you're not perfect either," I told her.

She nodded. "I know that."

"You're sad all the time, and you're secretive, and . . . and I feel like I don't even know you."

She sighed and deflated, and I wished I'd kept my mouth shut. I was lashing out at her because it was the only thing I could do.

Ahead, the mountains opened into fields. The road wound through an orchard and then past rows of grapevines clinging to posts. I spotted a few people—women with long, intricate braids and shaggy-haired men in tunics—picking fruit from trees and vines. As we drove past, their eyes followed us, stunned and apprehensive. I craned around in my seat to see what they'd do, and glimpsed Cyrus trotting along behind us on the road, the banjo slung onto his back. He waved to the people in the orchard, signaling that we were okay. I exhaled a pent-up breath, wondering what those people would have done if Cyrus hadn't waved them off. I remembered the sign by the fence. "Unwelcome visitors will be treated as such."

After what Mom had just told me, I wasn't sure what kind of visitors that made us. Would Rebekah, my surprise grandmother, turn us away? Maybe she would take one look at my mom and decide all had been forgiven.

I felt a thrill of wary excitement at the prospect of meeting a family member who hadn't existed to me until minutes ago, but the aching emptiness inside me sucked it away and left me feeling hollow.

The deeper into Eclipse territory we drove, the more attention we attracted, until we had a dozen Kalyptra following us. We passed a smattering of stone-cobbled outbuildings, greenhouses, gardens, storage sheds, a large A-frame barn, and an elaborate, patchwork yurt. There were fenced animal paddocks enclosing horses, cows, sheep, and goats, and several large chicken coops. Mom had to progress slowly because chickens and wild turkeys waddled into the road, unmindful of the tires about to flatten them.

Then we crested a grassy hillock, and I sucked in a breath as the house depicted in ink on my mom's lower back appeared before us: a sprawling, three-story chalet, like something you'd find high in the Alps. At the very top of the chalet, a broad balcony looked out across the valley.

A woman with thigh-length blond hair, wearing a long, lavender dress, stood on the balcony alone. She stared down at us a moment before turning and disappearing through the balcony door.

"That was her, wasn't it?" I said. "That was Rebekah."

"Yes," Mom said softly. "That was my mother."

We pulled up alongside an old pickup truck parked next to a shed. Mom killed the engine and we sat in silent awe for a moment as we gazed out the windshield at the wooden castle bursting from the middle of this remote valley, walled in by mountains on all sides.

"I forgot how big it is," Mom said, sounding breathless.

As soon as we stepped out of the car, we were surrounded. The people who'd been following the 4Runner converged on us, more heading in our direction from across the yard. With their proximity, the shuddering in my ears increased, and my fever ramped up several degrees. Sweat trickled down my back, and I went stiff. I could feel their energy, their life, like I was standing next to a bonfire. It was as palpable as steam in the air.

"It's all right," Mom said, sensing my tension. "They won't hurt us."

"That's not what I'm worried about," I muttered, my jaw aching from clenching my teeth.

My mom looked at me, her expression calmer than I expected. "You can't hurt them, Kenna. They're like you. Or you're like them, I suppose. You are Kalyptra."

My lips parted and a breath escaped. My eyes darted to the

assembled people and then back to my mom. I licked my lips nervously. "Are you sure?"

"Yes," she said. "But stay in control a little longer. You can still hurt *me*."

I blinked at her, confused, but my mom turned away, offering no explanation. Questions reeled through my head. My mom had lived here, and her mother was Kalyptra. So how was my mom not like me?

I surveyed the assembled. The Kalyptra represented a gamut of ethnicities—Asian, Latino, Indian, African-American—and ranged in age from early twenties to middle age, although they all possessed an ageless quality. The longer I looked at them, the more difficult it was to estimate their ages. But I didn't see a single child among them. Their clothing was somewhere between rustic and bohemian. Loose linen tunics with jeans. Peasant skirts and camisoles. Long dresses with bell sleeves. Cargo pants, brown boots, chambray and plaid flannel shirts. The women, for the most part, sported hair that draped to their waists, the men's to their shoulders. I remembered the droves of colorfully dressed, faux hippies who'd gathered en masse at Folk Yeah! Fest. At the time, I'd thought them stylish and reasonably authentic, but compared to the Kalyptra they seemed more like children playing dress-up.

What struck me most about the Kalyptra, though, was the glow of vitality they exuded, which I could not only see, but feel. They were otherworldly in their bright-eyed loveliness, like flowers picked at their zenith of perfection. Their skin was flawless and natural, their hair glossy, and their bodies lean and athletic in a way that even people who spent their lives at the gym could rarely achieve. Whatever naturalistic lifestyle they were living out here, it was working for them.

"Anya, is that you?" A man with thick golden hair, a pointy beard, and the physique of Thor shouldered his way to the front. I shrank from him and hid behind my mom. He looked like he could have picked both of us up by the backs of our necks, one in each hand, and tossed us like kittens.

"Stig," Mom said, smiling uncertainly and nodding. "You haven't changed a bit."

"It *is* you," the big man, Stig (pronounced "Steeg"), said in a tone of wonder, looking my mom up and down while the other Kalyptra gasped and whispered behind their hands. "I hardly recognize you. *Velkommen hjem*," Stig said in what sounded like a Scandinavian dialect, Norwegian or Danish. I had no idea what his words translated to, but I hoped not, *Get the hell out before we throw you out.*

Then he threw his arms around my mom in a hug and lifted her off her feet. "I knew you'd come back one of these days."

There was a singsong quality to his voice that made him sound like a cheerful bird. He released my mom and put his hands on his hips, still grinning. I released the breath I was holding, relieved that he wasn't about to toss us off Eclipse property. But when his eyes turned to me, the smile dissolved.

"You bring a stranger into our midst," Stig said, his musical voice going flat. "Why?"

"This is my daughter, Kenna," Mom said, her chin tilting up defiantly. "She may be a stranger, but she's still Kalyptra." Mom lowered her voice so only Stig could hear. "I need to see Rebekah. It's urgent."

She nodded to indicate me, and added, her voice barely audible, "She's culled the forbidden anima. She's going through catharsis."

"Catharsis?" I blinked at my mom, wanting to ask what she was talking about, but before I could open my mouth Stig clapped so loudly the sound stung my ears. "All right, everyone. Back to work. Plenty to do before sundown."

There were a few grumbles, but the crowd dispersed, heading back to the gardens and fields, most of them craning their necks to peer at my mom and me over their shoulders.

Stig ushered us toward the house. "Rebekah's inside. I'm sure she'll be happy to see you."

Mom snorted derisively. "No need to lie to me, Stig. I'm a big girl now. I can handle my mother."

Judging from the slight tremor in Mom's voice, I wasn't so sure she believed what she said.

REBEKAH

STIG LED US THROUGH CORRIDORS THAT TWISTED AND turned and split. The immense building could have been designed by a rabbit; it seemed more warren than house. The walls, floor, and ceiling were exposed wood, oily and aged. Ethereal paintings of moths with black circles on white wings crowded the walls in the hallways. The same species of moth that was inked on my mom's back.

"What kind of moth is that?" I asked.

Hearing my question, Stig glanced over his shoulder and gave my mom a look that I didn't know how to interpret as anything other than a warning.

"It's . . . an Eclipse moth," my mom said, and then quickly added, "But it isn't real. That is, it doesn't exist. It's like a fairy tale creature."

"Then what's with the obsession?"

Mom shrugged. "Eclipse moths are the Kalyptra's totem. Sort of a mascot or a family crest."

I guessed there was more to this story, but Mom didn't seem keen on talking about it in front of Stig, so I let it drop.

We turned a corner and Stig nearly collided with a girl heading fast in the opposite direction.

"Pardon me—" she started to say, and then she saw my mom and froze with her mouth open. She had skin the color of brown sugar, and long, silky black hair woven into an intricate braid that hung to her elbows. Her fierce eyes were small and dark, like black pearls.

"It's you," the woman said, breathless and flustered, blinking rapidly. "I thought . . . I mean . . . you're not supposed to be here."

"I know." Mom lowered her eyes, as though in shame. "Joanna, this is my daughter, Kenna."

Joanna's eyes cut to me and widened. For a long moment, all she did was stare at me. "She has gray hair," she said finally.

"It's not her natural color," Mom said, a sardonic crackle to her tone. She'd been coolly furious when she saw what I'd done to my blond hair.

"Why would anyone dye their hair *gray*?" Joanna asked in clear abhorrence.

Mom shrugged, as if to say, *Teenagers. Who knows why they do anything?*

Joanna continued to study me, and her brow furrowed.

"What's wrong with her?" she asked, but the apprehension in her voice told me she was not referring to my hair.

I shuddered and clutched myself. The respite I'd enjoyed was over, and my fever chills and aching body were ramping up again. I realized my teeth were chattering. My lungs felt hardened and shrunken, and my insides felt like they were caving in, like my rib cage would buckle and my organs and bones would fold into themselves like a collapsing universe. At the same time, parts of me seemed to be unraveling, trying to reach out for whatever—whoever—was near me, hair-thin veins trying to connect to something vital, something that could end my suffering. It hadn't been this bad after Jason Dunn. If it had, I didn't think I would have survived.

"Catharsis?" Joanna guessed before Mom could answer.

"I'm taking her to Rebekah," my mom said in confirmation. "She needs help, and I can't give it to her." Again, Mom lowered her eyes. "Not the way I am now."

Joanna's black pearl eyes darted to Stig, and then back to my mom. She seemed to be trying to decide something.

"You should leave," she blurted with sudden, forceful hostility. "Rebekah doesn't care about you or your mongrel daughter. Just get in your car and go."

My mom looked like she'd been slapped. Even Stig appeared surprised by the vehemence in Joanna's dismissal.

"Joanna," he said, shocked. "It's not your place to speak for Rebekah."

My mom shook her head. "I don't expect anyone to welcome me with open arms, least of all my mother." She fixed

104

her eyes on Joanna, and something unspoken passed between them. "I thought you might be different, Joanna. I guess that was too much to hope for."

Joanna's jaw clenched and her hands fisted at her sides, but what I saw in her eyes when she looked at my mom wasn't anger or loathing. There was affection in them, deep and unmistakable. And she seemed to be pleading . . . pleading with her eyes for my mom to take me and leave.

But I couldn't be sure, and a moment later she turned on her heel and hurried away.

My mom stared after Joanna with tears brimming in her eyes. I'd seen my mom sad. She was almost always sad. But I'd never seen her heartbroken, and that was how she struck me now.

I turned to my mom. "How do you know her? Or him for that matter?" I nodded at Stig. "How long has it been since you left Eclipse?"

"A long time," she answered vaguely.

"But you must have been back to visit?" Neither Joanna nor Stig looked older than twenty-five.

Stig and my mom shared another of those secretive glances. "No," she said. "Never."

I wanted to know more about this time discrepancy, but I had my own issues with time right now—mainly that I was running out of it. That reaching, unraveling feeling was getting stronger, and it seemed to be stretching toward my mom.

I wiped sweat from my brow with the back of a trembling hand, teeth still chattering as violently as if I'd just climbed out of a frozen river in January. "Fine. Whatever we're doing here, let's get back to it. I don't know how much longer I can hold on."

"Of course," my mom said, snapping back to reality and squaring her shoulders, as though she were about to go into battle.

Stig led us to a steep staircase and we began to climb. When we reached the third floor, we came to a closed wooden door, a pattern of branches and moons and fluttering moths carved on the surface.

Stig knocked softly. "Rebekah?"

"Come in." The response was immediate, as though she'd been waiting patiently for our arrival.

Stig pushed the door open, revealing cozy quarters that seemed to be part bedroom, part study, with a vaulted ceiling and exposed beams hung with colorful tapestries and lanterns. The walls were jammed with framed art, antique stringed instruments, and bookshelves. Fur rugs were scattered across the floor, the biggest lying in front of a fireplace with a stone hearth, surrounded by large, fluffy sitting pillows. Two large skylights let in shafts of lemony morning sun.

The first person my eyes locked on to when I entered was Cyrus, standing in front of a rustic birch wood desk, talking to the woman sitting behind it.

When I saw her, everyone else in the room faded.

I had to blink when she turned her face toward me, like I'd looked directly at the sun. Her smooth skin was the color of dark honey, and a cape of caramel-blond hair cascaded past her waist to the tops of her thighs. Her arms were slender, waifish, and multitudes of silver rings circled her fingers. Her face was almost too beautiful to make sense. Wide-set, pale eyes. Shell-pink lips. An aristocratic nose and chin, and high, round, peachy cheekbones.

She was nothing you'd think of when you think of a grandmother, but I knew on sight that this woman was mine.

She rose and glided toward me, smiling, but didn't spare so much as a glance for my mom. Her bare feet whispered across the wood floor and the gauzy fabric of her long, lavender dress fluttered around her ankles.

"You must be my granddaughter," she said. "I'm so glad to finally meet you."

I wanted to tell her to stay back, not to touch me. Even though my mom said I couldn't hurt these people, the Kalyptra, I didn't want to take any chances. But Rebekah smiled at me so gently, and there was a welcoming glow to her, like she'd been waiting for me all these years; like maybe, just by looking at me, having never met me, she *loved* me. This air of acceptance overwhelmed me and I couldn't speak.

She cupped my cheeks in hands as soft as baby skin. "I'm Rebekah," she said.

Then my ears filled with a shuddering roar, and my skin pulsed, one pounding heartbeat reverberating through me, before I felt myself unravel, strands of me reaching for her, for my mom, for anyone at all. Reaching to pierce their skin and drink the life inside them.

With an animal cry, I tore away from Rebekah, from all

of them, and backed against the wall. "I can't . . ." I said, breathing fast, though no oxygen seemed to reach my lungs. "I can't hold on any longer."

I looked down at my body and saw slivers of white filament extend from me, threads of pale light waving and twisting, seeking purchase.

With my back against the wall, I slid to the floor, arms wrapped tight around me as though I could hold myself together. But my body was rebelling, and no matter how hard I willed the veins of light to withdraw back into me, they refused.

Instead, they grew, reaching for my mom.

I shut my eyes tight and covered my head with my hands, unable, unwilling to watch what was about to happen. "Get away from me! All of you!" I shouted at them, and I hoped they listened, even though, knowing what I'd done to the land around my home, I didn't know if it would do them any good.

But I didn't hear any of their footsteps retreating from me. There was only Rebekah's voice, calm and assured and in control.

"Cyrus, fetch one of the jars. Quickly, please."

My entire body quaking, I dared to peek up at them and saw Cyrus throw open a cabinet on the far side of the room, removing a ceramic container. He handed it carefully to Rebekah, and she moved closer to me until I saw it was some kind of jar in the shape of an animal's head. A sheep's head, I realized when she was only a few feet away.

She continued to ease closer to me with the jar held out in front of her.

"Please," I begged, my words vibrating through my trembling throat, strands of me reaching to engulf her. "Get away."

She kept moving closer, her eyes never leaving mine. Then she knelt and set the jar in front of me.

I stared at the jar, and the sheep's head with its blank eyes stared back.

"Open it," Rebekah commanded, her voice filled with so much authority that I had no choice but to do what she said.

I opened the top of the lamb's head. Again, I felt that sense of unraveling, like a ball of yarn dropped down a staircase with someone still holding the string at one end. The pale veins extruded from me, stretching and surrounding the opening at the top of the jar as a fine, white cloud of light drifted from inside. The veins hoarded the light and wrapped around it, and as the white cloud diminished, the emptiness inside me was filled. My lungs eased and my bones ceased aching; the fiery itching on my skin stopped, and the shuddering sound in my ears quieted to blessed silence.

When the cloud was gone, the pale veins withdrew into me and I slumped against the wall and fell instantly, blissfully, asleep.

THIS SIDE OF THE RIVER

I DREAMED OF BLAKE.

I stood on one side of a river, its rippling waters tinseled with moonlight, and he was on the other. My bank was lush with blossoming trees and a carpet of white flowers bathed in milky moonlight. But Blake's side was dark, as though the forest behind him had recently burned, and the light did not reach it. He tried to tell me something, but the crashing roar of water drowned his voice. Then the river began to rise, pushing us farther and farther from each other until he was only a sliver in the distance, and I had forgotten his name.

I woke in an unfamiliar bed, and the dream lingered for a moment like a bad aftertaste before dissolving into the basement of my subconscious.

Though it was dark in the room and my eyes had not yet adjusted, I didn't need them to tell me I was not alone. I tensed, sitting up quickly, willing my groggy head to clear, and then realized that I wasn't groggy at all. My head *was* clear. My body felt normal. Better than normal, in fact. I felt freaking amazing, both physically and mentally. The pain and sickness that had racked me were gone. I didn't think I'd ever known such a sense of perfect, untroubled serenity. It was like every worry and fear and the mound of guilt I'd harbored had been locked away in a safe room inside my head, still there, but unable to touch me for the time being.

I recalled what had happened before I'd plunged into sleep. Meeting Rebekah. Losing control and coming undone. The sheep's head jar, and the white cloud of light that had been trapped inside it. The pale, glowing veins that had emerged from me and siphoned it into my body. What had that light been? Whatever it was, I could feel it inside me still, a crystal glaze over every thought and feeling. A soothing balm that filled up the emptiness and drove away my pain.

I was healed. The gnawing, aching, unbearable hunger that had been a constant torment since I'd woken in the basement was gone.

But where was I now, and who was in the room with me?

"Mom?" I tried. "Are you there?"

"She's gone," said the person in the room, who I still could not see.

I heard a scraping sound, and then an orange flame burst to life, illuminating Rebekah's stunning face in a warm glow. She lit an oil lamp on the bedside table, and the room filled with amber light. I took in my new surroundings. I was in a bedroom that was small but cozy. The bed was built into the wall, and the walls, floor, and ceiling were made up of planks of wood, like the inside of a cabin. There was a large cast-iron stove that looked like a potbellied steampunk robot next to the bed, and a colorful woven rug on the floor. The walls were bare, as though this room had never been occupied, or as if the former occupant had moved out and taken all of her things.

My eyes returned to Rebekah's. "What do you mean, she's gone?" I asked.

Rebekah sat in a chair across from me, but she leaned forward to take my hands in hers. Her proximity alarmed me until I remembered that whatever affliction I'd been suffering from for the last few hours was cured.

My grandmother—who looked to be no older than forty, although that couldn't be her true age since my own mom was near forty herself—tilted her head, brow furrowing in sympathy. "She went home. You're to stay here with us for the time being."

"She left me here?" How could she abandon me with a bunch of strangers, even if one of them was my grandmother? I was aware of a distant sense of distress, but it lay beneath the tranquil glaze that covered my emotions like a cool, silk sheet.

"For now," Rebekah said, reaching out and smoothing back my hair. She lifted a lock of it, and I saw that my hair was no longer the ash gray I had colored it, but a smooth, butterscotch blond.

I picked up a lock of my hair and studied it. "How did this happen?"

"Anima," my grandmother said simply, as though I should understand. But she saw my confused expression and smiled. "It has restored your body to its natural state. Well, not natural. I suppose *ultimate* is a more appropriate word. Your mother really never told you anything, did she?"

I started to shake my head, and then stopped and lowered my gaze to the patchwork quilt covering my legs. "She tried once," I said, remembering when I was ten years old, and my mom had found me in the yard, sobbing so hard I could barely breathe. She had taken me in her arms and comforted me until I'd calmed enough to tell her what was wrong. Erin was sick again and even though she was allergic, I had gone out to Mom's garden to pick flowers to make a bouquet for her. I thought I could tie it with a ribbon to hang upside down outside her window. Then the flowers would dry and she would be able to look at them every day until she got better. But when I'd reached to pick some of the wild lavender that grew around our house, white threads had wormed from my fingertips and reached for the plant. I'd been so scared I'd fallen over backward and screamed. When I'd looked at my hand again the threads were gone.

"What were they?" I had asked my mom, starting to cry again. "What's wrong with me? Am I going to get sick like Erin?" The thought would almost have been a comfort. I'd always felt guilty for being the healthy one.

I remembered my mom had covered her mouth with her hand, her eyes wide and frightened. I didn't understand until what happened with Jason Dunn that she was frightened of me.

I lifted my gaze to Rebekah's. "A long time ago, she told me I was different from other people, that I had a dangerous gift and I could never use it. She said I—" I stopped, hesitating. Though I had obsessed about what my mom had told me all those years ago, I had never, ever spoken the words out loud, and I was afraid to, as if hearing myself say them would be a turning point from which I could never go back. But then I thought about what I had done to the land around my house and how everything living had died, and I decided I'd already reached the point of no return.

"She said there were people in this world who could consume a living thing's energy, and that I was one of them," I said. "But that it was dangerous to do that because I might hurt someone, and if I did I might not be able to control my urges after that. She said if I ever felt the urge I should come and tell her right away." I stopped there, not wanting to explain to the grandmother I'd just met how I had killed my ten-year-old neighbor, drunk his energy like it was a delicious milkshake.

Rebekah's eyes darkened. "*Anima*," she said. "That's what we call living energy. In Latin the word means many things. *Life* or *spirit* or sometimes *soul*. It is all of those things and none of them. But your mom was right about one thing: taking anima can be dangerous and addictive, but only if you've never been taught control, and in that way your mother failed you inexcusably."

I winced, feeling instinctively protective of my mom, but at the same time a part of me wanted to side with Rebekah. In regard to my "dangerous gift," the only guidance my mom had given me was *Don't use it.*

Rebekah smiled gently at me, as though reading every thought that wound through my head. "Don't worry, Kenna. While you're here, we're going to teach you what it means to be Kalyptra."

I chewed my lip, feeling anxiety wriggle beneath that layer of calm. "How long do I need to stay here?"

"As long as it takes."

"Can anyone come visit me?" I asked, thinking of Blake and Erin. I'd never spent more than a few days away from home, and I wasn't used to being separated from my twin. And Blake . . . we were so new, the romantic side of our relationship only a day old. What would happen to us if I didn't see him for a week? A month? What if I wasn't the same person after all this? What if he wasn't either?

"I'm afraid not," Rebekah said. "We're not accustomed to visitors here, and it wouldn't be safe for you to be around normal people until you've . . . well, gotten used to your new circumstances."

"Not safe for them, you mean."

She smiled and stood, looking down at me. "We'll keep you so busy while you're here, you won't have time to miss anyone. Besides, you and I have a lifetime of catching up to do."

I nodded, thinking how much warmer Rebekah's demeanor was than my own mom's. She didn't feel like a grandmother.

She felt like the mother I should have had. The woman who should have raised me. But then I felt guilty for thinking such a thing, like I was betraying my real mom. But hadn't she betrayed me by raising me to be normal? By keeping me separated from the people who could have taught me how to be what I was without hurting anyone else?

"It's late," Rebekah said. "I'll leave you to sleep. You have a big day tomorrow."

"What will I be doing?"

She cupped my chin in her soft hand and tilted my face so I was looking directly into her eyes. They were the same color as mine, pale green. In the dim room, her pupils were large, crowding out the color of her irises.

"Tomorrow, you start over," she said.

Her skin against mine felt warm and charged. A wave of contentment swept through me, unwinding my muscles until I felt limp as a rag doll.

Then she released my chin and bent to blow out the lamp.

She slipped out the door, leaving me to the cool darkness with a sense of peace that felt wholly unfamiliar, but like something that should have been familiar. Like something I'd been missing for as long as I could remember.

As I drifted off, I heard strains of music coming from somewhere outside the house, melodic guitars and hypnotic drums that settled me into a trance-like state, and I thought about how far I felt from the horrors I'd experienced less than a day ago. Now they felt like someone else's nightmare.

CYRUS

WHEN I WOKE IN THE EARLY MORNING, THERE WAS still music playing, only now it was right outside my door. Someone picking softly at the strings of a guitar. With a jolt of alarm, I realized my own guitar was still in the back of Blake's 4Runner, and since visitors were not allowed at Eclipse, I would not have access to it until I went home again, whenever that would be. For me, that was like being separated from a limb or a vital organ or my twin or my asthma inhaler or—

Oh no.

My inhaler. Another thing I'd left behind. Another thing I needed to survive.

Anxiety pinched my airways, and I immediately began to wheeze. The tranquility I'd enjoyed during my conversation with Rebekah the night before was gone. All the old anxieties and fears and guilt had returned, and along with them came the knowledge that I had been forsaken by my own mother. She had dropped me off in this strange place and left me without so much as a goodbye. Without my inhaler. Without my guitar. Without my twin and without my boy.

Now it was just me and a colony of complete strangers.

Worst of all, the empty feeling that had plagued me yesterday was back, coupled with a straining sense of hunger like a wolf on a leash fighting to break free. It wasn't as bad as it had been yesterday. The physical symptoms—the aching, fever-chilled, shuddering madness—were still held at bay, but I had a feeling this respite wouldn't last. Whatever it was Rebekah had fed me from that jar—*anima*, she called it—I needed more.

Still wheezing, I climbed out from under the quilt, shivering at the chilly bite in the air. Someone had left a pile of folded clean clothes on the short dresser next to the bed, but I didn't bother with them, choosing to remain in the ash-gray T-shirt and dark gray jeans I'd been wearing since I arrived. There were flecks of dried blood on my shoulders from all that had soaked into my hair two nights before. I needed to wash my hair and brush my teeth. But did they even have toothpaste and running water at Eclipse? I scanned the room and saw no outlets. Clearly electricity was not a priority for the Kalyptra.

Whoever was outside my door playing the guitar must have heard the floorboards creak under my feet, because the music stopped and there was a tentative tap on the wood.

"Kenna? Are you awake?"

It was a man's voice with a slight Johnny Cash twang.

I pressed my ear to the crack between the door and the jamb. "Who's there?" I asked.

"Cyrus. We didn't officially meet yet."

Cyrus. The guy from the gate. The guy who made the back of my neck go hot when he looked at me.

"Just a sec," I said, my voice thin and hoarse from my narrowed airways. There was a pitcher of water and a bowl on a little table by the window. I hurriedly rinsed out my mouth, and then noticed a rustic-looking toothbrush and a jar of what looked like jelly. I opened the jar, sniffed it. It smelled like mint, so I dabbed my finger into it and tasted it, decided it was some kind of DIY toothpaste, and quickly brushed with it, hoping I hadn't guessed wrong, that I hadn't just washed my mouth out with lotion or shampoo.

There was no mirror in the room, so I ran my hands over my hair and clothes to try to make myself at least semi-presentable, and called it good enough.

When I opened the door, I found Cyrus leaning against the wall, cleaning his fingernails with a pocketknife. His guitar was propped against the wall next to him. He looked, if possible, even more beautiful than he had when I'd seen him the previous day, his shaggy mane all dark chocolate coils like he was Jim Morrison's hair twin, his eyes a stunning shade of jewel blue against his graham-cracker tanned skin. He must have been too busy to remember the top few buttons on his shirt, because it was open to the defined squares of his pectoral muscles. Looking at him made it even harder to breathe.

"Mornin'," he said, closing his knife and pocketing it in jeans that looked to have been worn as soft as an old T-shirt. He smiled a charming half smile and gave a little bow, one hand placed on his stomach, the other behind his back. "I'm Cyrus."

"I know," I said, wary. "Where's Rebekah?" I couldn't bring myself to call her Grandmother or Grandma or Nana or any of the things you were supposed to call a grandma. She looked too young for those labels. But remembering how much younger my mom had looked after I did whatever I did to bring her back from death, I couldn't believe Rebekah was actually the age she appeared to be, which probably meant that none of the other Kalyptra were, either.

"Asleep," Cyrus told me. "She had a long night and needed to get some rest. She asked me to keep an eye on you today, show you around and introduce you to some of the folks since you'll be staying here a while."

He must have seen my face change at the reminder of my sojourn sans expiration date, because he added quickly, "We're good people. Everyone's real excited to meet Rebekah's long lost kin."

"One of them," I corrected. "I have a twin sister."

At the thought of Erin, my breathing constricted again. I tried to take a deep breath to calm myself, but the air seemed to hit a wall inside my throat.

Cyrus's dark eyebrows scrunched together in concern. "Are you all right? You look like you might pass out or something. Rebekah won't be too happy if you keel over on my watch."

I shook my head, determined to relax and control my breathing. *It's all in your head*, I told myself, because that's what every asthma doctor who'd ever examined me claimed, despite evidence to the contrary. But it was true that the only triggers to my asthma seemed to be anxiety and panic, and I hadn't actually showed any symptoms until after Jason Dunn's death.

I took a breath through my nose and let it out slowly. My lungs eased a little, but only a little.

"I'm fine," I told Cyrus, and then chewed the inside of my cheek in hesitation. "But I was wondering . . . I think I would be more fine if—"

"I know what you're going to ask," he said, interrupting.

"You do?"

"Of course. We've all experienced what you're going through on one level or another." He winked at me and crooked his arm, gesturing for me to follow him.

I did.

Cyrus led me across the sweeping belt of field that surrounded Eclipse House, where wildflowers speckled the long grasses with tiny starbursts of color: patches of vermillion, tangerine, lavender, and lemon. We passed the old A-frame barn and a grove of trees where a colorful webbing of hammocks connected the trunks, a brightly painted wooden wagon that would have looked at home in a Romani caravan, and a yurt, the panels cinched up to reveal an interior filled with lounging sofas, floor pillows, and a number of acoustic guitars propped on stands. Any other day I would've made a beeline for those instruments. The way some people were with babies or puppies—needing to hold them, paw at them, fawn over them—I was with guitars.

Today, a more pressing need had replaced my usual compulsion, but even my craving for anima couldn't entirely overshadow the bohemian idyll of Eclipse.

"You know, I thought Eclipse was like some backwoods cult compound," I said to Cyrus. "But it's more like . . ." I trailed off, partly because I was out of breath, and partly because the word in my head seemed, for some reason, dangerous.

Paradise, I thought. *It's like paradise.*

"You sure wind easily," Cyrus commented when I didn't finish, taking note of the whistling rattle in my throat. My airways had begun to feel like they were wrapped tight with rubber bands.

"I have asthma," I said.

"Asthma . . ." he repeated, as though I'd spoken a word in another language.

"You've never heard of asthma?"

"It sounds familiar."

"It's a medical condition. Tens of millions of people around the world have it."

He shrugged, unconcerned in a way that irritated me. "Not here they don't."

"Good for you guys." I sighed and decided to admit the truth, both to myself and to him. "The thing is, I forgot my inhaler—my asthma medication—and I'm going to need it soon or I could be in trouble. Maybe someone could take me home, just to grab some of my things?"

He smiled, but shook his head. "I don't know what an inhaler is, but I'm pretty sure we can do better than that."

He waited for me to start walking again, which I did after a petulant pause.

"Tell me about yourself," Cyrus said, making me feel like we were on a blind date. Not that I'd ever been on a blind date. For some reason the thought of Cyrus and me on a date, even though we weren't, made flames bloom inside my cheeks. I had to turn my face away so he wouldn't notice and ask why I'd gone from pale to pink.

"Not really in a chatty mood," I said.

"It'll help get your mind off the catharsis symptoms," he urged. "What do you like to do? Do you have a job or go to school or something? Do you have a boyfriend? Who are you?"

Who was I? That was not a question I could answer truthfully. I was the girl who murdered a kid at the ripe old age of ten. I was the girl who almost did the same thing to her twin sister after bringing her back from the dead. I was the girl who was so out of control and dangerous her mom dumped her at a hippie commune and left without a goodbye.

"I'm a music snob," I told him instead.

"Oh yeah?" He raised a dark stripe of eyebrow at me, seeming intrigued. "What else?"

"I'm a songwriter and I play the guitar. It's probably the only thing I'm actually good at. This fall I start senior year, but I hate school, and I don't want to go to college. I want to be a musician. And I'm not sure about the boyfriend part. I might have one. We haven't really figured that out yet."

I wasn't sure why I decided to tell him any of these things. Once I started, the information poured out. Even though he was a stranger, I felt oddly comfortable around Cyrus. Maybe it was the southern accent, slight though it was. Southern accents just made the people who had them seem like they could be trusted.

And there was something about Cyrus's face, too. The more I looked at it, the more I saw. He wasn't quite as perfect as he'd seemed on first sight. His nose and chin were both slightly crooked, as though they'd been broken at some point. But the asymmetry only added interest and dimension to a face that would have been blandly flawless without it. My mom had claimed that true beauty was in the imperfections, but I'd always wondered if she only told us this because Erin and I were so very imperfect.

"Your turn," I said. "Who are you? What do you do? Do *you* have a girlfriend?"

"Sure," he said, grinning his crooked grin. "Lots of them."

Cyrus halted at a wooden fence, an enclosure several acres

wide and long, containing a flock of sheep and a herd of goats, and a dozen horses. He leaned his elbows on the fence and pointed.

"See that little one there?" he said, pointing to a shaggy, half-sized goat with brown and white fur. "He's our resident troublemaker. He keeps finding a way to jump the fence, then he gets into the gardens and eats as much as he can before we catch him."

I watched the goat race through an obstacle course of his young friends, knocking one of them over, and bounding over the top of another like it was a hurdle.

"What's his name?" I asked, smiling and chuckling a raspy laugh.

Cyrus snorted in derision, and then realized I was serious. "Oh, we don't name the animals."

"Why not?" I asked, and then decided it was a stupid question. This was a farm, and these animals were livestock, not pets. Did people eat goat? I was pretty sure they did, and the idea of anyone slaughtering this little goat was unthinkable to me.

"I'm going to call him Bully," I said decisively. "Bully the Kid. Baby goats are called kids, right?"

Cyrus frowned at me, ignoring my question. "That's not a good idea."

"Too late. It's already done." I called to the goat, "I hereby dub you Bully the Kid!" Maybe Bully's name would stick and the Kalyptra would start to think of him as a pet instead of just an animal. You couldn't eat a pet.

I watched Bully race across the enclosure and then spring into the air for the sheer joy of it, releasing a bleat of triumph when he hit the ground. I'd never envied a goat before, but at that moment I really, really wanted to be Bully, to feel what he was feeling. Even a few seconds of simple happiness would suffice.

I was comfortable existing in a mild state of malaise, and I'd always accepted that was who I was. My melancholia was like the vines that wrapped some decrepit structures, holding them up, fortifying them. Besides, I figured, not everyone had to be happy-go-lucky. The world needed miserable artists, too.

But after what I had seen in the basement—my family slaughtered, their blood, their death—I wasn't sure I wanted the darkness anymore. I wanted to tear off the vines that used to keep me from falling apart. To find some other way to exist, even if it meant becoming a whole new person.

Tomorrow you start over, Rebekah had said to me last night, like I didn't have a choice. Like that was just how it had to be, and I was both surprised and relieved to realize I was okay with that. I didn't want to be me anymore. I hadn't for a long time, but now that I was at Eclipse, separate from everything that made me me—my mom, my twin, my guitar, even Blake—I wondered if I could cast off the person I used to be and truly start fresh, like Rebekah said. The people here didn't know anything about me. I could be someone else to them. Someone better than who I'd been for the last seven years. For the last seventeen, for that matter.

I knelt and held out my hand to Bully the Kid, trying to get him to come to me. He started toward me.

"Best not touch him just yet," Cyrus warned. "You're still a bit raw. Wouldn't want you to cull him now that you've named him."

I withdrew my hand quickly, and Bully gave me an offended look and a frustrated bray, which sounded almost identical to a baby crying, before darting off to play with his friends again.

I straightened and turned to Cyrus, my lungs tighter than ever as anxiety swelled in me. "Is it always going to be this way?" I asked, terrified of the answer.

Cyrus turned his back on the animals and leaned his elbows on the fence, his posture relaxed and casual. All he needed was a wheat straw sticking out of his mouth.

"Nah," he said, seemingly unaware of my angst. "You learn to control it. The catharsis only comes after you cull too much anima."

"Cull?" The word sounded so much like *kill*, I wondered if I'd misheard him.

"Right. Culling is what we call it when we harvest anima from another living thing. Catharsis is what happens if you escalate the amount of anima you cull too quickly, and your body can't handle it. But we'll get you sorted in time, don't worry."

"But how?" I asked. "How do I control the need?" The need for more, always more.

As though sensing my agitation, Bully raced toward me,

braying a sound like insane laughter. This time I couldn't manage a smile, and he stopped at the fence, gazed at me with his black eyes, and then turned and raced away again.

I sighed.

Cyrus tilted his head to consider me, eyes squinted against the sun. "How much do you know about what you are?"

"Umm, let's see . . . pretty much nothing."

"So you're a clean slate, huh?"

I laughed humorlessly. "Yep. Squeaky clean. That's me." My laughter died, and I turned to him. "Tell me everything."

His eyes slid from mine. "I can't. Rebekah . . . she said she wants to be the one to tell you, but not until the time is right."

"When will that be?"

He shrugged, still avoiding my eyes. "You may be able to do what we can do, Kenna, but you're not one of us yet. You can't expect us to tell you the secrets we've kept from the world, and then release you back to that same world."

"You don't trust me," I said, shoulders sagging.

"We don't know you is all."

I heaved another sigh. "Can't you tell me anything? Are there other people out in the world like me?" I asked. "Like us?"

"It's possible, but if there are they aren't from Eclipse. Your mom is the only person who ever left."

"Do you know why she left?"

He scratched his neck, beneath his hair. "She wanted to be a part of the world. Eclipse wasn't big enough for her, I guess."

"The world?" I said, thinking that didn't sound like my mom. It wasn't as if she'd run off to Los Angeles to become an actress. She'd bought a house tucked in the woods, as far from town proper as she could get. "Is that what you call"—I made a sweeping gesture—"everything that's not here?"

He nodded, coils of dark hair dangling in his eyes. "This valley is our world. Staying separate is the whole point. If regular people knew what we could do, can you imagine what would happen to us?"

I pictured glass prison cells. Experiments. People in white coats carrying syringes and clipboards. I shuddered.

"But it's more than that," Cyrus said. "I've lived in the regular world, and it just feels wrong. Unnatural. Everything is artificial—the light, the music, the food. Your air is poison. You said it yourself. Millions of people have this 'asthma' now, including you. Your words have lost their meaning because you all talk too much, so you can't even understand each other. When you look at the sky at night, you're missing most of the stars. You live in an endless march of technology. A relentless forward momentum of progress. But here at Eclipse, our air is clean. Our food is pure. Our needs are simple." His voice seemed to go a little flat as he added, "We're happy."

I considered what he was saying and nodded in understanding. I often felt like I'd been born in the wrong generation, that I would have fit more comfortably in the sixties or seventies, before the Internet and smartphones and gaming systems and tablets turned everyone into cyborgs waiting to happen. Maybe because I'd never really belonged, I found myself in the role of constant observer. I watched, removed, as the people I went to school with texted more than they spoke, learned code faster than they learned how to write with their own hands, turned away from their physical reality for one that didn't actually exist. An intangible world of zeroes and ones. There was a pay phone outside a gas station in Rushing, a relic from another age, and once when Blake had stopped there for gas I watched as a girl I knew from school tried in vain to figure out how it worked before finally knocking on my window and asking if she could use my cell because she'd lost hers. It made me sad because at first I'd scoffed at her, and then realized I probably didn't know how to use the pay phone either, and if I did, I didn't have a single phone number memorized to call anyone.

A sudden tremor racked my body, and I felt that internal pinch again, as if each of my organs had simultaneously experienced some kind of vicious spasm. The shuddering sound in my ears, like palpitating wings, ramped up to a low roar.

Cyrus, watching my expression, seemed to recognize instantly what was happening. He smacked his forehead with the heel of his hand. "What am I thinking, keeping you waiting while I ramble on? Come on, let's get you some anima."

I looked around. "Where are we going to get it?" I was thinking of the sheep's head jar containing that white cloud of anima, and all I saw out here were actual sheep. Dread pierced my heart like a cold needle until Cyrus held out his arms and turned in a circle, as though to encompass all we could see.

"Anywhere," he said. "Anything living is yours to take."

"I don't want to cull any animals," I blurted, shaking my head rapidly. "I won't do that. Ever."

"You don't have to," he said, a sly smile on his face. He bent and picked a wildflower with a crown of plum-colored petals. "Here."

He held the flower out to me. I took it and raised my eyes to Cyrus.

"What am I supposed to do with this?"

"Cull its anima."

"But it's just a flower."

"I'm not saying it's going to tide you over forever, but it'll be enough. Trust me."

He smiled.

And I did.

I trusted him.

Then, before I knew what was happening, I felt that unraveling sensation. Pale veins as thin as thread emerged from my fingers and connected to the wildflower. Its energy— its anima—entered me like a deep breath of clean air after being held underwater. The anima infused and swam through me, chasing away the catharsis symptoms like dust scattered by a broom, before settling in my brain, enhancing my senses. Every color became more vibrant. Secret hues and shades that I'd never known existed bloomed in the sky, a variegated wash of blues and violets and blushes and sun streaks. The smell of the flowers and the earth and even the animals nearby was intoxicating. The sun and breeze on my skin made me sigh contentedly, and the air that entered my lungs tasted like powdered sugar and summer nostalgia.

I breathed deep. Deeper. Deeper. My lungs had relaxed and my airways were more open than they'd ever been.

"Better?" Cyrus asked.

Grinning, I nodded dizzily.

"Well, all right, then," he said. "Time to meet the others."

KALYPTRA

WHEN WE REACHED THE DINING ROOM, I WAS STILL enjoying the wildflower anima floating through my veins and bathing my brain, making everything soft and hazy, and at the same time vibrant and alive and *more* in some fundamental way, like a layer of dullness had been stripped from the world, revealing the beauty beneath. I thought of those camera phone filters that turned the crappiest of photos into works of art. This was like that, only a thousand times better, and encompassing every dimension of my being. Sight. Touch. Hearing. Smell.

Oh, lordy, the scents in the air. The layers and complexity to every inhalation.

Inside Eclipse House, the smell of cooking food was so intense and heavenly I almost started to drool. I caught the scent of sugar and mint, baking bread and warm jam, butter and cream and tea, strawberries and peaches. My olfactory senses separated each smell and appreciated it individually before combining them in a mouthwatering medley. I wondered if this was what it was like to be a dog.

We entered the kitchen, and Stig, covered in flour up to his elbows, saluted us from the massive butcher's block, shouted an enthusiastic *"God morgen!"* and then returned to kneading a mass of bread dough. Joanna worked alongside him, cracking brown eggs into a bowl with precise flicks of her wrist, but when she saw me she hit the edge of the bowl too hard and the egg exploded in her hand. She scowled in my direction as she snatched up a towel and wiped away the yellow yolk dripping from her fingers. Beneath the sensory euphoria I was experiencing, I was dimly aware of a twinge of disquiet. Many of the Kalyptra seemed wary of my presence, but Joanna was downright hostile. What had I done to make her hate me so much?

The kitchen and dining hall were filled with people. When Cyrus and I entered everyone stopped what they were doing and stared at me in silence. I shrank under the weight of so many eyes, but a girl with a waist-length, volcanic eruption of lava-colored hair cut through the crowd toward us. She veered past me and planted a wet kiss on Cyrus's cheek with her cushiony lips.

"Where have you been all morning?" she asked, batting tawny eyelashes at him. She had curves that would have put a Victoria's Secret model to shame, and she flaunted them unabashedly in a low-cut dress with bell sleeves that looked to have been pieced together from several hundred scraps of mismatched fabric. Somehow the look worked on her, but I could never have pulled off so much color, so many different patterns and textures. I was a one-note kind of girl.

Cyrus jerked his head at me. "Rebekah asked me to keep an eye on our guest."

"I bet you enjoyed that." The girl narrowed her eyes first at Cyrus, then turned to me with her hands on her hips. "She's pretty. Scrawny, but pretty. We need to put some meat on your bones, Kenna. You're wasting away."

Even through the anima haze, I was coherent enough to be embarrassed at having my body assessed by someone who could have filled out Scarlett Johansson's dresses. My cheeks burned so hot they probably matched the girl's cinnamon hair.

"Cut it out, Illia," Cyrus said, a note of hostility in his normally cavalier voice. "You're making her uncomfortable."

Was I that obvious? "It's okay," I said. I didn't want to cause any trouble while I was here. The Kalyptra weren't used to visitors invading their space, and I wanted to be as inconspicuous as a shy ghost if I could manage it.

Illia was suddenly flustered. "I'm so sorry," she said to me. "Cyrus will tell you I say whatever it is I'm thinking, even if I should keep my mouth shut. Everyone here is used to me, but, well . . . it's been a long time since we had company."

"It's been never," Joanna put in snidely. She had finished cracking eggs, and now she leaned against the kitchen island with her arms folded, glaring at Illia with those small, oil-drop eyes. They were like snake's eyes, I realized. Black and beady. And dangerous.

Illia ignored her. "Welcome to Eclipse, granddaughter of Rebekah," she said, and then hugged me so tight I heard my ribs creak. But with the wildflower anima enhancing my senses, it felt good to have her body pressed so tight against mine. I found myself hugging her back, relishing the warmth radiating from her skin. Her smell—honey and ginger and lemons—filled my head like a fog. After seven years of keeping people at a distance, I realized how much I'd missed human touch, and this was human touch to the hundredth power.

"Don't worry," she said softly into my ear. "We accept you."

I almost melted into a puddle on the floor. I didn't know these were words I'd been waiting to hear. That I had *needed* to hear for so long. My mom had told me to hide what I was, and so I did, but every day had been a struggle. A white-knuckle grip of self-control. I was exhausted by restraint. I felt stretched thin enough to rip apart.

Or I had.

Now I felt full and buzzing and relaxed all at the same time.

I felt alive and I felt free.

Illia untangled herself from my arms and held me back. I could tell by the sympathetic smile on her face that she understood what was going on in my head.

"Since Rebekah isn't here yet, I'll make the introductions," Illia said, sliding her hand down to mine and squeezing it, which caused a rush of tingling pleasure to swim up my arm. Her touch felt so good I had to fight not to swoon. I wondered dreamily if this was merely the effect of the wildflower anima, or if maybe I had a thing for girls and never realized it until Illia pressed her chest to mine. I knew people around town speculated that my mom was a lesbian. She was beautiful in a scrubbed, unadorned sort of way, and men asked her out all the time, but she always said no.

The previous summer, I'd worked part-time in Mom's bakery after she had to fire an employee and didn't have time to hire someone else. I would have liked to work there more, but one of us had to be home with Erin to keep an eye on her, and since Mom had to make a living that responsibility fell to me. But during that summer at the bakery, I'd witnessed firsthand the way men looked at my mom, and the polite disinterest she showed toward them. It was like she didn't see them, even the good-looking ones, like they all had the same face, and she didn't need to look at it to know them.

"Why don't you date?" I had asked her at the end of my first day working in the bakery, during which I'd seen her hit on by three different men.

Her answer was a shrug and an unsatisfying, "I just don't."

"Well, don't you think our lives might be easier if we had a dad?"

She had sighed an extraordinarily long sigh. "In some ways, maybe. But then we'd have to let someone new into our lives. Someone who would want to know everything about us. I don't know if either of us wants that."

She was right. I never bothered her about dating again.

There were too many names and faces for me to remember when presented with them all at once, but some of the Kalyptra were unforgettable. There was soft-spoken Hitomi with her milk-pale, porcelain skin, who stood out from the rest of the sun-browned Kalyptra. In a sweet, girlish voice, she thanked me for coming, as though I'd been invited to tea, and then kissed me on both cheeks before introducing me to Rory, a tomboy with a smoky voice and a thick collection of dreadlocks that hung to her waist with little bells and stones and bits of feather woven into them. There was Sunday, who sported the most glorious thunderhead of an afro I'd ever seen, and whose laugh was so loud and raucous it infected everyone who heard it. Illia referred to her as "the artist."

"Of course, there is no shortage of artists at Eclipse," Illia said. "But everyone knows Sunday is the real prodigy among us. She did the paintings in the hallways, and all of our tattoos." Illia slipped her dress off one shoulder to reveal a small piece of a much larger tattoo of a moth wing.

"You did my mom's, too?" I asked Sunday.

She nodded, but didn't elaborate, and I got the impression the Kalyptra may have been instructed not to talk about my mom. Nearly everyone told me I was the spitting image of Rebekah. No one mentioned my mom. I wondered how much power Rebekah wielded over them. She definitely seemed like she was the one in charge, with her imperious tone and her expansive room with the balcony that looked out over the valley.

I was greeted next by Diego and Yuri, who argued loudly in Portuguese when speaking to each other, but lost their accents completely when talking to anyone else. Though dressed in jeans and cowboy boots, Diego, the older brother, had a dignified elegance about him, like he'd enjoyed a privileged life. He was the only male among the Kalyptra with his hair cut short. He bowed over my hand and kissed it. "Eclipse welcomes you, *bela*." Yuri, his hair a mop and his mouth in a perpetually wry smile, possessed none of his older brother's sophistication. He elbowed Diego aside and, as though in competition, gave an even more enthusiastic— but mocking—bow as he said, "It is an absolute pleasure to meet you, Kenna. You ever need anything, anything at all, I am your man."

Illia hooked an arm around my waist and whispered in my ear, "Don't be fooled by those two. They may flirt with you, but, well . . . let's just say you don't possess the equipment to play their game."

"You mean they're gay."

She blinked at me, taken off guard, and then gave me a distrustful look. "Is that a problem for you?"

"No. Why would it be?"

Illia put a hand to her forehead as though she'd experienced a wave of dizziness. "Things must have changed quite a bit since my day."

I wanted to ask her when that day might have been, but that seemed rude, like asking a woman's age. Illia looked twenty, but in her eyes she appeared much older than that.

She shook her head and waved at the air with one hand. "Regardless, there are plenty of other men here for you to choose from."

"Oh, no, I have a boyfriend back home. Sort of."

"Well, we live by a different set of rules when it comes to fidelity, and while you're here, you're one of us." She glanced at Cyrus. "Truthfully, if you're going to have a dalliance with anyone at Eclipse, it should be Cyrus." She reached up, took a lock of my hair, a lock of hers, and began to braid them loosely together. "He's a very good kisser."

I darted a look at Cyrus, who caught my eye and smiled questioningly, as though to ask, *Are you okay?*

Without losing a beat, Illia went on with the introductions, but I was so rattled I didn't remember a single name after that.

The Kalyptra must have been instructed by Rebekah to welcome me with open arms. Whereas when I'd first arrived I'd been treated with outright suspicion, now—with the exception of Joanna—they behaved as though I were their long lost sister. They hugged and kissed and fawned over me, but as the effects of the wildflower anima in me dwindled, their affection began to make me uncomfortable. I missed the intensity of my enhanced senses. I started to tense as I felt the pull of anima swirling inside each person who touched me, the craving to sip at it like a mosquito sucking blood. I wanted to go outside to cull another flower, but I wasn't sure how to ask to be excused without offending anyone, and I didn't want to seem like some kind of anima junkie, so I tamped down my craving and forced a smile.

Rebekah was the last to enter the dining hall. By that time everyone was seated and waiting for her, and a feast lay steaming on the table. Eggs flavored with recently picked herbs, topped with blistered tomatoes and mushrooms sautéed in butter. Fresh goat cheese and jugs of velvety milk. Baskets of apple and berry muffins. Crunchy bread full of seeds and nuts, with butter so rich and sweet it was almost like whipped cream. Berries drizzled with honey and sprinkled with mint. And several pots of tea that tasted like vanilla and lemon and almonds.

Rebekah made her appearance just as I was about to crack and start digging into the food with my bare hands. I hadn't eaten since the stale hospital Danish I'd picked at during my interview with Detective Speakman. I'd been so distracted by hunger for anima over the past twenty-four hours that I'd forgotten all about food.

My grandmother wore a long, white dress just transparent enough to show her lithe, long-limbed figure. Her hair was spooled on top of her head in a messy bun. She flicked a hand at us. "Eat, please. What are you waiting for?"

She poured herself a cup of tea while the rest of us filled our plates. Rebekah ate sparingly, her knees up under her, revealing bare feet and ringed toes. She sipped her tea, gazing at me as though she were casually observing a new animal that had been introduced to an established family in a cage at the zoo, wondering how I'd get along with the natives. But she didn't speak to me, or anyone for that matter. She merely watched us. I got the impression there were things she wanted to say to me, but not in front of the rest of the Kalyptra.

"Kenna, will you join our circle at the fire tonight?" Illia asked, spreading herbed butter on a thick slice of seed bread.

"Your circle?"

"Most nights we play music around the fire," Stig explained. "Did your mother teach you to—" His words cut off, and he glanced at Rebekah with an expression that reminded me of a dog afraid it had incurred the wrath of a strict master.

I looked from Stig to Rebekah. "I don't know," I said, ignoring the aborted question so as not to get Stig into trouble. "I don't have my guitar."

Stig waved his hand at that. "If there is one thing we have plenty of at Eclipse, it's guitars," Stig said. "I should know. I made most of them."

He pushed his chest out proudly when he saw my eyes pop with wonder. It was like he'd just told me he was responsible for erecting Stonehenge.

"You make guitars? Will you show me how?"

Stig grinned. "Of course."

"Do you write music, Kenna?" Rebekah asked.

I looked over to find my grandmother staring at me intently.

I nodded. "I don't know if I'm any good," I said, which wasn't exactly true. I knew I was good. I just didn't know what these people considered good.

"Your mother used to write songs," Rebekah said, sounding far away, lost in memory. She sipped at her tea. "We don't sing them anymore, but they were lovely. Sad, but lovely."

This news was nearly as much of a shock to me as it had been to discover I had a grandmother I never knew about. My mom had never told me she wrote music. She had never even alluded to the fact. There was so much she could have taught me, about music, about myself, but instead she had hoarded secrets, and asked me to do the same. But I remembered when I was very young, there was a song she used to sing to Erin and me to get us to go to sleep, a sort of lullaby.

Sweet girl, don't cry.
Sweet girl, I hear you sigh.
I'll never let you go,
But you still must dream alone.
Sweet girl, don't cry.
Sweet girl, I hear you sigh.
I'll be here when you wake,
So you won't be afraid
to dream alone.
To dream alone.

I'd thought it was a tune all parents knew and sang to their children, but now I wasn't so sure. Maybe that lullaby had been one of hers. It was certainly sad and lovely, as Rebekah said my mom's songs were. I wished she had told me who she was, or who she had been. I'd always known my mom was aloof, but I was coming to understand that it was more than that. She was a complete stranger.

I feel like I don't even know you. That was what I had said to her in the car, but I had immediately regretted my words. Now I was glad I had said them, gratified that she knew how I felt before she abandoned me. *I'll never let you go*, my ass.

"Maybe you could teach us some of your songs," Rebekah suggested.

I bit my lower lip, not sure I was ready to share my music again so soon. My performance at Folk Yeah! Fest seemed like it had happened to someone else.

"Then it's settled." Illia clapped her hands excitedly. "You'll come to the fire tonight and we'll learn some of your songs."

When breakfast was finished, most of the Kalyptra departed to work in the fields and orchards and gardens, while a few stayed to clean up after the meal. I started to help clear the dishes, though I was desperate to get outside again and sample more anima. But Rebekah had other ideas.

"Kenna, come to my study," she said, her tone leaving no room for argument. "I need to speak with you."

"Did I do something wrong?" I asked when we were alone in Rebekah's room. Maybe it was my perpetually guilty conscience doing my thinking for me, but it seemed like I had displeased Rebekah.

Instead of answering my question, she said, "Have a seat," indicating an arrangement of large pillows arcing in front of the fireplace.

I lowered myself awkwardly onto one of the pillows and

folded my legs, biting my lip to keep myself from rushing to apologize when I still didn't know how I had offended, or even if I had.

Rebekah took the pillow across from mine, lounging comfortably. After a pregnant silence that would have driven Blake crazy, Rebekah finally spoke.

"How do you feel today?"

"Fine," I said.

She smiled the kind of knowing smile that told me she could see right through me to the back of my brain, into the dark cellar where I stored my most appalling secrets. "Be honest."

I took a breath and sighed. Lying to Rebekah wasn't going to get me anywhere. She was too perceptive.

"When I woke up this morning the withdrawal symptoms or whatever you call them were back," I told Rebekah.

"Catharsis," she corrected, and nodded for me to continue.

"They weren't as bad as they were yesterday, but I knew they would get worse," I said. "Cyrus had me take anima out in the field, and after that I felt great again, but—"

"But once it wore off, the hunger returned."

I nodded, averting my eyes in shame. "I don't know how to control it."

"You can't."

I blinked at her, wondering if I'd heard her wrong. "But isn't that why I'm here? To learn how to control it?"

"That's what your mother would like," Rebekah said. "But the real reason you're here is because you can't cull another

Kalyptra. You're here because your mom doesn't want you to hurt her or your sister or anyone else. She understands how thorny your situation has become. It is one thing to experience catharsis after culling too much anima in too many forms, as you did. It is another to undergo catharsis after culling the most potent form of anima, which you also did."

I raised my eyebrows in question.

"Human anima," she clarified.

I swallowed hard. So my mom had told her what happened in the basement. Had she also told her about Jason Dunn?

Rebekah leveled her green eyes on me, her gaze intent and penetrating. I felt like she was peeling back layers of me using only her stare.

"Have *you* taken human anima?" I asked, looking down, unable to maintain eye contact any longer.

"Yes," Rebekah said without hesitation, and I was surprised to hear no trace of guilt in her voice, and equally surprised that I was relieved at her lack of obvious culpability. She didn't explain the circumstances that led to her taking human anima, and although I was desperate to know what had happened I didn't ask. I had never spoken of what I did to Jason Dunn, and I guessed Rebekah would prefer not to talk about her experience either.

"Unfortunately, the very nature of anima is addictive," Rebekah said, "and the more potent the sources of it that you take, the more your cravings will escalate. The amount of anima in a nonsentient living thing like a plant is minimal and wears off quickly. The amount in an insect or spider is

146

slightly more potent, and in a creature like a reptile or bird or mammal, more efficacious still, because those sorts of anima bring with them a trace of the vessel."

I shook my head, not sure I understood. "The vessel?"

"The container. In some cases, a body. But there are other things that can hold anima, if one knows how to capture it."

I glanced toward the cupboard from which Cyrus had taken the sheep's head jar. Rebekah saw where my eyes went and nodded.

"We call them culling jars," she said. "We use them to store anima."

I pictured the rows and rows of jars I'd glimpsed inside that cupboard, and I couldn't suppress a shudder of desire. I unconsciously licked my lips like a dog salivating at the sight of meat.

"What kind of anima?" I asked, hoping Rebekah couldn't detect the grasping neediness in my voice.

Rebekah cocked her head to study me a moment before answering. "Mostly animal," she said.

I swallowed hard, thinking of Jason Dunn killing Erin's cat, Clint Eastwood, and its entire litter. Then I thought of the animals that had perished in the circle of death surrounding my house, the chaotic furor of sensations and impulses that had poured into me and flowed through me into the bodies of my mom and Erin. That had saved their lives. Lastly, I thought of Bully, the rambunctious little goat I'd named earlier that morning.

"You kill the animals to take their anima?" I asked,

horrified, and beneath that horror, desirous in a way I could not ignore or suppress.

"Cull," Rebekah corrected. "We don't kill. We *cull*. We harvest. There is a difference."

"But if the animal dies—"

"Kenna." She spoke my name sharply, a reprimand, and I shut my mouth. The way my grandmother shifted from serene to commanding was going to take some getting used to.

"Do you eat meat?" she asked.

I shrugged. "Sure."

"So do we," Rebekah said. "The animals at Eclipse live good, happy lives, and when we need their meat we slaughter them humanely, and we preserve their anima in one of the culling jars so we can ration it over time and share it among the entire commune. The meat feeds our bodies, and the anima . . . well, it feeds everything else. Do you know what the word *Kalyptra* means?"

I shook my head.

"A Kalyptra is a veil. We call ourselves this because we know of the existence of a veil that obscures the divine world all around us, and we know how to lift that veil and see beyond it. Anima is *how*, Kenna. Anima heals our bodies and keeps us young, but more importantly it connects us to nature and expands our minds and our experience of the world in a way no one who is not Kalyptra can ever understand."

"Like a drug," I said.

"It is simply energy, but, yes, the experience can provide

a dreamlike experience and enhance your senses, similar to certain drugs. And, as I said, the ability to cull anima comes with the potential to become addicted if you take too much, or if you take anima that is too powerful for your mind and body to manage."

"What kind of anima did I take yesterday?" I asked, thinking of the tranquility that had washed over me, so heavy that it had carried me straight into sleep. "It was lamb, wasn't it?" I guessed before she could answer, remembering the shape of the jar.

Rebekah nodded. "We craft the jars accordingly."

"But how?" I asked. "How do you get anima into the jars, and why are they able to contain it? It seems like the anima would just . . . leak out."

She waved one long-fingered hand in a dismissive gesture. "It's not something I can explain. You have to experience the process for yourself in order to learn. I was taught by a *bruja* in Mexico how to make the jars." She smiled. "Perhaps someday I will teach you, too."

She sat up and crossed her arms on top of her knees. "As to how we transfer anima from one vessel to another, I believe you already know something about that."

I looked down at my hands, picturing those strange, white threads that emerged from them when I took anima. "I guess so."

"You have nothing to be ashamed of, Kenna. What we are is something to be celebrated, not repressed or despised.

Never be ashamed of who you are, sweet girl. You are Kalyptra. It doesn't matter that you were raised apart from us. We are what we are, regardless."

"Does that mean you still consider my mom Kalyptra?" I asked her.

Rebekah's eyes shifted past me, as though my mom had just entered the room and interrupted us. "No," she said finally. "She gave up her gift. She's lost to us."

My heart tripped over a few beats. "You can give up being Kalyptra? How?"

My grandmother turned her gaze back to mine, her eyes slightly narrowed, her mouth a flat, humorless line. For an instant she appeared decades older. Or perhaps it was just that her sudden bitterness wiped away her beauty.

"Why would you ask such a thing? Did I not just tell you that being Kalyptra is a glorious privilege?"

"I'm sorry." I immediately regretted my question. "I was just curious. I mean, I'm way more curious about how we became, you know, the way we are to begin with."

Rebekah schooled the venomous expression from her face, and once again she was the stunning woman I'd first laid eyes on yesterday.

"Of course you are, dear. Of course you are. There's so much you don't know about us. But we can't cover it all in one day. I wouldn't want to overwhelm you after the hell you've been through. What happened to your mother and sister . . . how horrible that must have been."

Tears seared the backs of my eyes, and I felt a hot pressure in my head like I was going to sneeze. My throat clamped down around my rising anguish, but it was no use.

I had lost my entire family. I had lost them because of something horrible I did.

I had brought them back, but that didn't change the reality of how they had died.

I broke then. Broke wide open, and all the tears I'd held back, all the sobs I had bottled, came bursting out.

"My poor, sweet girl," Rebekah said, and she came to me and wrapped me in her arms and held me for as long as I needed her to. At some point her hair loosened and fell from its bun on top of her head, and I felt a nostalgic rush of warmth for this woman I barely knew as her long, blond hair draped over my arms like a blanket of silk threads. It made me feel like a child again, the child I had been when my mom's hair was long like Rebekah's and I had hidden myself in it like I was hiding behind drapes while she sang me to sleep.

Sweet girl, don't cry.

I was a child again, and I wanted to be taken care of.

I wanted Rebekah to take care of me.

LISTEN CAREFULLY

I HAD ANTICIPATED I WOULD GET TO SPEND THE DAY WITH my grandmother, that maybe she would take me on a walking tour of Eclipse, during which we could cull another wildflower or two, or, even better, that we might sample from some of the jars in her cupboard. But when I had finished crying and pulled myself together, she rose from the pillows and held out her hand to help me up.

"Now, sweet girl, I have work to do, and I imagine you'd like to get yourself cleaned up. Cyrus can show you to the bathhouse and bring you whatever you need."

"Oh. Okay," I said, failing to hide my disappointment.

Rebekah touched my cheek, and as I had last night when she touched me, I felt a pleasant charge on my skin, like a little bit of her anima had transferred to me. I didn't know if that was possible, but that was what it felt like. She leaned forward and kissed me on the forehead. "We'll have plenty of time together. Don't worry about that."

I nodded and tried to smile as Rebekah led me to the door and guided me out. "I'll see you at dinner," she said, and started to close the door, then paused with a look that said she'd just remembered something. "Kenna, one thing . . . you met Joanna?"

I nodded, but didn't elaborate on what Joanna had told my mom, that we should leave and not come back.

"I would ask that you steer clear of her for now," Rebekah said. "Joanna and your mom have a complicated history, and I worry that she might take some old grievances out on you."

"I'll do my best," I told Rebekah. I didn't mention that I wondered if Rebekah might do the same thing.

"Promise me that you will."

"What?"

She stared at me with unblinking, expectant eyes. "Promise me that you will not talk to Joanna, even if she seems friendly."

"I—I promise," I said faintly.

"Good girl," she said before closing her door, making me feel a bit like a puppy that had just been left at home alone for the first time.

As I descended the stairs, I wondered what it was Rebekah was so busy doing alone in her room, while the rest of the Kalyptra worked in the fields and gardens, or tended to the livestock, or took care of the house. Maybe she saw her position as more managerial. Or royal. Regardless, the Kalyptra didn't seem to have a problem with the way things were done at Eclipse. They gave the appearance of perfect contentment and satisfaction with their lives. Joanna might be the exception to that, though. There was something different about her. She didn't possess the same blissful tranquility as the others. Or maybe it was just my presence that was disrupting her sense of well-being. I wished I knew more about what had happened between her and my mom, but now that I had promised Rebekah I would avoid her I couldn't exactly ask her to tell me all of my mom's old buried secrets.

So, of course she would be the first person I ran into when I got lost trying to find my way back to my room.

"There you are," she said when she saw me. "I've been looking for you."

She carried a guitar by its neck. Just looking at the instrument stole my breath. It was small and delicate, made from what I guessed was rosewood, and carved on the back was a design of moon phases and moths.

Joanna held the guitar out to me. "Here," she said. "It belonged to your mom."

"Really?" I accepted the guitar, cradling it against my chest and running my hands over the wood. This guitar was special, an instrument that might have a mind of its own. A voice it had earned from years of play. But I sensed it was a voice that had not been heard in a very long time.

"Rebekah wanted me to get rid of it after your mom left,"

Joanna said. "But I couldn't do it. Your mom loved that guitar more than . . . well, more than a lot of things."

I opened my mouth to ask her to tell me more about my
mom and how she'd been when she was Kalyptra, but then
I remembered my promise to Rebekah and I closed it again.

"Thanks," I said simply.

Joanna shrugged, as if it was no big deal, but I could tell
by the intensity in her expression that it was. "She would have
wanted you to have it. Your mom, not Rebekah."

I wondered if Rebekah would be angry if she found out I
had it, and even more angry if she found out who had given
it to me. I momentarily considered handing it back to Joanna,
telling her I couldn't take it. But who was I kidding? My
hand felt fused to the guitar. I couldn't give it back now if I
wanted to.

Joanna read my mind. "It would be best if you kept it in
your room. Don't bring it to the circle tonight. Don't let Rebekah know you have it. Stig has plenty of others you can
choose from." Her dark eyes darted left and right, as though
to make sure we were alone. "I suggest you play it right away,"
she said in a lowered voice. "And listen carefully to what it
has to tell you."

She brushed her hands over the front of her dress as
though to wipe away some invisible trace of dust, and walked
past me without a goodbye.

Eventually, I found my way back to my room, went inside,
and shut the door. I forgot all about taking a shower, and even
my hunger for anima was pushed to the back of my mind as

I sat down on my bed with the guitar perched delicately in my hands.

I strummed the song I'd played at Folk Yeah! Fest. It seemed like a thousand years had passed since I'd stood on that stage and played my song in front of all those strangers. The festival organizers had said they'd let the contest participants know within a week who had won. Did it even matter anymore if I ended up the winner? After the festival, I'd entertained a few brief hours of optimism that my life might be headed in the right direction, but now everything had changed.

The notes of my song twanged sweet and buzzy, and I felt their vibration in the air, across my cheeks, and in my fingertips. But there was something a little discordant about the sound, a subtle wrongness. I remembered what Joanna had said about listening carefully to the guitar's voice, and I tuned it several times, trying to get the sound perfect, but the slight flaw remained. Still, it was an imperfection I could live with. *True beauty is in the imperfections*, as my mom liked to say.

I played through my song once from beginning to end, and then stopped, pressed my palm over the strings to quiet them, and closed my eyes.

The song I played at Folk Yeah! Fest was the song I'd been playing when Blake saw me the first time after moving to Rushing, before he ever knocked on our door and brought us a plate of his famous oatmeal raisin surprise cookies. I'd taken my guitar into the woods behind our house to practice. There was something divine, almost holy about the bare-bones resonance of an acoustic guitar surrounded by forest and running water. I'd had no idea I wasn't alone that day, not until a month later when Blake admitted that he'd been spying on me. He said he would have come to talk to me then, but he didn't want to interrupt, didn't want me to stop playing.

It occurred to me that the woods where Blake had stood when he first heard me play were the same woods I had destroyed. So much of my old life was gone now, or felt like it was fading, like a dream after waking. I missed Blake terribly. The longing to see him was so deep it made it hard to breathe, like he was a kind of medicine, same as my asthma inhaler or the anima that had eased my lungs that morning. But at the same time I was glad to be away from him, from my mom, and even from Erin. I didn't want them to see me the way I was now. I'd read once that you were only truly yourself when you were alone in the woods with no one watching. I wasn't alone at Eclipse, but I felt, for the first time in a long time, like I was closer to my true self here.

I didn't mean to, but I spent the rest of the day holed up in my room, playing quietly. I remembered the tune of the lullaby my mom used to sing to Erin and me, and I played that and expanded on it, giving it my own spin, adding to the lyrics until the lullaby became a full song. I missed lunch. I missed dinner. Suddenly I looked up and realized the sun had set and the sky was the color of blueberries sprinkled with sugar.

My fingers ached. I held them up in front of my face and saw deep, red grooves in the skin from making chords. I bit my lip and groaned. This was not the first time I had gone into a kind of dissociated state while playing guitar. When I was in the zone, everything else faded into the background. But now that I'd come back to reality, I was fully aware of the empty hunger in me, the beginnings of cramps in my muscles, and a feverish chill across my skin.

A knock on the door startled me and I shot to my feet, scanning the room wildly for a place to hide the guitar. I lifted the mattress and quilts and stowed it beneath, then arranged my pillows and blankets into a haphazard mess so the shape wasn't noticeable. Hopefully whoever had come to call on me would simply assume I was a slob.

When I opened the door, I found Cyrus outside, arms crossed tightly over his chest and a glower on his face.

"Where have you been?"

"Here," I said.

His eyes narrowed and he scrutinized my face as though suspicious that I might be lying. "You've been in your room all day? Doing what?"

"Thinking." I shrugged, and raised my eyebrows at him. "Why did you look for me everywhere but in my room?"

"Because . . ." He trailed off and shook his head. "I don't know. I just thought you might've gone off on your own. You have to be careful. It isn't safe to go into the woods alone. There are coyotes, wolves even."

"Oh, I get it. You thought I tried to escape." I was kidding, but then I saw Cyrus avert his eyes. "You did, didn't you?" I said.

"The thought crossed my mind."

"Why would I want to run away?" I asked, leaning against the doorjamb. "What aren't you telling me?"

"Oh, there's plenty you don't know about us yet," he said, relaxing and cocking a wolfish smile. "So come with me and I'll teach you a thing or two."

I hesitated in the doorway. The hunger inside me for more anima was insistent, but not yet an emergency. What did seem like an urgent situation was the fact that I could smell my own body, and I had to pee.

"Mind if I get cleaned up and change first?" I asked.

Cyrus grinned. "I thought you'd never ask."

Heat sizzled on the back of my neck. "That bad, huh?"

"Let's just say I've been trying not to breathe through my nose when I'm with you."

"All right, all right. You don't have to look so amused." I tried to curve past him, giving him a wide berth, but he hooked an arm around my waist and whirled me back. I found myself in a sort of half embrace with my face only inches from his. The fever on my skin moved to my stomach, and the ravenous hunger in me woke up like a startled bear, roaring to life.

"Let me go," I said, trying to pry myself from Cyrus's grip. He held on, planting his hands on my hips. "What are you doing? Let me go!"

I started to panic as I felt myself begin to unravel and reach for him.

"Hold back, Kenna," he said, his voice calm and serious.

"You can't hurt me, but that's no reason to let yourself lose control. Don't let your appetite rule you."

I tried. I did. I held on, and just when I thought I couldn't stand it any longer, when I felt like I would burst apart at the seams, Cyrus let me go.

I was breathing heavily, my heart rioting in my chest.

"See?" he said, giving me a nod of approval. "You're learning already."

I rounded on him. "Don't ever do that again."

I grabbed clean clothes from the pile in my room and stormed past him, not looking to see if he followed, but knowing that he did.

Moonflower
and Moth

After showering in the thankfully non-coed bath-house and changing into clean clothes, I joined Cyrus on the front porch, where he was sitting in a wooden rocking chair, watching moths bat themselves against the lanterns that hung along the covered porch. I was still irritated with him for the little "lesson" he'd sprung on me earlier.

The porch spanned the length of Eclipse House, long enough for two picnic-style tables, a dozen rocking chairs, and a swinging bench. Patchwork quilts waited on many of the chairs, like anxious pets anticipating their owners' return, and lanterns hung on tiny hooks every few feet along the porch. Moths with moon-colored wings gathered around the light, hovering tentatively before knocking themselves against the glass. I thought of the bug zapper my mom put outside during the summer to keep the insects from overwhelming us. Most of the insects, when they flew into the humming bulb, elicited tiny bursts of electricity as they died, but whenever a moth found its way to the buzzing light the sound of its demise went on and on. Moths didn't die quickly or easily. They kept on fighting to get at the light, even as the life was seared from them.

I'd never been a fan of moths, maybe because I felt a certain empathy for them with their obsessive natures, their disposition to destroy themselves to get at the thing they craved.

I didn't sit down in the chair next to Cyrus, but went to the porch railing and leaned against it, my back to Cyrus.

"Where is everyone?" I asked. The yard and fields were empty of Kalyptra.

"Dinner," he said.

I revolved to face him. "That wasn't cool, what you did."

He nodded acceptance. "I see that now."

"I know I can't hurt you, but it feels like I can, and I don't want that. I don't *want* to want to take your life. So from now on can you just warn me when you're about to, you know . . . touch me or get close to me or whatever?"

"I can do that." He stood up and took a step toward me. "How close is too close?" he asked. Even from a couple of feet away, I could sense the anima murmuring its siren song from the other side of his skin.

My body felt flushed, like I'd been standing in the sun too long and was close to heatstroke. My stomach fluttered with either giddiness or anxiety, I wasn't sure which.

"You could probably get closer than that," I said, and swallowed. "But not much."

He took another half step toward me, and my heartbeat pounded until I could feel it all through my body. "That's far enough," I said.

Cyrus nodded and moved back. "Good to know," he said, and then turned and started down the porch steps. When I didn't immediately follow, he paused and glanced back at me. "What's the matter? You don't trust me anymore?"

"I never said I *did* trust you."

"Ah. Well, Rebekah trusts you with me, so how about it?" He held out his hand as though for me to place mine in his, but then curled his fingers. "Follow me."

As Cyrus led me around the side of the house, I wondered what the deal was between him and Rebekah. There was a closeness and intimacy between them that I didn't sense between Rebekah and any of the other Kalyptra, almost like a mother-son relationship.

"Are you and Rebekah related?" I blurted out, and then felt my cheeks go hot.

Cyrus glanced over at me, brows drawn together. "Why do you ask?"

"Answer the question," I insisted, growing impatient and nervous for reasons I didn't want to admit, even to myself.

His mouth quirked as he read something in my eyes that seemed to amuse him. "She's my mother," he said.

My stomach dropped, and so did my jaw. That would make Cyrus my—

"At least, that's how I think of her," Cyrus continued. His eyes darkened momentarily, like he was recalling an unpleasant memory. "My own mother wasn't the kind any kid hopes for."

I sighed, relieved, and nodded. "I get that," I said.

He studied me, curious. "Anya wasn't a good mother? I find that hard to believe."

"In some ways she was." I shrugged. "In others, not so much."

We came to a halt in front of a leafy vine that climbed the outer wall. Large white flowers in the shape of trumpets bloomed on the vine. I could smell their sugary sweet fragrance from a few feet away.

"This is our climbing moonflower," Cyrus told me. "It's night-blooming, which means its petals unfurl after dark to emit its fragrance. During the day their leaves absorb sunlight, and in the dark their fragrance attracts moths that feed on the nectar and pollen."

Cyrus reached up and plucked a moonflower the size of my fist from the vine and held it out to me. I accepted it and breathed in its scent until I felt dizzy.

"You don't want to take straight from the vine, or you'll end up culling the entire plant. Touching the source of the anima you're trying to cull directs the flow. Culling wildly from multiple sources is dangerous because you risk taking too much, and the more anima you take, the more you'll want. Until you learn how to control your vena, you should always touch the thing you want to cull. *Always*," he said again for emphasis.

"Vena?" I said, shaking my head.

164

"That's what we call them, the threads that emerge when you're going to take anima," he said. "*Vena* means veins in Latin, only these are more like extensions of your own anima."

"Vena," I repeated, spinning the moonflower between my thumb and forefinger like an inverted parasol. Then I closed my fist around it, crushing its satiny petals and releasing a pungent waft of its scent, and at the same moment, without thinking, I opened myself to the moonflower's energy. A dim glow flickered inside my palm. My skin tingled as my "vena" emerged and attached to the flower. A tiny amount of anima trickled into me, and then stopped. In my hand, the flower wilted, and its sugary scent vanished from the air.

The flower's anima didn't fill me, but it narrowed the emptiness inside and made my head go swimmy and my skin come alive. I swayed on my feet as the anima concentrated in my vision. The land took on a surreal quality, more like a painting than real life. Moonlight seemed to hover over the ground like fog. The sky was the color of crushed blackberries, the stars bursting huge and white like popcorn.

Moths began to flutter toward me, alighting on my clothes. One landed on my cheek and I felt its feathery antenna brush my skin.

"It must think I'm a moonflower," I said to Cyrus.

Cyrus reached out tentatively, his eyes asking permission before he touched me. His strong, warm fingers wrapped around my wrist and he raised it toward his mouth. I tensed, thinking of Blake, of how he would feel if he saw another guy touching me. He wasn't a jealous type that I knew of, but then I'd never given him any reason to be jealous. I wasn't even sure if what was happening at that moment was cause for jealousy. But this worry was fleeting. It evaporated and was replaced by serenity. Anima left no room for anxious thoughts.

Cyrus inhaled. "You do smell like the moonflower."

I felt an easy smile play on my mouth. "Can I have another?" I asked.

Cyrus plucked a new blossom from the vine and handed it to me. I promptly culled its anima, and felt the energy sink into the cracks inside me. I tilted my head back and spread my arms out wide, gazing up at the expanse of stars, blinking at their brightness. The sky seemed to revolve slowly. Or maybe it was the earth. The ground beneath my feet throbbed. I could feel the world inhaling and exhaling. It had its own slow, steady heartbeat. And its breath was everywhere. The universe gathered around me, stardust falling on me like lazy snow.

This was the world behind the veil, I thought. This was the world that no one but the Kalyptra got to experience.

Another handful of moths touched down on my hair, my forehead, their fuzzy legs scratching softly at my skin, their curled proboscises licking at my pores. That's what the vena looked like, I thought. Like the proboscises of these moths, curling and searching.

"One more," I said, laughing. "One more flower."

Cyrus picked another moonflower and handed it to me, and I culled it, too.

My head rolled on my shoulders, and I had to fight the urge to let myself fall backward as though a cloud would catch me. Auroras of emerald and sapphire light whirled languidly above me. I wanted to go on feeling this way forever, drawing down galaxies and heavenly bodies and swimming in the turmoil of color and fire.

Moths surrounded me like I was made of light. I reached for one of them, feeling the vena come loose and search for the moth.

"Kenna, no!" Cyrus's voice was like a whip crack and startled me even through the anima haze.

I yanked my hand back. "What did I do?"

He was shaking his head roughly, a look of alarm on his face. "I'm sorry, it's my fault. I forgot to tell you that we don't take moth anima. It's forbidden."

"Why?" I asked, my brow furrowing until I remembered what my mom said about moths having some kind of spiritual symbolism to the Kalyptra.

"Did Rebekah tell you how certain types of anima are tainted by their vessels, that they carry properties of it?"

I nodded, and then shook my head. "She did, but I'm not sure I understand."

"If you cull the anima of a squirrel, you'll be filled with energy. The anima of a bear, you'll feel mighty and powerful. If you were to cull the anima of a wolf, you would have the urge to run and hunt. The lamb's anima Rebekah gave you when you first arrived made you peaceful. But if you take moth anima, you become a slave to your impulse, and your only imperative will be to seek light at any cost. If there is a light on the other side of a glass window, you will smash your hand through it to reach it. If there is a fire, you will walk straight into it."

"Why is it so strong?" I asked. "Rebekah said insect anima isn't that potent."

He hesitated. "Because we're not meant to cull moth anima, so we would be punished for the transgression. Moths are our kin, in a sense. To take the anima of a moth would be . . . well, a kind of sacrilege. Just remember . . . no moth anima. Not ever."

Moths are our kin? We would be punished for our transgression? To take the anima of a moth would be a kind of sacrilege?

I wasn't sure if these statements were as odd as they sounded, or if it was the anima twisting through my brain that made them sound so . . . archaic. So eerie and unsettling, bringing to mind religious zealots and cult leaders dressed all in white.

I wondered if Cyrus knew that I had culled thousands, possibly tens of thousands of moths the night my family was murdered. But that was before I knew better.

"Okay," I said. "No moth anima. I promise."

MODERATION

EVERYTHING IN MODERATION. THAT WAS MY MOM'S favorite maxim. Or maybe it was the one she quoted most often to me because, well, I'm not a moderation kind of girl. Not when it comes to the things I love. Then I'm all about extremes. I don't have a medium switch. If I'm going to eat my favorite dessert, I'm not going to have a few dainty bites. I'm going to scarf the whole cake. If I'm going to play music, it's going to be my life. If I'm going to get angry enough to hurt someone, well . . . they'll probably end up more than hurt.

Blake called this black-and-white thinking. It was all or nothing with me.

I'd spent the years since I killed Jason Dunn in a state of constant restraint. I'd tried to maintain an interest in school even though the only thing I wanted to do was spend my days in the woods with my guitar and a notebook. I'd tried never to get close to anyone, never to touch anyone, for fear I would lose control. I had kept my feelings for Blake locked in the cellar in my mind. I had tried to be the good daughter. A middle-of-the-road, temperate, normal girl. I'd done my best to be easy, to balance out the stress of Erin's health problems.

After Jason, I had tried never to take anima again. Now I had to take it every day to keep from losing myself to catharsis.

Where had these years of attempted moderation gotten me?

Right back where I started. Always wanting more.

The morning after I culled the moonflowers, I woke to find my anima haze had evanesced, leaving behind one overriding thought that eclipsed every other: *more*.

The hunger for anima wasn't as all-consuming as it had been in the days after I culled Jason Dunn, or in the hours after I'd culled everything within a hundred foot radius of my house. This hunger was more of a low, background murmur in my head, in my blood, in my fingertips. But it was harder than ever to deny, because now I knew there was so much anima to be had in the world, and culling it did not require hurting anyone.

I could take and take and take a little at a time and there would always be more.

I wanted to start right away. I practically leaped out of bed, stopping only long enough to brush my teeth and change into a soft linen tunic and a pair of jeans covered in holes and patches. There was no mirror in my room, but I didn't really care about my appearance. I had more important things on my mind.

After breakfast, the Kalyptra went to work, while Cyrus and I decamped to the fields. By afternoon, I had culled a dozen different varieties of plant, and their combined anima mingled inside me, making me feel at once like I was rising toward the sun and rooted to the ground, immobile and connected to the earth beneath me like I'd grown roots. It was a strange sensation, and I wanted it to go on and on, but the high never lasted long, and each time it wore off I was left craving more. Not only more anima, but more potent forms of it.

I didn't admit that to Cyrus. I told myself I would get used to it. I'd just started taking anima regularly, so the novelty of it was sure to wear off at some point. I could stick to plants and maybe a few insects, despite the fact that there were thousands upon thousands more types of anima to try. Despite the way my mind kept returning to those jars locked away in Rebekah's cupboard. My natural tendency, which I had denied for so long, was to indulge with abandon, but I could maintain control. Eventually, it would get easier to abstain from anima. It had to.

In the wildflower field, Cyrus culled a variety of plants with me, and for the first time I experienced what it was like to be blissed-out on anima with another person who was feeling the same things I was feeling. With Cyrus also on anima, the connection I felt with everything around me extended to him. I detected his heartbeat through the ground.

I could see every gradation of color in his eyes. I could smell the oatmeal-and-honey soap he'd used to wash his hair. His face was that of a glorious god against a backdrop of sky as radiantly colored as the blanket of flowers that surrounded us.

Cyrus culled a wild poppy and its sanguine petals turned black and crumbled to dust. He flopped back on the picnic blanket he'd brought to the field and covered his eyes to shield them from the sun.

I stayed sitting up so I could gaze at the wonder surrounding us, the colors so vibrant they almost burned my eyes. The air so soft, so scented, it seemed tangible, as though I could run my fingers through it like water. My skin throbbed with pleasure as it drank in the sun's heat.

I got up and walked toward the animal enclosure, where I could see Bully rampaging on the other side of the fence. I stuck my hand through the posts and called to him, and he charged toward me with such reckless abandon that I thought he would ram the fence. But he stopped inches from my hand and shoved his head against my palm.

"Hey, Bully the Kid," I murmured to him, scratching at his coarse fur. "How's my little wild man? Are you getting into plenty of trouble?"

Bully made a contented, babyish cry in response and rubbed his head harder against my hand. With my senses enhanced, I would have thought his animal smell would be too much, but his scent, when magnified, was earthy and green, like lawn clippings and good soil. I inhaled him, digging my fingers through his fur. Lost in sensation, I didn't notice when that unraveling feeling began, but when I saw a glow ignite around my hand I yanked it back, startled and horrified. Bully, equally startled, darted away from me, bleating in disappointment that his petting session had cut off so abruptly.

"What is it?" Cyrus asked behind me.

Panting, heart racing, I turned to him. "I almost culled him."

"Who?"

"Bully. My goat."

Cyrus made a face. "Who said he was *your* goat?"

"I named him," I said. "He's my responsibility now, and I almost . . ." I covered my mouth with a hand. "I thought if I had enough anima in me, if I wasn't feeling withdrawal, then I'd be under control."

Cyrus shook his shaggy, glossy hair. "It'll take longer than a day to get a handle on what you can do."

"How long?"

His expression was blank, confused, as if I'd asked him something so obvious he was having a hard time coming up with an answer. "Forever," he said, and lowered his eyes, as though he didn't want to look at me when he said what came next. "What you did to save your family, the amount of anima you culled, that's more than any of us has ever attempted to take at one time. Even Rebekah. Have you ever eaten a meal so big it made you sick, but then an hour later you're hungry again?"

"Yeah, every Thanksgiving. But won't I eventually go back

to normal? I mean, I'm not eating huge meals anymore, or meals period. I'm, like, sampling. I'm tasting."

Cyrus held his hands up in a helpless gesture. "It might get easier, Kenna, but you're always going to be hungry. You're always going to want more."

I returned to the blanket and flopped down on my stomach. Cyrus followed and sat beside me, close but not too close.

"You okay?" he asked after a long, empty silence.

I shrugged, not looking at him. "How am I ever supposed to go back to my real life?" I asked.

"Are you sure you want to go back?"

Now I did look at him, blinking in surprise. "Of course I want to go back."

"Why?" He sounded truly baffled as to why I would ever want to leave Eclipse.

"My whole life is there," I said, growing agitated. "My family. My twin. Do you know what it's like to be separated from your twin?"

"No," he said. "I had two brothers and I couldn't wait to get away from them. Rebekah had a twin though," he added as an afterthought, as though he'd just remembered.

"Really?"

"Yeah. Long time ago."

"Where is she now?"

Cyrus's eyes darkened, and he glanced back toward Eclipse House. "She died. Not sure Rebekah would want me to tell you about that, though. Might be best if you didn't mention

I said anything." The side of his mouth curled up and he changed the subject. "You didn't mention your boyfriend."

"What?"

"The guy you said was waiting for you back on the other side of the mountain."

"Oh. Yeah." I bit my lip, feeling vaguely guilty beneath the cloak of anima. I wasn't sure why I hadn't mentioned Blake, or why I didn't want to talk about him with Cyrus now. He just felt so far away. Barely two days had passed since I'd said goodbye to Blake, and already it seemed as though I hadn't seen him in a month. I recalled the dream I'd had my first night at Eclipse, about the rising river dividing Blake and me. His side of the river had been so bleak, and mine so lush and alive.

"Do you miss him?" Cyrus asked. "Is he a reason not to stay here?"

I picked a blade of grass, then watched a thin filament of energy extend from me and attach to it. In my hand, the blade of grass went limp, and the air around me took on a shimmering quality, like it was filled with tiny, crystalline insects. The flowers in the field went electric with color, and the sky began to undulate like a vast ocean. The clouds appeared to breathe, expanding and morphing into nebulous shapes.

"You didn't answer my question," Cyrus said, raising an eyebrow.

"I know."

If I went home—*when* I went home—I would still need

to take anima, the same as I did here, but it would not be the same as it was here. I would be surrounded by dead, gray forest, not living green and gold and every other color of the rainbow. In my house, I would be haunted by memories of blood and pain and sickness and sadness. And I would be alone. There would be no other Kalyptra to guide me, or cull with me, or understand me.

But the anima of that blade of grass wound through me, and made it hard to care about the future when everywhere I looked the veil of mundane that concealed the real world had dropped, revealing the divine world hidden beneath. Like earth was actually heaven, but no one could see it unless they drank the magic elixir.

I lay on my back and stared up at the morphing, rippling ocean of sky.

"Two brothers, huh?" I said to Cyrus, changing the subject.

"Yep."

"Do you ever see them?"

"Nope."

"Do you want to?"

"Nope."

I rolled onto my side and propped myself up on my elbow. Cyrus mimicked my posture, so we were face-to-face. Looking at him made it hard to breathe. He was as mesmerizing as the evolving sky. I could have sat there for hours, interpreting his features like a work of art, a priceless sculpture.

"How long have you lived here?" I asked.

"A long time."

"How many years?"

"Lost count."

"How old are you?"

"Can't remember."

"Who were you before you came to Eclipse?"

He smiled, but his eyes darkened and shifted sideways. "Someone who doesn't exist anymore."

Days passed in a blur. Time meant something different at Eclipse. No one checked a calendar. No one bothered naming the days of the week. A Monday might as well be a Saturday might as well be a Wednesday. It made no difference. All that really mattered was the season, and we were in the best one: the pinnacle of summer. Every day started crisp and ended golden warm. The nights were clear, and I spent them around the fire with the Kalyptra, playing music late into the night, filled with anima so my fingers never tired.

I stopped thinking about the past or the future, only dwelled in the present moment. Impulse and sensation were all that mattered. Ego didn't exist, because *I* didn't exist, not as a single being with a single consciousness. I was part of something far larger than myself, connected to a vast network of energy that existed all around me.

Most days, after culling anima with Cyrus, I joined the Kalyptra and worked alongside them, learning skills I never would have thought to acquire at home, and probably never would have used because everything I'd ever needed was available in a store, or was just a phone call or a car ride away. Yuri introduced me to carpentry, and I found a strange kind of satisfaction in working with tools and wood. Hitomi taught me how to recognize and treat sick plants, how to judge the perfect time to pick a tomato or a cucumber from the vine, how to taste grapes and decide when their sweetness and acidity levels were prime for winemaking. Diego educated me in the care and feeding of livestock, and Rory gave me lessons in making wine and beer, in pickling vegetables and preserving fruit and meat, and in making cheese. I disappeared into Stig's workshop for an entire day, and when I came out I had a brand-new guitar, one handcrafted by Stig, although he let me help him when I could. When I was alone in my room, I played my mom's guitar, even though it still didn't sound quite right. But I brought my new guitar to the circle that gathered around the fire at night.

Flame-haired Illia tried to teach me to sew, but it turned out I had no appetite for needlework. So instead I hung out with her while she worked, the two of us chatting easily about everything and nothing.

It was Illia who designed and made all the beautiful dresses and caftans and intricate tunics the Kalyptra donned in the evening, after the day's work was through. The walls of Illia's studio on the second floor of Eclipse House were lined with colorful fabric swatches, bolts of lace, cabinets filled with buttons and thread and ribbons.

"Where do you get all this?" I asked her while I clumsily helped with mending. "You can't make it here."

"No, no. Once a year, Rebekah allows me to make a run into town with Cyrus so I can buy what I need."

"Do you hate it out there as much as Rebekah and Cyrus do?" I asked, expecting a tirade against the world like the one Cyrus had laid on me my second day at Eclipse.

She frowned, her eyebrows knitting together in concentration. "I don't think I ever hated the world, but I didn't like who I was when I was in it. I didn't like what I had to do to survive. I was . . ." Her cheeks went pink and she lowered her eyes. "Let's just say I did some things I'm not proud of. I made terrible mistakes, the kind that make it hard to look at yourself in the mirror every day. But I've put all of that behind me now. That was another life. Another me."

I felt a rush of warmth for Illia, so strong it brought tears to my eyes. I understood her, and I felt like she understood me. Aside from Erin, I'd never had any close girlfriends, and I wasn't sure being friends with your twin counted. This was one more element, one more key to happiness that I'd been missing.

Illia cupped my chin and raised my face. I didn't resist her touch. At Eclipse, I was a different person. A person who didn't have to keep other people at a distance because I was afraid of what I might do to them.

"You like it here, don't you?" she asked.

"I more than like it."

She smiled her broad, mischievous smile. "And what about you? Do you like yourself when you're here?"

I opened my mouth to answer, and then closed it again, afraid to hear myself say the words that were in my head: *I hated myself at home, but I don't hate myself here.*

"There's a saying," I told her. "'Wherever you go, there you are.' I guess that means you can't escape yourself, you just drag all your baggage around to every new place."

Illia's smile began to fade.

"But the thing is," I said, shaking my head in consternation, "every day I'm here, I feel lighter, like I'm getting rid of the baggage one piece at a time."

"Soon you'll be light as a feather," Illia said, and held up against my face a length of mint green fabric almost the same color as my eyes. "This is perfect. I'm going to make you a dress you'll never want to take off. Until you meet the right guy, of course." She winked and gave a bawdy laugh that made me blush.

"Oh, I don't wear a lot of green," I said.

"Then you're making a mistake. With that hair and those eyes, you should be wearing greens and blues and lavenders. Maybe orange? But color, always color."

"What about gray?"

She laughed and began cutting the fabric. "Gray isn't anyone's color, silly."

* * *

The Kalyptra sang while they worked, songs I'd never heard because their music had been born at Eclipse and had never left. I listened carefully when I was with them, memorizing the lyrics and practicing the melodies on my mother's guitar when I was alone in my room. But every time they asked me to teach them one of the songs I had written, I balked, worried they wouldn't fall in love with my music the way I'd fallen in love with theirs. Afraid my lyrics would tell them too much about who I was outside of Eclipse and remind them that I was a stranger in a strange land, not one of them.

I played guitar, and sometimes took up one of the drums or tambourines, or just clapped and stomped my feet to create a rhythm, but I didn't dare to sing with the Kalyptra, whose voices were always harmonious. I didn't want to disrupt that harmony. I was content simply to be a part of the music, jam sessions that sometimes went on for hours without pause, fueled by the anima that turned every sound to syrup and heartthrob, melodies evolving as we played, veering from energetic to languid and back again.

After these sessions, we were usually too elated to sleep, so we retired to the yurt—what the Kalyptra referred to as the "dreaming tent"—to lounge and talk and take anima. We let the night lead us where it would. Although Rebekah often attended the nightly musical assemblies, she always excused herself to bed instead of accompanying us to the dreaming tent. I began to get the impression that she felt separate from the rest of the Kalyptra, like a parent to all of them, never able to be their friend for fear of losing their respect or giving up some of her authority. The Kalyptra, in turn, were eternal children with their enthusiasm and playfulness.

Joanna was the exception, always hanging back from the rest of the Kalyptra, always with a sour expression on her face and cool reserve in her dark eyes. As I had promised Rebekah, I steered clear of Joanna as much as possible, which wasn't difficult because Joanna hadn't approached me since the day she'd given me my mom's guitar. Still, I got the impression she was watching me, waiting for something, although I had no idea what that might be.

I basked in Rebekah's company when she was with us, but I didn't mind that she abstained from nights in the dreaming tent. Her presence might have altered the bacchanalian group dynamic, made it more formal. Everyone would be on their best behavior.

Sometimes after our jam sessions there was dancing, or late-night feasts of fresh breads and cheeses and fruit and honey. Some nights Sunday, the artist, painted temporary tattoos on our arms and shoulders and backs. She preferred to paint on me because I was a blank canvas, not a single tat to my name. She offered to give me permanent ink, and I almost said yes, but then I thought of what Blake would say. Blake loved art, but was not a fan of tattoos. Erin, too, had strong opinions against them. Still, I told her I would think about it.

There were nights when the Kalyptra began to partner off into couples, and I would slip away and return to my room, blushing furiously and missing Blake, wishing I could walk over to his house like I used to and knock on his window, lure him out for a walk in the woods. I replayed the memory of our kiss over and over like a favorite song, the kind that never gets old.

In her sewing studio one day, I asked Illia the question that had been nagging at me. "Why aren't there any kids at Eclipse? I mean, you guys have plenty of sex. Do you make your own condoms here or something?"

Illia, threading a needle, jerked and accidentally poked herself, drawing a bright bead of blood. She sucked at it and cocked her head to study me, seeming bewildered by my question.

"We can't have children," she said. "Not with each other, anyway."

"Why not?"

She hesitated, and I wondered if this was a subject she and the others had been instructed not to get into with me. There seemed to be a lot of those subjects, deemed off limits by Rebekah. No matter how many times I questioned the Kalyptra about the origin of our power, I never got a straight answer.

"Kalyptra can only have children with normal people because our power is passed down to the child. Our power is what makes us Kalyptra. None of us is willing to give that up, even for a child." She lowered her eyes, as though she didn't want to witness my reaction. "Except for your mother. Her power passed to you."

My mouth dropped open, and for several seconds my mind went completely blank as I absorbed what she was telling me.

"My mom lost the ability to cull because of me?" I said after a moment of silence.

Illia raised her eyes tentatively and nodded. "I'm sorry. I shouldn't have been the one to tell you."

"No," I said, my voice cold and my shoulders trembling with quiet rage. "My mom should have been the one. She should have been the one to do a lot of things."

MIDNIGHT GLORY

THERE WAS A GAME THE KALYPTRA LIKED TO PLAY. A game they'd invented that was similar to Truth or Dare.

The game was called Dominus, and it worked like this: we rolled a set of homemade dice to decide who was the Dominus. The Dominus was basically the master of the game, and got to decide the punishment for those who chickened out of their dares. He or she also got to wear a crown and a velvet cloak that Illia had made, and had to sit with a chicken in his lap.

The first time I played, Yuri challenged me to stand on my head for an entire minute. I could barely do a cartwheel, but I had no choice but to try. I made it about three seconds before toppling over onto a pile of pillows to the triumphant laughter of the others.

"Punish her!" the Kalyptra crowed in unison. "Punish her! Punish her!"

Diego, that night's Dominus, held his chicken up for silence, and spoke to me in a grave tone, although I saw a smile twitching at the corner of his mouth. "Kenna, you failed to complete your challenge, and must therefore be punished." Diego whispered something to Stig, who looked appalled.

"Oh, she won't like that," Stig said, stroking his pointy beard. "Choose something else."

"She's not supposed to like it," Diego reminded Stig. "That's the whole point."

"What?" I said, getting nervous. I thought they'd go easy on me since it was my first time playing the game.

"You'll see," Diego said, and to Stig, "Go on." Diego jerked his head toward the door to the yurt, signaling for Stig to go and retrieve something. Stig was gone for less than a minute before he returned with a wriggling, muddy earthworm dangling from his fingers.

"No," I said, appalled. "I am not eating a worm."

"You don't have to eat it," Diego said, and couldn't suppress his grin any longer. "You have to cull it."

"Oh. That's all?" I held out my hand for the worm. "Not a problem. I thought you said this was going to be a punishment."

Although I'd stuck to plant anima since I had arrived at Eclipse, I didn't see much harm in culling the anima of a worm. As Stig laid the squirming invertebrate in my open palm, I found I was actually looking forward to taking from a slightly more potent source of anima than plant.

But I should have known better. The worm, after all, was supposed to be my punishment.

The instant the earthworm's anima hit my brain, my thoughts became sluggish and senseless. I tried to speak, but when I heard the garbled nonsense coming out of my mouth I didn't even have the capacity to be horrified. Then things got worse. I flopped onto the floor and began to writhe and squirm, desperate for soil and moisture. I didn't want to do it, but the impulse was undeniable. Instinct took over.

I was vaguely aware of laughter from the Kalyptra. Distantly, as though I were underground, I heard Cyrus telling the others, "It's not funny."

The game continued around me, and by my next turn the worm anima had worn off enough so that I could yell at Diego.

I punched him on the arm, riling his chicken, which flapped its wings and tried to escape. "You're a mean Dominus."

"Careful," Diego said, a wicked grin on his face. "It's your turn again."

I remembered what Rebekah and Cyrus had told me about the anima of certain creatures being tainted by their vessel. Now I understood what they meant, and I filed earthworm anima away in my head as off the menu, along with moth and human. I made a mental note to ask Cyrus if there were any other types of anima I should avoid, but I got caught up in the game again and forgot all about it until three nights later, when things went very wrong.

*　*　*

We were in a post-jam afterglow in the dreaming tent, lounging and chatting and eating strawberries and goat cheese on
rye bread, when Rory burst in, holding a ceramic bowl of
filled with black-petaled flowers.

"Look what I found!" she called out, holding the bowl
above her head and shaking her hips like a belly dancer in
her harem pants and a cropped shirt that showed her flat,
firm stomach. The bells tied to the ends of her dreadlocks
jangled. "I went hiking in the woods today and discovered a
patch of these beauties."

"Oh my." Hitomi rubbed her hands together, her tone
awed. "My favorite."

"What are they?" I asked, peering into the bowl. I'd never
seen flowers with black petals, not real ones anyway. With
their trumpet-shaped petal arrangement, these looked almost
identical to the moonflowers that grew on the side of Eclipse
House, except for the color.

"Midnight glory," Hitomi said. "Sister to the morning
glory, but quite rare. Its anima is uncommonly potent for a
flower. Shamans and diviners chew the seeds to give themselves prophetic dreams. For us, the effect of its anima is like
a lucid dream. You close your eyes and whatever you imagine becomes real."

Hitomi placed her hand over the bowl. A thread of vena
extended from the tip of her finger and connected to the

rim of an ink-black petal. A subtle glow filled her eyes as she drank the flower's anima, and then her pupils expanded, dark and bottomless. The flower shriveled and crumbled to powdery dust.

Rory offered the bowl to me.

"Kenna, I don't know if that's such a good idea," Cyrus said, shaking his head at me.

I hesitated, my hand halfway to the bowl. "Why not?"

"Oh, Cyrus, don't scare her," Illia said, and then to me, "It's something every Kalyptra should try at least once."

Hitomi smiled at me, eyes hazy and distant, as though she were looking at me, but not seeing me anymore. Or seeing some other fascinating version of me. Then her eyes drifted closed and she sighed and melted onto a pile of pillows in a state of obvious ecstasy.

Diego moved to my side and draped an arm around my shoulder. "You don't have to do anything you don't want to do. The anima of these flowers can have an . . ." He looked at the ceiling, searching for the word. "An *unpredictable* effect."

"Like moth anima?" I asked.

The Kalyptra all looked at one another in alarm.

"No," Cyrus said. "Not like moth. It's just . . . kinda bizarre."

"Ah, she can handle it," Yuri called out. "Do it, Kenna. It'll expand your consciousness and take you to places you've never been before and whatnot."

"Leave her alone," Cyrus growled at Yuri.

"I can make up my own mind," I told Cyrus. I wasn't sure if I found his protectiveness irritating or endearing.

"Do what you like," Rory said. "I'm partaking." She fished a flower out of the bowl, and a moment later her pupils had expanded to the size of pennies. One by one, the others, including Cyrus, culled midnight glory until their eyes were as black as its petals and they were in another realm of rapturous consciousness, while I was on the outside, alone and separate.

I looked down at the flowers with no small amount of trepidation. From what Hitomi described, midnight glory could provide a kind of hallucinatory experience for normal people, not just Kalyptra, which made it a drug, something akin to mushrooms or mescaline or ayahuasca. I'd never done a real drug, not even marijuana, but I supposed when it came down to it anima was a drug. It was a mind-altering substance that I couldn't get enough of. I needed it every day to sustain me. Did the fact that I craved it constantly make me an addict, or was anima more like food and oxygen and water, things my body couldn't thrive without? Was a person an addict for breathing or wanting lunch or getting thirsty?

I took a determined breath and let it out, peer pressuring myself. *Everyone else did it, so I might as well, too.* I reached for a flower. But I released my control too soon and whip-thin tongues of energy unwound from four of my fingertips and attached to several of the flowers, instead of just one.

Their anima hit me like a slow-motion wave, rolling

through my body until it crashed into my brain. I closed my eyes and sank backward on the sofa. When I opened them and stared up at the roof of the dreaming tent, which was hung with a patchwork canopy of drapes and tapestries, the colors seemed to melt toward me like dripping paint. They pulsed and kaleidoscoped and pinwheeled and seeped. Color swallowed me and spit me out. Swallowed me and spit me out. Then sucked me down into an oozing vortex, where I spun inside a wormhole, traveling deeper and deeper.

It was dizzying and surreal, definitely one of the best anima trips I'd been on.

But then everything changed.

"Kenna. Look at me. Look at what you've done."

The guttural, rasping voice sent a surge of chills across my skin.

I sat up and found Jason Dunn standing in front of me, Jason Dunn as I had last seen him. He resembled a human in shape alone. He had arm and legs, a head and a torso. But that was where the similarities ended. His skin was wizened like that of a rotting pumpkin, his eyes black pits sucked deep in his face. His mouth puckered against toothless gums, and his fingernails were long, brittle, and yellowed, grasping a mason jar filled to capacity with what appeared to be dead moths.

Jason's caved-in mouth moved and the voice it produced made me want to clap my hands over my ears.

"Look what you did to me, Kenna."

My heartbeat slowed, but I could hear it in my ears, a

sporadic, thunderous *ka-thunk! Ka-thunk!* I closed my eyes tight and told myself that when I opened them again Jason would be gone. This was only a hallucination. Nothing more. I was tripping out on the midnight glory anima. None of this was real.

But when I willed my eyes to open again, Thomas Dunn stood next to his son, wearing the same mummified features. The shriveled skin. Sockets and mouth like sinkholes in his face.

"Look what you did to my boy," Thomas Dunn said, staring at me with those black pits that should have been eyes. "You were supposed to pay. Your family lives and my boy is dead."

I clawed at my mouth and my eyes bulged so hard it felt like my retinas might detach. I searched around wildly for help, thinking Cyrus would know what to do. Cyrus would fix this. But Cyrus and the rest of the Kalyptra were gone. In their place were my mom and Erin, but they were as dead as Jason and Thomas Dunn. As dead as they had been in the basement, slashed and bloodied, Erin's face a swelling mass of black bruises.

"No, no, no." I cowered against the wall of the yurt. "No, I saved you. I brought you back. I brought you back!"

"For now," Erin said, her mouth pulled down at the corners in a hideous grimace, as though she'd had a severe stroke that paralyzed her face. "But nothing lasts forever. Not death and not life."

The colors dripping from the ceiling bled to red, and

began to rain down on my family until they were painted from head to toe, cocooned in blood. Jason and Thomas Dunn were washed red, as well. And then the blood found me. It drizzled down on me, hot and slick. I huddled with my knees against my chest, trying to hide from the crimson deluge.

"Nothing lasts forever," Jason mimicked in his rasping raven's voice. "Not death and not life."

Jason opened the lid of his mason jar, and the dead moths inside began to jitter and twitch, returning to life. With sudden velocity, they burst from the jar and flocked toward my face like off-kilter bullets, the combined murmur of the wings a roar in my ears.

I screamed, a sound that tore my throat, made it raw.

With the moths converging all around me, I bolted from the dreaming tent that had turned into a nightmare haven. I didn't know where I was going because I couldn't *see* where I was going. The moths surrounded me like a dark, trembling cloud, their wings shuddering and obscuring my vision. I ran and ran and I didn't know I had entered the forest until branches raked my skin and snagged my hair. I pushed through them, arms out in front of me, eyes blind with the palpitation of dusty wings.

I ran and didn't stop until I smacked headlong into a low tree branch that knocked me flat on my back.

Pain exploded in my head, turning my vision white, and then gray, and then black, and then starry.

Dazed, I stared up at the sky through a mesh of leaves and

branches, and saw that the stars had all turned crimson and the sky, too, was shifting to the color of blood. My body clenched in expectant horror, waiting for the sky to turn to blood as the roof of the yurt had and fall on me. Then I felt warm wetness seeping over my cheeks, and I realized the blood was coming from my head, not from the sky. I touched the place on my brow where I'd hit it on the branch. An ache radiated down through my nose and cheekbones, and I felt a swelling lump and a deep, open laceration. I wiped the blood from my eyes and realized, suddenly, that the thrumming of the swarming moths' wings was gone.

And a far worse sound had replaced it.

Now there was only one set of wings beating the air, distant, but moving closer and closer. A sound that was at once as soft as a whisper and as loud as an approaching helicopter. My eyes, filling with blood again, searched the sky and found its source.

A single moth, its wingspan as wide as my outstretched arms, descended through the sky, wings bone white with bloated black moons floating in their centers.

I tried to scream. To move. To do anything.

My body was frozen.

It's not real, I told myself. It's not real. *It's not real!*

But I felt the wind of its wings on my face, made out specks of dust shimmering in the air around those massive wings.

Then its tongue—its proboscis—unfurled, a glowing white whip as thick as my pinky finger, a swollen, tangible twin of the strands of energy that uncoiled from me when I took anima.

It wasn't real.

It was not real.

It was so close now I could reach out and touch it. If I had not been paralyzed with fear, I would have batted at it with my arms. Pummeled it. Clawed at its furry thorax. Instead, I lay prone and immobile, waiting for the moth to do what it would to me.

It touched down on my chest, heavy as a soaking wet pillow, its eyes black and empty as a crow's. Its wing beats slowed and its long lash of a tongue probed at the gash in my forehead, pressing into it like a man-eating vine, slipping beneath the skin. Then, without warning, as though it had tasted something it didn't like, the behemoth of a moth withdrew its tongue and beat its wings like a bellows.

It lifted into the sky and vanished into the treetops.

"Kenna!" I recognized Cyrus's voice, calling from somewhere nearby. Then he was at my side, falling to his knees. His hands checked my head wound, fingers gentle, but I shuddered at the memory of the moth's tongue worming through the seeping laceration.

"I'm so sorry," Cyrus said, removing his shirt and pressing it to my bleeding forehead. "I never should have let you try that anima."

"I should have listened to you," I said, my voice weak, barely audible. I wondered vaguely how bad the injury on my head was, how much blood I had lost.

"Did you see it?" I asked.

Cyrus shook his head. "What?

"The moth. It was just here."

Cyrus's brow furrowed, and he raised his eyes to search the sky. "No," he said. "I didn't see anything."

"It was as big as me, Cyrus. It . . . it was real."

Even in the dark, I could see the concerned expression on his face. He said nothing, only gathered me in his arms and lifted me like I weighed no more than a sack of fall leaves.

He carried me all the way to Eclipse House. I hid my face against his chest, eyes shut tight, afraid to open them. Afraid the monstrous moth would change its mind and return for me. For my blood.

AWAKE

THE NEXT MORNING I WOKE BEFORE DAWN, BUT NOT IN my bed. I sat up, blinking in the hazy, predawn light, the previous night's events shuffling into place in my brain.

The dreaming tent.

The midnight glory anima.

The dead.

The blood.

The moth.

I remembered everything. I wished I didn't.

I was in Rebekah's room, in her bed. Cyrus had carried me, fading in and out of consciousness, all the way back to Eclipse House and up three flights of stairs to Rebekah's room, where she had opened up her cupboard and brought out one of her culling jars for me. I didn't see the shape of this jar, didn't know what kind of anima was inside. Instead of letting me cull the anima herself, she culled it and channeled it into me, the way I had done for my family. Like she wanted to take care of me. And she had.

The ache in my head had vanished instantly, and I felt the flesh of my forehead knit itself whole—such a strange sensation, like closing a zipper on your own skin. And then my bad trip had turned into a euphoric, waking dream, my blissed-out body seeming to float several inches above the floor as color and light and soft sensation embraced me. I drifted on a warm river and eventually ended up in a sleep filled with safe, impregnable dreams.

I swung my legs over the side of the bed. Cyrus was crashed out on floor pillows, shirtless, one arm flung over his face. He snored faintly, which I found endearing. I resisted the urge to kneel down beside him and touch the bare skin of his back to experience the smoothness of it again. The warmth that radiated from him. As he'd carried me from the forest, I had kept my face nestled against his chest, breathing in his scent, warming my shivering body against his.

Seeing him so soundly asleep, I felt a surge of affection for this hippie cowboy. He had tried to protect me from myself last night, and I'd ignored him. But still he'd come after me. If he hadn't, I might still be alone and lost in the forest, afraid to move for fear of calling the attention of that *thing*. That moth with its curious, probing tongue.

But that monstrosity hadn't been real, had it? Certainly the hallucinations of Jason and Thomas Dunn, and of my family and the blood raining down on me weren't real. The moths in Jason's killing jar weren't real. So why should the mega-moth, that impossibly huge creature, be real?

Rebekah stood on her balcony, looking out at the green mountains and the silver sky, speckled with a few tenacious stars. She turned her head when I stepped outside. The morning air was dewy, and clung to my skin like wet silk.

I came up beside Rebekah and leaned against the railing. For a moment neither of us said anything. I wanted to thank her for healing me and bringing me fully out of my bad trip, for taking care of me like I was her responsibility, her own child. But I was embarrassed to bring it up, embarrassed that I couldn't handle the midnight glory anima. I didn't want to be a burden to Rebekah.

Rebekah saved me the trouble of figuring out what to say by speaking first. "Cyrus tells me you saw the Mother last night," she said.

I blinked at her, thinking I must have heard her wrong. "No, I didn't see my mom," I told her. A hallucination of her, yes, but not my actual mom.

Rebekah shook her head. "Not your mother. *The* Mother. The Mother of the Kalyptra." She smiled. "In a vision, of course."

I shook my head at her, utterly confused. "Who is the Mother?" I would have thought she considered herself the mother of the Kalyptra.

"Our goddess," Rebekah said. "She is our maker. The Eclipse moth, the Kalyptra anima."

I noticed that Rebekah's pupils were slightly enlarged, and wondered if she was on anima. She sounded dreamy and slightly disconnected. But it was early in the morning, so maybe she was just groggy.

"I saw a moth," I said hesitantly, not sure whether I wanted to admit what I had decided could not be possible. "It—she tasted my blood." I touched my forehead, where the laceration had been. "But she didn't like it."

"That's because you're Kalyptra. The Mother doesn't drink the blood of her children."

"But it wasn't real," I said, sounding a little desperate, wanting Rebekah to agree with me. "It couldn't have been real."

"When the veil comes down, you see what others can't," Rebekah said, which didn't really answer my question. "Did you know a group of moths is called an eclipse?" she asked, and I was somewhat relieved that she diverted the conversation away from the reality or unreality of what I'd seen.

I shook my head at Rebekah's question. "Why are they called that?"

"Because moths are obscure. Their coloring helps them blend with their surroundings so they can hide in plain sight, like the silent sun when the moon masks it in an eclipse. The sun is still there, only you can't see it. Moths are expert at disappearing, just like us. We disappeared right in the middle of the world, yet people rarely happen upon us here, and when they do they don't know who or what we are. To them, we're merely people. They have no idea they've just encountered superior beings."

The disdainful tone she used when talking about regular people put my back up, but I tried to brush it off. She probably didn't mean to sound as condescending as she did.

"Do you know why I built this place, Kenna? Why I gathered this family and introduced them to a new way of living?"

I said nothing, only looked at her expectantly and shook my head.

"When I was a little girl, I had a large family," she said. "Three brothers and four sisters, one of whom was my twin, Anya. She was your mother's namesake."

Her stiff tone told me she considered naming my mother after her twin a mistake.

"Anya and I were the eldest of our siblings," she went on. "Our mother and father were quite wealthy, so they could afford to give us the kind of lives most people only dream of. We lived in San Francisco and attended school there, but we spent our summers at our mother and father's country home, where we passed every day playing together from sunup to sundown, swimming in the river, riding horses, gardening, caring for animals, reading fairy tales beneath shade trees, taking music lessons. During those summers, it was as though we existed in a place without time, another world separate from the one that waited for us in the fall. Our own daydream realm where we would be young forever. Young and happy and free."

She paused, her mouth quivering at the corners.

"When I was seventeen, my youngest sister, Gillian, came down with influenza. We did all we could for her. My mother and Anya and I nursed her night and day, and my parents called in the best doctors, but it made no difference. Gillian died, and soon after, my mother came down with the fever. And then my father fell ill. One by one, my brothers and sisters sickened and their fevers drowned them in sweat, and they coughed until their throats tore. They writhed and twisted in their sheets, fraught with delirium, as I tried to hold them down and pour medicine into their throats, which they only coughed up, along with blood. I was there with each of them when they died, because by the end I was the only one still well enough to care for them. I took care of them. But it made no difference."

I swallowed hard, thinking of Erin, of the helpless dread I felt every time she caught a cold. "Anya got sick, too?" I asked, although I wasn't really asking. I already knew. If Anya were alive, wouldn't she be here now?

Rebekah nodded, and the tears in her eyes slid free and trailed down the sides of her nose. She wiped at them absently. "I haven't talked about Anya in a long time, but I think about her every day. I write down every memory I have of her to preserve her. She was brilliant, my sister. Brilliant and fascinated with learning and kind to everyone. If there were any fairness in this world, she would have lived, not me. She was by far the better of the two of us."

"I'm sorry," I said, my own voice thick with emotion. Rebekah's twin sounded so much like Erin. And the way she felt about her twin was the same way I felt about mine. That she was the better of the two of us. That she deserved life, not me.

I wondered why Rebekah had never mentioned a desire to meet Erin.

"I lost my entire family in the space of a month," Rebekah continued. "For a long time after, I wished the influenza had taken me, as well. But when I married and became pregnant with your mother, all of that changed. The marriage didn't last, but I had my Anya. I had a reason to live again." She wiped at one eye with her long, elegant fingers, naked of their silver rings. "I created Eclipse for her, and I gathered a family for her, so she could have the kind of childhood I remembered. The kind I lost. A beautiful dream that would never end."

Rebekah's mouth closed and she turned back toward the mountains just as a sliver of sun appeared, spreading honeyed light across the farm.

"Do you hate her?" I asked, fearing the answer, because I didn't want to believe it was possible to hate your own child. I didn't want to believe it was possible for my mom to hate *me*, even though I'd taken something intrinsic from her. Because of me, she was no longer Kalyptra. How could she not hate me for that?

Rebekah stared straight at the sun as it rose, her gaze unwavering, not even squinting against the brilliance. It was like she'd trained herself to look directly into the searing light.

"I used to believe love was not a choice. That a sister must love her sister. A child must love her parents. A mother must love her children. But now I know that you always have a choice, in everything you do and everyone you love and everyone you hurt. And so I no longer consider your mother my child. That is my choice."

My heart lurched like I'd been punched in the chest. "Then you must not consider me your granddaughter."

She shook her head and turned to me, her skin and hair the color of champagne in the new light of day.

"You're Kalyptra. That makes you family."

Then I understood why she had never asked about Erin, never mentioned a desire to meet my twin.

Erin wasn't Kalyptra. She didn't have our power. She meant nothing to Rebekah. Nothing at all.

During my time at Eclipse, I had formed a bond with Rebekah that obscured what I felt for my real mom. Even before Jason, she had kept me at a distance, and now I thought I knew why. Because I had taken her power and made her ordinary. But the idea that Rebekah cared nothing at all for my twin chipped away at my fledgling love for my grandmother, weakening it at its foundation.

"Do you miss them?" Rebekah asked.

She didn't have to say their names. I tapped my fingers on the balcony railing, creating a nervous rhythm. I didn't know how to answer her question. At first, being away from Erin and Blake felt like being separated from two of my limbs. But the longer I was at Eclipse, the less I thought about my mom or Erin or Blake. I was so busy immersing myself in the world of being Kalyptra, in music and anima and unconditional acceptance, that I hadn't had time to miss them.

"It's complicated," I answered finally, and quickly changed the subject. Rebekah's story had brought up something, yet again, that I still didn't understand.

"Rebekah, where did we come from?" I asked. "I assume no one else in your family was Kalyptra, or they would have been able to heal themselves, or be healed by you. Did you not know you were Kalyptra back then?"

I thought of her use of the word *influenza* instead of simply calling it the flu. I tried to remember the last time there'd been an outbreak of the flu that killed entire families of people. I was pretty sure that hadn't happened in a really long time. Rebekah looked no older than forty, and a youthful forty at that. My first night at Eclipse, she had said anima was the ultimate panacea, a vitamin that could cure any disease, heal any wound, as well as expand our consciousness, tearing down the veil between the mundane world and the ethereal. It made sense that anima extended life, but for how long? Were we to become immortal? Would any of us ever die?

On and on. Every time I learned something new about the Kalyptra, it opened the door to a hundred more questions.

Rebekah shook her head. "I wasn't always Kalyptra. None of us were. We chose what we are, and *became* Kalyptra, all of us, including your mother. And then she chose to cast off her

205

gift." She smiled fondly at me, but something dark glittered in her eyes as she said, "You are the only one of us who was born Kalyptra, who never had a choice."

She started to turn away, and I grabbed her sleeve. "Why are we like this? Why can we do what we can do? What does any of it mean? Please, Rebekah, I want to understand. I want to know everything."

She raised an eyebrow at me. "You want to know things that only a true Kalyptra can know."

"You said I *was* Kalyptra. That I was family."

"Do you want to go home?" she asked.

The question jarred me. "Y-yes. No. I mean, I do, but I want to be here, too. I want to be in both places."

She shook her head slowly, disappointed and clearly hurt. "Until you choose us, you aren't one of us. I can't tell you what you want to know, and I can't let you live in our world."

I sucked in a breath as though I'd been hit in the stomach. "Rebekah . . ." I said, not wanting to believe she'd meant what she had just said.

I can't let you live in our world.

Rebekah turned her back on me and went inside, signaling that our conversation was finished. If there was one thing I had learned about my grandmother, it was that once she decided something was over, there was no changing her mind.

Feeling hollowed out and emotionally drained, I followed her inside, where Cyrus was now sitting up, rubbing his eyes like a drowsy toddler who'd just awakened from a too-short nap. But when he saw me his eyes cleared and he stood up, a hank of dark curls tumbling over his brow.

"Are you okay?" he asked, searching my face.

I touched my brow where I'd split my scalp open before realizing he wasn't referring to the wound. I felt another undeniable rush of warmth for him, but Rebekah's icy response froze my blood.

"She's fine," Rebekah answered for me. "In fact, I think she's ready to go home."

LAST DAY

BULLY RAN AT ME FULL TILT WHEN I CALLED TO HIM FROM the fence, and then bounced and bleated when I offered him the parting gift of an entire bunch of carrots.

"I'm going to miss you, kid," I said as he munched distractedly on his treat. I tousled the wild tuft of hair between his ears, trying not to cry and not really succeeding.

It had been twenty-four hours since Rebekah had decided to send me home, and I was still in shock. Every time I broke the news to another Kalyptra that I was leaving, I had to white-knuckle my emotions to keep from bursting into tears. The next morning, Cyrus would drive me home.

I should have been elated at the prospect of being reunited with Erin and with Blake and my mom and my guitar, but mostly I just felt anxious. I wasn't the same person I'd been when my mom had dropped me off at Eclipse. I didn't know if I would fit into my old space in my old world anymore.

"I don't understand why you have to leave all of a sudden," Cyrus said, leaning against the fence beside me, arms folded tight across his chest. He'd been nearly as upset as I was when Rebekah told me I had to leave. We'd spent a lot of time together, and I'd grown attached to him, to his easy smile and his country-boy charm. I woke up every day looking forward to seeing him, to taking anima with him and feeling the connection between us grow, like we were sharing the same dream, the kind from which you never want to wake up. But I hadn't realized the feeling was mutual.

Cyrus went so far as to question Rebekah's decision that morning after the midnight glory disaster, earning a sharp rebuke before my grandmother sent us away.

"I must have done something to make her mad," I said.

"What were you talking about before she said it was time for you to go home?"

"A lot of things. She told me about her twin, and why she founded Eclipse. And I asked her some questions she didn't want to answer because . . . I guess because I'm not really one of you."

He nodded, eyes veiled, and I could see that a part of him agreed with Rebekah. Whatever secrets the Kalyptra had, they didn't trust me with them yet, and maybe they never would.

I gave Bully one last scratch behind the ears as he finished his carrots. He bolted back to the herd, feet barely touching the ground.

"I'm going to miss him." I wiped at a tear leaking from

the corner of my eye. "I'm going to miss everything about Eclipse. Except maybe the midnight glory."

I thought Cyrus would laugh, but he turned to me, his face serious. "I'm going to miss *you*, Kenna." He raked a hand through his tangled curls and looked at the toes of his boots. "More than I know how to say. Eclipse is better with you as a part of it. As a part of us," he added softly.

For a moment the air between us was charged, almost crackling with electricity. I felt myself pulled toward him, a kind of horizontal vertigo.

"Kenna!" Cyrus and I both jumped at the sound of my name, and turned to see Sunday jogging toward us through the field, afro bouncing and bracelets jangling. She had legs like an Olympic runner and her dark skin practically glowed under the bright sunlight. She wore one of Illia's creations, a short yellow sundress with tiny, crystal buttons. She grabbed me by the wrist and tugged me away from Cyrus, toward Eclipse House.

"What's going on?" I asked, scrambling to keep up with her. I glanced over my shoulder at Cyrus and saw him standing next to the fence, arms hanging heavy at his sides and an abandoned-puppy-dog look on his face.

"I have to draw you before you leave," Sunday said. "Your face begs to be immortalized."

"It does?"

"Oh yes. Those eyes of yours. The cheekbones. Exquisite, just like Rebekah's."

Sunday led me to her studio and shut the door. Her studio

was next to Illia's, but I'd never been inside. It seemed to have been designed with her particular skills in mind, as it was almost all windows and skylights, letting in light from every direction. There were stacks upon stacks of painted canvases covered in cloth leaning against the walls. Eclipse House was enormous, but clearly there was only so much wall space on which to hang her art. If I'd known she had so many unhung works lying around, I would have asked her for a few to decorate the bare walls of my room.

"Is it okay if I look?" I asked Sunday, lifting the sheet that covered a row of finished canvases. Her back was turned to me. She was busy setting up for my portrait, gathering her paper and charcoal and arranging a stool in the light, and merely grunted a reply that I took to mean yes.

I peered beneath the sheet, expecting paintings like the rest that adorned the hallways and walls of Eclipse House, colorful, surreal depictions of what the world looked like through the lens of anima, when the veil was lifted to reveal the true splendor that most people would never know. But these paintings were nothing like the other works of Sunday's I'd seen. These I could only describe as troubling.

My lips parted and I forgot to breathe as my eyes roamed the first painting, a disturbing depiction of bodies writhing in a pit, ringed by people with Eclipse moths the size of baseball gloves perched on their faces, hiding their eyes, replacing them with black moons. The next painting was of an Eclipse moth with its proboscis unfurled and inserted into the pupil of a small child. The third was of Rebekah. I knew it was her, even though a moth the size of a hardcover book had alighted on her face and concealed her eyes. I knew her by her mouth and her chin and her glorious hair. Where her eyes would have been, the Eclipse moth's black moons represented them. In the painting, Rebekah was naked, her arms held out to her sides and her palms turned upward. In each palm she held a flaming moth, and a huge pair of powder-white wings extended from her back. There were more paintings—dozens more, all of them grim and disturbing, most featuring faces obscured by Eclipse moths with flaming wings and naked men and women with moth wings and oil-black eyes—but I didn't get a chance to peruse them.

"What are you doing?"

I whirled around to find Sunday staring me down, her hands on her hips and an expression on her face that was angry, but also fearful, as though she'd been caught stealing. I'd never seen her anything but happy and smiling and laughing that raucous, infectious laugh of hers, so this sudden change in her was as jarring as the sight of these grim, unsettling paintings she kept hidden away.

She marched toward me and snatched the sheet out of my hands, lowering it over the paintings and obscuring them from view.

"Those are private," she said sternly, though her voice was trembling slightly.

"I—I'm sorry," I stammered. "I asked you if I could look, but I guess you didn't hear me."

She took a breath that lifted her shoulders and let it out in a loud huff. Then she smiled and waved her hand. "It doesn't matter," she said, all evidence to the contrary. "I just don't show my darker work to the others."

I thought of the dozens of songs I'd written that I'd never shared with the Kalyptra. They were too joyless, and the Kalyptra were all about joy. I could see why Sunday kept these paintings to herself. I kind of wished I hadn't seen them at all.

"Okay, are you ready to get naked?" Sunday asked, jerking me from my thoughts like a fish on a line.

"What?"

"Take off your clothes," she commanded.

My hands automatically crossed over my chest. "I thought you wanted to immortalize my face."

"Yes. Face. Body. The whole you. Come on now, don't be shy, girl. You ain't got nothing I don't have." She laughed—she was always laughing. I'd never met anyone who found so many reasons to laugh as Sunday did. God, I was going to miss her and all the rest of the Kalyptra. The idea of being separated from them after so many weeks of bonding made it hard for me to breathe.

"Kenna," Sunday said, tapping her pencil impatiently. "Strip."

I hesitated. I'd never been comfortable with my body, not because there was anything wrong with it, but because it had always felt like a secret, something I was supposed to keep hidden until I found someone I trusted completely to let him see it. Was Blake that person? My answer should have been an immediate *yes*, but it was Cyrus's face that swam into my mind.

Sunday sat at her desk with her pencil poised and a large piece of paper ready on her easel. I sighed and stripped off my dress. What could it hurt? We were both girls.

Sunday's sharp eyes scrutinized me a moment before she instructed me in how to pose. I ended up sitting on a stool with my back to her, my face turned toward the window so she could draw my profile and the lines of my shoulders. My hair lay long and loose on my back, my face bare. My skin and hair had become luminous since I started taking anima, and my body, which had always been scrawny and a bit brittle, all joints and angles, had put on muscle, giving me curving hips and leanly rounded shoulders and hard, smooth legs.

Sunday sketched in silence for several minutes, her focus complete and unwavering.

"How does it look?" I asked.

"Great," she said, smiling up at me. "Thank you for doing this. I've sketched everyone else here about a thousand times. It's nice to have a new model."

"Everyone? Naked?"

"Mmhmm."

"Even the men?"

"If you're wondering how Cyrus looks with his clothes off, the answer is: he does not disappoint."

"I wasn't," I said, blushing.

"Okay," she said, chuckling.

"No, really!"

"I believe you, honey." She was still laughing.

Cyrus chose that moment to open the door and poke his head in. Sunday didn't even glance over to see who it was, just kept scratching on the paper with her pencil, but I scrambled for something to cover myself with, yanking the quilt off Sunday's bed and cocooning myself inside it.

Cyrus lowered his gaze until I had the blanket securely covering me. But the desire I saw in his eyes made a fever of echoed lust roll across my skin.

Sunday glared first at me, and then at Cyrus. "Kenna, you better be able to find that exact pose again or I'll have to start over. Cyrus, why are you bothering us?"

"I, um . . . I don't know," Cyrus mumbled, then shook his head. "I mean, Rebekah wants to see you, Kenna."

"She'll be along shortly," Sunday said, and shooed him away.

Cyrus withdrew, and I released my breath and slumped into the chair. "I think I'm done for the day," I said.

"No, no, I'm almost finished. Look how gorgeous you are." Sunday turned her sketchpad so I could see what she'd drawn.

I didn't realize I'd stopped breathing until my lungs began to plead for air. Sunday's talent was undeniable. In the space of fifteen minutes, she'd brought a version of me to life on the page. The girl in the portrait was earthy and confident, even sensual. She was none of the things I was used to seeing.

The girl in Sunday's drawing was some other version of me entirely.

And I liked her. I wanted to stay *her.*

"You wanted to see me?" I asked, hesitating in the open doorway of Rebekah's room.

Rebekah stood and came out from around her desk, her expression somber. "I've arranged a going-away party for you tonight. Nothing fancy. A small feast. A little singing and dancing afterward."

"You didn't have to do that," I said, even though I was touched.

"We wanted to see you off properly."

I lowered my eyes and shifted from one foot to the other. "Maybe I can come back in a couple of months."

Hopeful, I raised my eyes to find my grandmother shaking her head. "I thought I made myself clear. You can't live in two worlds, Kenna. You have to choose one." Her tone was laced with bitterness. I wondered if my mom had made the same request.

"Fine." My cheeks flushed with anger. What Rebekah was asking of me wasn't fair. I couldn't write off Erin and my mom and Blake like they meant nothing to me. I couldn't simply say goodbye to the world. It wasn't that cut-and-dried.

I turned my back on her. "If you ever want to see me again, you know where to find me."

*   *   *

Stig was in charge of the "small" going-away feast, which turned out not to be so small. When I entered the dining room that evening, I found it packed with so much food there was barely room for plates and silverware on the table.

Rory, her dreads bound up in a scarf on top of her head, thrust a goblet filled with scarlet wine into my hand and tilted the glass to my lips. The wine went from my belly to my bloodstream fast, and I immediately started to feel looser and more relaxed. I glanced around and saw that Cyrus was nowhere to be found. He'd been MIA ever since he walked in on Sunday sketching my nude portrait. I wasn't sure I could look him in the eye now, and maybe he felt the same way about me.

"Do you know where Cyrus is?" I asked.

Rory shrugged, the spaghetti strap of her camisole slipping off her shoulder. "I'm sure he'll turn up."

For once Rebekah arrived before everyone was seated, while we were still mingling. She glided into the dining room then, and poured herself a glass of wine. She raised it in a toast. The room, which had previously been filled with chatter, quieted in an instant.

"To my granddaughter, Kenna," Rebekah said. She met my eyes, and smiled. "Who is welcome to return to Eclipse anytime she wants."

My lips parted and a silent breath escaped. Murmurs sounded throughout the room.

217

Then Rebekah raised her wine glass a little higher, and the rest of the Kalyptra said, "To Kenna!" Everyone drank except for me. I couldn't take my eyes from my grandmother.

Rebekah set her goblet on the table, stepped close to me, and wrapped me in a warm hug. For a moment I was too stunned to hug her back.

"I can really come back?" I asked.

She nodded against my hair. "Just promise me one thing: no more questions. Not until you choose our world and our way over all others."

"I promise," I said without hesitation. It was an arrangement I could live with if it meant I got to return to Eclipse.

She held me back and took my face in both of her hands. Her skin carried the most minute charge, and I felt it sink into me and galvanize my brain so I wanted to jump up and down and whoop with joy. I could come back to Eclipse anytime I wanted. Rebekah loved me. She wanted me to be with her.

I had never felt such elation. I wanted to dash into the yard and run with abandon like Bully did, and sing at the top of my lungs.

Instead, I ate, and ate, and ate. Each bite was more delicious than the last. There was so much food, it took almost two hours to eat it all. Spicy carrot soup. Salad with peaches and goat cheese. Rosemary bread and roasted turkey, sautéed mushrooms over mashed potatoes, flaky, lemony trout, and asparagus and zucchini slathered in butter. For dessert there was lemon cake with blueberry sauce. Throughout the meal, someone kept refilling my goblet when I wasn't looking, so by the time I took my last bite I wasn't sure how much I'd had to drink, and I wasn't sure I cared. My head was swimming. I was dizzy with love and acceptance and a happiness so pure it was thrilling.

I was young and alive and free. Free to return to the place where I belonged.

Rebekah announced that cleanup could wait until the morning. The Kalyptra piled from the house and congregated around the fire pit. Rebekah brought out a culling jar wrapped in a colorful scarf, and one by one the Kalyptra took from it, strands of vena sipping at the effervescent energy that sparkled around the lid. When it was my turn to take, I opened my mouth to ask what kind of anima it was, but Rebekah gave me a warning look.

"No more questions, remember?"

I nodded, and took.

And the life inside me amplified to a hundred. The world around me lit up with night colors, vibrant indigos and lavenders and emeralds, and the stars became shattered crystal fireworks. Yuri and Diego had built up a raging bonfire that reached toward the moon, flames dancing to the music that filled the air. And the Kalyptra danced too. I joined in the fray, the night whirlpooling around me, a swirling mixture of navy blue sky and orange firelight and streaks of white stars.

When the anima wore off, I slipped away from the group

to find something else to cull, though I wanted more of what-ever was in that jar. I hungered for it in a way that reminded me of the days after Jason Dunn's death.

I didn't realize someone had followed me until she spoke at my back.

"Did you find it?"

I spun around to find Joanna standing a foot behind me. I clutched my chest. "You almost gave me a heart attack."

I'd nearly forgotten about Joanna and my promise to Rebekah not to talk to her. Rebekah was big on asking for promises, it seemed. I glanced toward the fire to see my grand-mother watching me, eyes narrowed as though in warning.

"I should get back to the fire," I said, easing away from Joanna.

She grabbed my arm and held me in place. "Did you find it?"

I shook my head. "I don't know—"

"In the guitar," she broke in. "Your mother's guitar."

"You put something in there?" That could explain why the sound had never been right.

Her fingers tightened on my arm until they dug in, and I saw her teeth were clenched behind her lips. "Don't come back here, Kenna."

I pulled gently away. "Look, I understand that you don't like outsiders—"

Again, she cut me off. "You think you know us after a few weeks, but you don't. You'll never be one of us, and it's better that way. Believe me. Your mom was smart. A lot smarter than me."

I felt like the ground had dropped out from under my feet. "Look, I don't know what I did to make you hate me. Whatever it is, I'm sorry."

"I don't hate you. I'm trying to help you." She stepped back from me, searching my eyes. "But maybe it's too late for that."

She stared at me for a moment before saying, "Tell your mom something for me, okay?" Her voice began to tremble with emotion. "Tell her she was right, and I was wrong, and . . . tell her I wish I'd come with her. I wish it more than I can ever say."

Then she turned and walked quickly toward the house, leaving me standing on the grass, staring after her. I forgot about finding something to cull. My brain was buzzing with uncertainty and bewilderment.

When I felt a hand on my shoulder, I startled and whipped around.

"Did I scare you?" Cyrus stood behind me, holding a piece of rope that was tied to a leather collar around Bully's neck.

"A little." I blew out a breath and laughed off Joanna's cryptic words. She didn't like me, that was all. She was trying to scare me into staying away from Eclipse because of whatever had happened between her and my mom. And something had definitely happened. All that stuff about my mom being right and her being wrong . . . about wishing she'd come with her. There was history there. Maybe I could get my mom to tell me what had happened between her and Joanna.

"I wanted to show you something," Cyrus said, breaking through my distracted thoughts. He crouched behind Bully and motioned for me to do the same.

"Look." He turned the leather collar on Bully's neck so I could read the word embossed on it: BULLY. "Now everyone will know who he belongs to."

"Thank you." My heart swelled like an inflating balloon, and I threw my arms around Cyrus's neck. He hugged me back, burying his face in my hair, and I thought how amazing it was to be able to touch other people. This person in particular. I let my body relax into the embrace. Cyrus's body was warm as an oven, and his hair was soft as rabbit fur against my cheek.

"Do you want to dance?" he said close to my ear, lips brushing my skin, making me shiver.

"What about Bully?"

Cyrus released me and tied Bully's makeshift leash to the nearest fence post. Bully immediately began chewing through his leash.

"Yeah, that's not going to hold him," I said.

"Not forever, but it'll last long enough for a dance. Come on." He took my hand and led me toward the fire.

The music slowed to an undulating, sultry rhythm, and Cyrus pulled me snug against him. My chest pressed to his as we rocked side-to-side; Cyrus's hand branded the center of my back, his breath warm on my ear.

"Eclipse isn't going to be the same without you," he said. "I forgot what it was like to get to know someone I've never met."

Before I could stop them, the words that had been balanced on the tip of my tongue all day fell.

"I'm not ready to go home," I told him. "I want to ask Rebekah if I can stay a little longer."

Suddenly the music was replaced by a shout of alarm as two neon-bright high beams cut through the night, headlights moving fast toward Eclipse.

"Trespasser!" Hitomi cried, pointing at the lights. She clutched at Diego's arm, her eyes wide and filled with fear, as though the arriving car signaled an invasion. Maybe it did.

For a moment the Kalyptra remained collectively paralyzed, me included. My heart was galloping and my feet seemed frozen to the ground. But that lasted only a few seconds before Cyrus shouted to the crowd, "You know what to do!"

I turned to him, blinking. Maybe the Kalyptra did, but I didn't.

Cyrus seemed to sense my distress and took me by the arms. "It's okay," he said. "We'll find out what they want and deal with them. There are far more of us."

I nodded, though this didn't exactly make me feel better.

The Kalyptra reacted to Cyrus's shout the way well-trained students do during a fire drill. After an initial moment of disorder and uproar, they formed a line (or in this case, more of a wall) and waited for further instruction from their leader.

Rebekah stepped up beside Cyrus and me. Her expression remained as composed as ever, but her back was rigid and straight. She glanced at Cyrus. "How did this trespasser get through the gate?"

Cyrus shook his head. "No idea. Bolt cutters on the padlock, maybe. Or they drove straight through it."

"Then whoever's driving must want something from us very badly." Rebekah's eyes cut to me, and I realized what she was implying. Whoever was driving toward Eclipse had come for me.

I experienced a moment of panic, but it evaporated when I recognized Blake's 4Runner.

"Blake!"

I bolted toward his SUV before he'd even come to a full stop. Then he was out the door and crushing me in a hug. I hugged him back fiercely, realizing this was the first time I'd been able to touch him without fear of hurting him.

His mouth next to my ear breathed my name, "Kenna," as though he wanted to remind me of it. Remind me who I was.

I buried my face in his neck.

"Are you all right?" he asked.

I nodded against him. "What are you doing here?"

"I'll tell you in the car. We have to go." His tone was grim.

I pulled away from him. "Why? What's wrong?"

He hesitated, but only for a moment. "It's Erin," he said. "She's sick again. She . . . she needs you."

I stopped breathing, and when I started again it was too fast. I hadn't had an asthma attack since I'd culled that first wildflower with Cyrus. I'd barely even thought about my asthma. Every day I had grown stronger and healthier. Meanwhile, back at home, Erin had been doing the opposite.

I didn't hesitate. Before I knew it, we were in the 4Runner, and Blake was driving us away from Eclipse.

I realized too late that I hadn't said a single goodbye. I craned around in my seat and saw Rebekah through the back windshield, her expression furious and frustrated, and Cyrus at her side, his mouth turned down and his eyes forlorn.

They quickly disappeared from view behind us, but I couldn't stop seeing their faces every time I closed my eyes.

ETURNED

IT WAS PAST MIDNIGHT WHEN BLAKE TURNED ONTO THE long drive that led to my house. It was strange to be aware of time again. There were no clocks at Eclipse. Things happened when they happened. Would I spend the rest of my life comparing life at Eclipse to reality?

The woods around my house were as dead as they'd been when I left. Deader, even. There was no color in our forest, only shades of gray. Ash and charcoal and slate and smoke. Juxtaposed against Eclipse, with its vibrant green and amber grasses and wildflower fields, my home was the color of a funeral dirge. I wondered how Erin and my mom could stand to be here, surrounded by such bleakness.

How would I be able to stand it?

It doesn't matter, I reminded myself. Erin was all that mattered right now.

We found Erin asleep in her bed, the blankets pulled to

her chest. Mom sat beside her, holding her hand. There was a bandage wrapping Erin's head and another wrapping her right wrist.

"Mom?" I said when I entered. Blake hung back in the hallway behind me.

My mom turned her head, and I saw her cheeks were streaked with tears. The youthful radiance had faded from her face and she looked more like herself again—beautiful, but like a regular person. Not like the Kalyptra, with their angelic glow.

I didn't know what to expect from the reunion with my mom. She stood and came to me, studied my face for a long moment, and then held out her hand to me tentatively, like I might bite.

"I'm okay now," I assured her. "I swear." Ever since my mistake with the midnight glory, I'd been that much more focused on control.

Mom nodded, but didn't close the gap between us. "Thank you for coming home," she said in an odd, formal tone, as though I were a stranger. A guest. Had she written me off already? Had she expected never to see me again? The thought made a searing concoction of anger and dejection boil in my stomach.

Mom lowered her hand instead and turned back to Erin, launching into an account of my sister's deteriorating condition.

"She was fine until this afternoon. Or I thought she was. Then she went out for a walk, and she didn't come back.

I found her by the river, unconscious. She was bleeding from a cut on her head, and her wrist was broken. When she came round, she told me she was hit with a wave of fatigue, the way it used to happen. She passed out and hit her head. She broke her wrist when she fell."

"You didn't take her to a hospital?"

My mom's answer was bitter. "Why? So they can set her bone and tell me there's nothing more they can do, and then send me on my way?" Mom took a breath and let it out, trying to compose herself. "After I found her by the river, she admitted the old symptoms had started to manifest. She said she'd been short of breath. She'd felt heart murmurs. She tired too easily. She hadn't wanted to tell me in case it was nothing. She wanted to be normal for as long as she could, didn't want me to start fussing over her and taking her to doctors again."

Mom covered her face and her shoulders shook as she began to cry. "I can't do it all over again. I can't wake up every day knowing I'm going to lose my sweet girl."

I felt distant as I watched my mom cry, separated from my emotions even without anima inside me. All I could think about was what I now knew about my mom, that she had lost her power because of me. That if she hadn't had me, she would still be Kalyptra, residing in paradise. If loving people was truly a choice, as Rebekah claimed, then my mom must hate me. And I had to admit, I hated her a little bit, too. All these years, I could have been healing Erin with anima. She could have lived a normal life instead of the pitiable existence she'd been born into. She had nearly died more times than I could remember, and my mom had never asked me to help her. Never guided me.

My mom would have rather let Erin die than let me be what I was and help my twin, and I hated her for that.

"Can you help her?" my mom asked, but too late for me to ever forgive her.

Instead of answering her, I turned to Blake and motioned him into the room. He stepped forward tentatively, like he wasn't sure his presence was appropriate. That was Blake. Always considerate. Always thoughtful. My feelings for him were still there, but they seemed subdued now, like they'd been shot up with a tranquilizer.

"Blake, can you carry Erin?" I asked him dubiously. Blake looked like a little boy compared to Cyrus. I wasn't sure he was strong enough.

But Blake nodded, eyes wide with curiosity. "Of course. Where are we going?"

"Into the forest," I said, and then turned back to face my mom. "Wrap her up in a blanket and keep her arm stabilized. We're going for a walk."

Erin roused briefly when Blake picked her up out of bed and cradled her against his chest. Her lids fluttered open, and when she saw me a sleepy smile curled the corners of her mouth, and my heart ached with grief for the healthy, transformed version of her she'd been when I saw her last. She wore an old pair of her glasses with a crack in one of the lenses.

"I'm so glad you're here," she said, her eyelids sagging closed again. My mom had given her pain medication for her broken wrist, and it had made her drowsy.

"Me too," I said, and hoped she didn't hear the lie in my voice. I wasn't complete without my sister, but that didn't mean I was happy to be home, surrounded by reminders of death. Of the terrible things I'd done and the terrible consequences those things had garnered. But Erin, more than any person I would ever know, was my soul mate and always would be. There was a reason I hadn't been able to say goodbye to her in the hospital the time she'd been so certain she was about to die. Without her, the best part of me would be gone, and I didn't know if I could live like that. I thought of Rebekah and her twin, the two of them so much like Erin and me, and my heart ached for my grandmother. I understood why she felt the need to create a place like Eclipse, to try to recreate what was lost and make it last forever. And I understood why my mother leaving her was such a betrayal.

Erin drifted back to sleep, and I brushed at the tears leaking from the corners of my eyes.

I took the lead as we marched through the dead woods toward the river. My mom and I carried flashlights. I shone mine around the forest where I used to spend so many hours with my guitar. Now the fragile, leafless trees were blackened and haunting, like skeletons made of needles and splinters.

While we walked, we heard frequent crashes as heavy branches fell and burst into dust.

As soon as we stepped into the living part of the forest, the air felt lighter, easier to breathe. I drew in a lungful and let it out slowly, turning in a circle. I didn't know how much I would have to cull to heal Erin again, but I couldn't cull wildly the way I had last time and risk losing control this time. If only I had one of Rebekah's jars, this would be easy. But I doubted Rebekah would ever sacrifice one of her precious jars to save a non-Kalyptra, even her own granddaughter.

"Blake, will you lay Erin down in this clearing?" I said, kneeling to pat an area soft with pine needles.

He did as I asked, panting with the exertion of carrying her. Then he and my mom stood on either side of me, waiting for my next move and giving me stage fright. I didn't think I could cull with them watching me, especially Blake, since he'd never seen what I could do. I wondered how it would look to him, if he would find the vena beautiful or terrifying. Either way, I wasn't ready to find out.

"I need privacy so I can concentrate," I told them. "Will you wait for me back at the house?"

"I'd rather stay close to make sure everything is okay," Mom said. Translation: she didn't trust me to keep Erin safe. I narrowed my eyes at her. If anyone didn't trust anyone at this point, it was I who didn't trust her. All the secrets she'd kept from me . . . all of the ways our lives could have been better if she'd only taken me to Eclipse to learn about myself sooner.

No, it was she who couldn't be trusted.

"I can't do it with you watching me," I said plainly, and held up my hands as though to say, *That's all there is to it.*

Finally, Mom nodded. "We'll come back in twenty minutes to check on you."

"Fine. Good." I was growing impatient.

My mom knelt and kissed my sleeping sister on her forehead and then disappeared into the woods, her flashlight beam cutting the dark. Blake lingered a moment longer, crouching down beside me.

"Hey," he said. "Are you okay with this? You seem a bit . . . uncertain."

"I'm okay," I lied. "Just worried about Erin."

"I don't understand much of what's happening, but I know you'll help her." Blake leaned forward to kiss me and I almost let him. For an instant, all the old feelings roared to life and I was ready to forget Cyrus and adore Blake and only Blake. Then the memory of Cyrus's warm skin against mine as we danced beside the fire ghosted through my mind.

I turned my face away, denying Blake's kiss, and hated myself for the hurt and confusion that furrowed his brow.

"Sorry," I told him. "I just . . . I have to concentrate."

"I'll leave you alone." He looked back over his shoulder at me as he walked away, the pain of rejection still in his eyes, reminding me of how Cyrus had looked as I'd driven away from Eclipse.

I covered my face with my hands. "Shit," I said under my breath. "Shit. Shit. Shit."

Nearby, I could hear the low gurgle of the river. Normally, I found the sound of the river soothing, but not today. What could I cull to heal Erin? I didn't want to destroy any more of the forest. That would attract suspicion. But I needed something potent. Something sentient.

Taking deep breaths to calm myself, I glanced around and saw a small pile of river stones and realized I had unconsciously guided us to the place where I'd buried Erin's cat and its litter so many years ago. *Would the anima of a living cat be enough to heal Erin now?* I wondered, and then felt guilty for thinking it. I didn't want to cull a cat or a dog or any other creature. But what choice did I have?

"Are you going to fix me again?" Erin asked, startling me from my thoughts.

I looked down to find Erin's eyes were open, gazing up at me.

"Is that why we're out here?" she said.

I smoothed her hair off her forehead. Her hair had thinned again, her scalp showing through. "That's the plan."

She frowned. "Is it safe for you?"

I nodded and forced a reassuring smile that I didn't feel. "Don't worry about me. I know how to stay in control now."

Her eyes moved across my face as though she were reading a map. "You're different, Kenna."

I couldn't meet her gaze. "A little. Yeah."

"A lot," she said, sounding troubled. "But you look beautiful."

I couldn't miss the note of disdain in her voice, and guilt

233

wrenched at my heart. A lot of people don't know this, but twins often balance each other out. When one is up, the other is down. When one is rebellious, the other tends to be obedient. When one is sick, the other becomes healthy. While I was away at Eclipse becoming the ultimate version of myself, Erin had been at home, withering with illness.

"Do you know why I'm sick again?" Erin asked. She'd always been better at reading my mind than I was at reading hers.

"I guess the fix wasn't permanent." I remembered what the dead version of Erin had said to me during my bad trip the other night.

Nothing lasts forever, not death and not life.

My sister's gaze moved to stare past my shoulder and she murmured, "'All that lives must die, passing through nature to eternity.'"

"What did you say?" I asked sharply, chills dotting my spine.

"It's a line from *Hamlet*," Erin said. "It's what Gertrude tells Hamlet when his father dies." Her eyes darkened behind her cracked glasses. "I've told you that line before. Remember?"

And then I did. She had quoted it to me when she'd come so close to dying. My mind had retained the meaning of the quote, but not the exact words, and had tormented me with it during my bad trip on the midnight glory.

"I remember," I said, nodding. "You're about a thousand times smarter than me, you know that?"

"That's because all I could ever do without hurting myself was sit in the house and read." Her eyes drifted past me and she sighed. "That time in the hospital, when I asked you to say goodbye to me . . ."

I swallowed hard, choking on emotion. "I couldn't do it. I still can't."

She nodded, as though we agreed on this. "I don't want to go back to the way I was," she said. "I know this sounds terrible, but I think I'd rather die than do that." Her eyes grew watery. "You want to hear something ironic?"

"Sure."

"Before I died, I wasn't afraid to die. I hated my body for being so frail. I wanted out of it. It was a prison. But then you brought me back and gave me a new body, and while you were gone I tried to do as many of the things I'd missed out on as I possibly could. I walked for hours in the forest. I ran on the trails. Kenna, I climbed a tree. I know it's silly, but I'd never done that before. And you know what? It was one of the most amazing things I've ever done. Why didn't you tell me what it was like to climb a t-tree?" Her voice hitched. "Now I'm terrified to die. I want this life, but not the old way. I want all the things I've been missing."

I nodded. I knew exactly what she meant. "I'm going to make sure you get what you want."

From the woods came a crack of twigs. I looked up, expecting to see another branch falling, but instead I found a stag with an impressive cradle of antlers striding through the trees less than ten feet from us.

235

I didn't think. Didn't hesitate. It was like that night in the basement all over again. Instinct took over, only this time instinct didn't lead me to cull everything in sight.

Only the stag.

I thrust out my hands, and my vena whipped from my palms and attached to the stag. It moaned like the hull of an old ship hitting rough water as its anima siphoned into me. I wanted to hold on to the anima, to experience what it was like to be the stag, this regal, dignified creature, all power and purpose and nobility.

But this anima was not for me.

I culled until the stag was sapped, its body a withered casing that fell to the forest floor with a hollow *thunk,* like a heavy sack of flour being dropped. I didn't realize until I turned my attention back to Erin that she was saying my name. Saying it again and again in horror.

"Kenna, no! Please stop!"

Her eyes were wide, and she was trying to sit up, to scoot away from me. She cried out as she jarred her broken wrist. Distantly, I was aware that she was afraid of me, repulsed by me, but with the stag's anima blanketing my mind I couldn't be concerned.

"Give me your hand," I said. My voice sounded like wind blowing through an old house, low and resonant.

Instead, Erin yanked her good hand away, so I planted both of my hands flat on her chest and pushed with all my might, as though trying to shove my way through a stuck door. The strands attached to her like IV tubes and anima poured from my body to hers. She released a hissing gasp, her eyes bulging from her head, light surrounding her whole body. Her back arched and her legs convulsed and her gasp became a scream. I saw her change before my eyes, watched her hair thicken and her skin go from chalky pale to a warm honey glow. Her muscles filled out and her wrist straightened.

And all the while she screamed.

And then silence.

It was over. The glow around her body faded, and inside I felt dark as a cave.

Erin sat up abruptly. She shot to her feet and I stood too, watching as she ripped her arm from the sling. Then she charged at me in fury and shoved me hard.

"I told you to stop! Why didn't you listen?"

I was breathless, my mind spinning like a top right before it goes out of control. "It worked. Your arm, all of you . . . I healed you."

To show me her arm was healed, she shoved me again.

"Why didn't you stop?" She was crying now, and I was bewildered.

"You said you'd rather die than go back to being sick."

"I—I didn't know how it would be! I didn't know you'd do *that*." She pointed an accusing finger, not at me, but at the corpse of the deer. "You were hurting it. It was horrible, Kenna. Is that what you did while you were at Eclipse? Killed animals? Sucked the life out of them like you did to Jason Dunn?"

I inhaled a sharp breath and shook my head rapidly. "No. No, of course not."

"I don't believe you."

Voices from the woods. My mom calling our names. She must have heard Erin shout.

Erin pushed me again, lighter this time, not to hurt me or knock me down. It was like she was lashing out, only in defeat.

"I can't let you do that to me again," she told me. "I was wrong. I want to live, but . . . not like this. Not like you."

My sister whirled around and ran from me.

"Erin, wait!" I charged after her.

Through the trees, I saw two figures with flashlights. Erin threw herself into my mom's waiting arms and started sobbing. Blake headed straight for me.

"What happened?" he asked. "Why is she crying?"

I opened my mouth to explain about the deer, and then closed it again and shook my head. The emptiness in me was all-consuming. I needed to take anima, and I knew I couldn't do it with Blake watching, not after Erin's reaction.

Her words cut me, as sharp as any knife.

I want to live, but not like this. Not like you.

"We'll talk later," I said to Blake, my voice coming out flat and deflated. "There's something I have to do."

I walked to the river, culling plants along the way, but for some reason their anima didn't satisfy me the way the anima at Eclipse had. Maybe that was because I had so recently culled a much more potent source of anima, and now everything in comparison seemed inadequate. What I wanted was another stag, to be filled with anima that made me feel mighty, formidable. To taste that experience again, if only temporarily.

But Erin was right. What I had done to that deer was horrifying. Necessary, but still it must have come as a shock to her to witness it firsthand. I must have seemed like a monster, every bit as repellent as the moth creature I'd imagined in the forest.

Would she ever see me the way she used to? Would my own twin turn away from me now that she knew what I was?

She had brought up Jason Dunn when she railed at me. So she had figured it out . . . She knew I had killed him.

I sank down by the bank of the river and bent to look at myself in the water. The moon was behind me, and the water reflected its light like a mirror. The smell of pine and the mossy scent of river water perfumed the air. I thought of the day I'd found Clint Eastwood's kittens, their bodies limp and their fur matted with mud. And Clint Eastwood's body, mutilated. Her head missing entirely. To this day, Erin still didn't know what Jason had been, but now she knew what I was, and she hated it.

A cloud moved over the moon, turning the river dark. A drop of cold water landed on the side of my nose, and more peppered my cheeks and forehead. Seconds later, a deluge began.

I stood and ran back toward my house. I'd just entered the barren perimeter of trees when a flashlight beam stopped me in my tracks.

"Kenna, is that you?" It was Blake.

I stopped running. He didn't have an umbrella or a raincoat, and his hair was plastered to his head, his T-shirt drenched and sticking to his skin.

Blake lowered the flashlight so it wasn't shining in my eyes. "I know you wanted to be alone, but I got worried when it started to rain."

"It's okay," I said, hugging myself to keep warm. "I'm finished out here."

"You're shivering. Come on, let's get inside."

I didn't move. "How's Erin?"

He hesitated. "She's freaked out, but your mom is handling her. She's just happy whatever you did worked."

I clenched my fists, my palms slick with rain. It worked, but if Erin wouldn't allow me to heal her again then ultimately it wouldn't matter. Unless I forced anima on her. I could do that, sneak into her room while she was sleeping and dose her with a little anima every day. Maybe that would be enough to keep her healthy. Maybe I didn't need to cull such potent anima to sustain her.

I didn't know. All I knew was that Erin was disgusted with me, and it made me feel disgusted with myself, too.

Blake tried to take my arm to pull me in the direction of the house, but I yanked away. I could feel the anima flowing inside him like a self-contained river. And I wanted it. I wanted *him*.

I didn't know what I was doing. One second I was pulling away from him. The next I had knocked the flashlight from his hand. It fell to the ground, pointing away from us. Then I grabbed the back of his neck and pulled his mouth to mine. For a moment he was too stunned to react, but when he did there was none of the politeness that had been present in our first kiss. This one was all fervor and need. Rain poured down our faces, caught in our lashes, and wet our lips. I relished the feel of Blake's mouth moving on mine, and the sense of anima flowing just on the other side of his skin.

His lips tracked down over my rain-drenched chin to my neck. He kissed my collarbone. My fingers disappeared in his hair. I drew him down onto the soggy ground on top of me. The forest floor was soft with the ash of crumbled trees, silty like the dust from a moth's wing. And there *were* moth wings beneath us. Hundreds, thousands of them. They blanketed the ground like fall leaves.

Blake hesitated, refusing to put his full weight on top of me. He looked bewildered, eyes wild, breathing as hard as if he'd just finished a marathon.

I yanked him down again, needing to feel his anima.

"We can't, um, you know," he said, knuckling his forehead in a way that made him seem too young, too innocent to be doing this.

"We won't. I just want to be close to you," I said. "As close as I can be."

He bowed over me and grazed my lips softly with his, holding back. But I needed more urgency. I needed more *need*.

I rolled him over and straddled him so I could be in control, and found myself pinning him with his elbows over his head as I crushed my mouth down on his. I moved my hands to his chest, planted my palms there.

A memory flashed into my mind. Images. Fragmented perceptions. Jason Dunn's empty eyes. My hand grabbing his arm. A vein of energy reaching out from the center of my palm to connect me to him, so I could drink his life. His light.

I sat up, rain pouring down my back, blinking at my hands still flat on Blake's chest. The dropped flashlight pointed into my eyes, seeming accusatory. A tickling sensation had started in the center of my palms, hair-thin strands of my vena uncoiling like tenuous bridges.

I shot to my feet and Blake sat up, dazed, chest heaving. "What's wrong? Did I do something?"

I backed away from him, holding up my hands as if to ward him off like a wolf I'd happened upon in the woods.

"Stay away from me, Blake," I told him. "You're my best friend, and I love you, but stay the hell away from me."

SPLINTERS AND STAINS

WHEN THE DOORBELL RANG THE NEXT MORNING, I knew before answering that it would be Blake. The rash of texts I'd received from him since I'd left him last night foretold his visit.

He lifted the black guitar case he carried by his side. "I thought you might want this back now that you're home."

"Oh, right. Thanks." I hadn't even thought about the guitar since I got home. My mind was still struggling to wake up from the dream that was Eclipse. I felt like I'd been ripped from the deepest sleep.

The rain had ceased sometime during the night, and morning dawned bright as sunflowers, although no amount of sunlight could turn the land around my house into anything other than a circle of depressing gray. How could gray have ever been my color? It was a miserable color. But, then,

I'd been a miserable person. That had changed at Eclipse, and now I felt the pull of that place like a tide drawing me back. I missed my other bed, missed my room with its potbellied stove and my mom's antique guitar, even though I had to keep it hidden beneath my bed, where it still lay. I missed the Kalyptra, and the air that seemed to carry every scent and sound farther than the air in the rest of the world. If someone were baking bread inside Eclipse House, I could smell it from the field. If someone sang in the orchard, I could name every note. Even the sky there seemed different—deeper and bluer and more dramatic, regardless of whether my view of it was enhanced by anima.

"Want some coffee?" I asked Blake, raising my mug. I'd always drunk it black, the sharpness of its taste almost like a daily punishment for my past mistakes, but now I was used to Hitomi's tea blends, and in comparison the coffee tasted too bitter. Or maybe it was just me who was bitter. I'd done time in paradise and come home to a dead forest, a dying sister, and a mom who felt like someone I'd never met.

But there was still Blake. Even though I knew he'd be better off without me in his life, I wanted him in *my* life. Like twins, we'd balanced each other out, finished each other. He was my light and I was his darkness. But in the end, maybe that just created more gray.

"No, thanks," he said to my offer of coffee. He set the guitar case down on the porch. "Can we talk?" he asked, squinting in the sunlight. He'd forgotten his sunglasses, and I could see his eyes were bleary, red lidded. He looked like he hadn't slept. I hadn't either. Too many thoughts twisting and tangling inside my brain like fast-growing vines.

We sat on the porch, keeping several inches between us. So much for not reverting back to old patterns.

"I'm sorry about last night," I said. "I didn't know what I was doing."

He entwined his fingers, keeping his eyes on his knees. "No, I'm glad you stopped us. I mean, it's not like I don't want to . . . you know. But we didn't have protection, and it was muddy and raining and—" He shook his head. "It just wasn't how I imagined it should be with us. Not that I thought there'd be silk sheets and chocolate strawberries or anything, but . . . well, you know."

Blotches of red appeared on his neck and he cleared his throat and adjusted his collar like it was too tight.

I stared at him, uncomprehending, until it hit me: he thought I was talking about sex. He had no idea that, when we were kissing, I had been a hair away from taking his anima. And if I'd started to do that, I had no idea if I could have stopped. Then I would have added one more dead person to the list of people I'd culled, only this time it would have been someone I loved.

"Blake," I said, my stomach filling with acid. "I have to tell you something."

I started with the truth: I killed a boy named Jason Dunn.

I ended with another truth: I almost killed Blake.

In between, I did my best to leave out no details. Rebekah would be furious if she found out what I'd told him, but I felt like I owed him an explanation. Besides, if there was one person in the world I trusted completely it was Blake, and it was time he understood who I really was. Then he could decide for himself whether he wanted someone like me in his life.

"So that's it," I said after talking for over an hour with few interruptions from Blake. My coffee was cold now, and more bitter than ever. I finished it anyway and cringed, setting the mug aside. "I've never told anyone else."

He looked at me, and the expression on his face made me want to sink into the ground. In his eyes, I saw what I always feared I would see if someone knew the truth: revulsion. It was fleeting, but I saw it in the downward turn of his mouth and the pinch of his eyes. Then Blake covered his face with his hands, dragging them down over his cheeks.

"You were just a kid," he said. "You didn't know what you were doing."

"I did know," I insisted. "He was bad. He made my sister suffer, so I decided to make him pay for it. It was murder, Blake, and it was intentional. I might as well have put Jason in a killing jar of my own. I *am* a killing jar, Blake. A living, breathing killing jar, and I almost put you inside, too."

Blake stared out at the crumbling, gray woods.

"You want to go back to Eclipse," he said, speaking my thoughts for me in a voice that sounded weary and defeated.

"I don't know what I want." After all those truths, I was starting with the lies again. I knew exactly what I wanted.

Blake stood and turned to me. His expression morphed from betrayal to heartbreak to loss, finally arriving at anger.

"You may not know what you want, but I do," he said. "I want you here with me. When you decide that's where you belong, I'll be waiting."

He shoved his hands in his pockets and walked away, his shoulders hunched and his head bowed slightly. It was the posture of someone trying to protect himself, and that's why I didn't run after him or call him back. I'd hurt him too much already. I didn't want to hurt him anymore.

I didn't want to hurt anyone.

I picked up my guitar case and went back inside the house with the intention of holing up in my room and practicing some of the Kalyptra songs I'd learned. I didn't want to forget them. It occurred to me that I hadn't written any new music since I'd gone to Eclipse, and that I didn't actually feel any need to. I only wanted their music now. My own was too dark, too mournful. I wanted the brightness and vivacity of Kalyptra rhythms, the bone-rattling throb of Kalyptra drum beats.

But my mom waited for me in the foyer. Her eyelids were red, so I guessed she'd been crying.

"We need a family meeting," she said, her voice just raspy enough to confirm that, yes, she had definitely been crying.

I sighed, my body sagging. I felt so tired I could barely stay upright. I needed to take anima soon. At Eclipse, I was constantly sampling anima. I rarely went more than a few hours without it.

"Can it wait?" I asked.

She shook her head. She looked even more tired than I felt. "Now would be better. There are things we need to . . . resolve."

Resigned, I set my guitar down in the foyer, and followed her to the dining room, where Erin was already seated at the table.

I sat across from my sister, who kept her eyes trained on the surface of the table, as though it were the most interesting thing she'd ever seen. I tried to get her to look at me, but she only drew more tightly into herself like a potato bug. Her rejection did more than sting: it crushed. It flattened me like roadkill.

And it pissed me off.

I had saved her. I'd healed her broken, useless, prison of a body, and this was how she treated me?

I folded my arms over my chest, clenching my fists and glaring at her so she would feel my anger, even if she didn't see it in my eyes.

"So." Mom cleared her throat, glancing between the two of us. "Our family has been through hell. I think we can all agree on that. But I have a feeling the worst is behind us now, don't you, girls?"

Erin ignored her. I raised an eyebrow and waited for her to get this over with.

"As we move forward, we need to establish some guidelines," she went on.

Mom launched into what was clearly a prepared speech.

I tried to listen, but at some point I became fixated on her hands. I couldn't stop looking at them. They were identical to Rebekah's, the fingers long and slender. How could my mom have betrayed Rebekah the way she did? How could she abandon a mother who loved her so much that she built a new world for her? Rebekah had given her a freaking utopia, and she had shunned it. What was wrong with this woman?

"Kenna, are you listening?" Mom said.

I raised my eyes. "Yep. Keep Erin healthy, but don't cull animals, only plants. Keep what I am a secret. Never do what I do in public. I got it."

"Do I even get a say in this?" Erin asked, finally looking up. Her chin thrust out defiantly. She looked beautiful and strong, and I hardly recognized her.

Mom's brow furrowed in confusion. "Erin . . . you understand that we don't really have a choice in all this. If you want to stay healthy, you have to let Kenna help you."

"Then maybe I don't want to stay healthy. Maybe I wasn't meant to be healthy."

"Honey," Mom said, trying to maintain a reasonable tone, though I could tell she was panicking inside. "You don't mean that."

"I don't? Tell me, why is it so important for Kenna to save me now? How long has she been able to do this . . . this *thing* she does? Her whole life? And only now you want her to start playing witch doctor to me?"

I raised my eyebrows at Erin. I had never heard her speak to our mom with such venom in her tone.

"She makes a good point," I said. "I've been wondering the same thing myself."

Mom looked helplessly from me to Erin, and then lowered her eyes. "I—I told you in the car, Kenna, I made a mistake, and I realize that now. I should have taken you to Eclipse a long time ago, but I was afraid."

"Afraid of what?" Erin and I asked in unison.

Mom shook her head, her hair hanging around her face. I saw a tear drop from her eye and land on the table. "That you would turn out like me. That you would be too weak to control your gift."

Cold fingers of dread traced my spine. "What did you do, Mom?"

She didn't answer, only shook her head, more tears dripping onto the table. I should have felt pity for her, but instead disgust writhed through me like a serpent.

I stood abruptly, my chair shrieking across the hardwood. "You don't even want me here. The only reason you sent Blake to pick me up was because Erin needed me. Otherwise you would have left me at Eclipse forever."

My mom looked at me like I'd slapped her, raising her head and blinking in stunned surprise. "That's not true. I—I only wanted to give you time. You know why I couldn't stay there with you, why it was dangerous for me to bring you home."

"I also know how easy it is for you to turn your back on family. You did it to your own mother. You were the only real family she had, and you just abandoned her. The same way you abandoned me."

"You think that was easy?" She stood to face me, but when she spoke her voice was trembling. "Nothing about what I did back then was easy, Kenna, so don't accuse me of things you don't understand. I left because I wanted a real life, a decent life, and I want the same thing for you."

"No," I said. "You want me to be something I'm not. You want me to be normal and safe and mundane. But guess what? I'm never going to be, but lucky for you I can keep Erin alive and healthy, so you can have a normal daughter after all."

I hated myself for the things I was saying, but I couldn't stop. So many unsaid words had built up inside me, and now it was all pouring out like lava, consuming everyone in its path.

Erin stood, too, glaring at me as though I were the lowest thing on the planet. A worm. A fungus. A virus.

"And whose fault is it that I was born defective, Kenna?" she said. "Is it a coincidence that I shared a womb with you and came out sick? Is it a coincidence that Mom almost died before she could bring us to term? Or does it all revolve around *you*?"

"Erin, don't," Mom said. "Please, just stop."

"No," Erin said sharply. "Kenna needs to know what she did to us."

My mouth opened, but all of my harsh words had dried up and blown away. My heart, too, seemed to have shriveled in my chest. Illia had told me Kalyptra didn't have children because if they did, they lost their gift. The only reason Rebekah had been able to have my mom was because she'd given birth before she became Kalyptra. But she hadn't said anything about this. Was it true? Had I nearly killed my mom and Erin simply by existing?

My sister, my twin, fixed her eyes on mine. "You ruined me," she said. "So don't act like you're doing me any favors by saving me now. If it weren't for you, I wouldn't have needed saving. If it weren't for you—" She hesitated, but only for a moment. "We'd all be better off."

My brain went numb. My skin felt as cold as a corpse's and I started to shake.

I didn't argue with Erin because I didn't disagree. Instead I nodded, turned my back on my family, and walked out.

I grabbed my guitar case in the foyer and headed toward my bedroom, wanting to be alone, but then I found myself standing at the foot of the stairs that led down into our unfinished basement. I hadn't been down there since this whole nightmare began. I'd told myself I would never go into the basement again, but my feet had different ideas. They moved me forward and down, into the darkness.

It's not easy to get blood out of cement. Cement is porous. It absorbs. It stains. It keeps.

Someone had tried to clean the blood from the storage room in our basement where Thomas Dunn had killed my family. The blood itself was gone, but the stain remained, a permanent shadow cast by that night's events. A permanent bruise on our lives.

I stepped into the room and set my guitar case down. It

smelled metallic, like pennies. All of the boxes and odd bits of furniture that had been stored inside were gone. It was just an empty, tainted room now.

I moved to the one corner of the little room where blood hadn't reached and sat down with my guitar case laid on my legs. My fingers traced the lyrics I'd scrawled on the case in silver pen.

Ghosts crowd the young child's fragile eggshell mind. The Doors.

I love you. I'm not gonna crack. Nirvana.

There's someone in my head but it's not me. Pink Floyd.

Why had I chosen these scraps of lyrics? They had spoken to me, but that had been another version of me. These words were so hopeless, so dark. I wished I could wash them away and start with new lyrics, bits of the Kalyptra's songs, which were the kind of optimistic poetry I had never before imagined myself writing.

And no wonder I had been depressed. Not only had I murdered a kid, but by simply existing I had destroyed my twin's body and nearly killed my own mother.

I unsnapped the brass clasps on the case and opened it, revealing my acoustic guitar. I lifted it out, cradled it in my arms like a sleeping child. For the last seven years, when I'd been unable to touch anyone, I had held on to this guitar. When I was so lonely I could barely stand it anymore, I had my music.

I began to play, brushing the strings, arching my fingers to form chords. I sang, but my voice came out hollow and toneless. I hadn't taken anima yet today, and I felt vacant, like my soul had taken a vacation from my body.

"You shouldn't be down here."

My hands froze on the strings. Erin stood in the doorway, her face pale, as though she might throw up. Her eyes were wide open, staring at the broad stain on the cement.

"I figured this was the one place where no one would come looking for me. Not that you'd want to see me."

"I'm sorry for what I said up there," Erin said, holding up her hands and shaking her head miserably. "I was upset and everything just poured out."

"I'm sorry I ruined your life."

She looked stricken. "You didn't," she said, but there wasn't much conviction to her words. We both knew they weren't true.

"Erin, seriously, it's okay," I told her, but my hand clenched involuntarily on the guitar strings until I felt them cutting into my fingers. "I'd rather know the truth. When did Mom tell you?" I asked.

"She didn't tell me anything," Erin said. "I analyzed the facts and I guessed. I guess I guessed right." She shrugged. "But it's not like it's your fault, Kenna. You are what you are. You didn't choose to be born this way."

A monster. A killer.

No. I was Kalyptra. Rebekah had told me there was no shame in what we were, and that was what I wanted to believe, but it was getting harder to do that with every passing hour.

I nodded. "Now that we're all on the same page, it—" *It*

makes my decision easier, I almost said, and then stopped my-self. "It's something I can deal with," I finished.

Erin hung her head. She picked at a loose string on one sleeve. "I feel like I've lost you," she said in a quiet, defeated voice.

I swallowed what felt like a wet sock jammed down my throat. "You haven't lost me. We're just different, like you said. I was born the way I am, and you were born the way you are. We didn't get much choice in the matter. We're kind of the worst twins ever, you know?"

She laughed dryly at this. "Yeah, we're the worst."

Her laughter died off quickly, and an uncomfortable si-lence stretched between us. I had never once in my life felt uncomfortable around my own twin. Maybe she *had* lost me a little bit. Or we had lost each other. If Erin didn't need me to keep her alive—if, that was, she would let me—would it even matter if I disappeared into Eclipse forever?

I cleared my throat. "I need to be alone, okay? I have a lot to think about."

"Okay." She sniffed, turned around, and I knew she was crying. She paused, but didn't look at me as she said, "You should check out Blake's blog. It might remind you of what you've been missing."

When I was alone again, I sat for a long time, clutching my guitar, my muscles straining with tension until they trembled. I stared at the bloodstain on the floor, my teeth clenched. My problems hadn't started here, but this room, with its stain that wouldn't wash off, was a perfect metaphor for my life.

I stood abruptly, holding my guitar by the neck. Then I swung it over my head and smashed it into the wall. The strings twanged and the wood snapped and cracked like the trunk of a falling tree. I beat the instrument against the wall until it splintered to a hundred pieces, and then I fell to my knees among its remains and grasped them, squeezed them into my palms until they pierced skin and blood welled up around sharp shafts of wood.

I wanted to cry, but instead I bled.

For a long time, I only knelt there, watching my palms fill with crimson, thinking there was nothing I could do to wash away the stain. The only way to escape it was to leave.

ANYA

MY MOM KNOCKED ON MY BEDROOM DOOR AROUND midnight, which was late for her. She woke at five a.m. every day to drive to her bakery, so her standard bedtime was a sensible ten p.m.

Sensible. That had always been a word I used to describe my mom. But now she made no sense to me. Why would she leave Eclipse for this? Why would she have children when she knew it would strip her of her power and might even kill her?

I remembered the message Joanna had given me to deliver to my mom.

Tell her she was right, and I was wrong. Tell her I wish I'd come with her. I wish it more than I can ever say.

Why did Joanna wish that? What was I missing?

It was then I remembered, too, what Joanna had told me about my mom's guitar, that there was something hidden inside it. So much had happened since my hurried departure from Eclipse that I'd forgotten all about this new revelation.

Mom sat on the edge of my bed. She seemed drained of energy, like she hadn't slept in days. I thought idly how much better I could make her feel with a small infusion of anima, but I had a feeling she would decline an offer to help her even if I made it.

I was afraid that you would turn out like me. That you would be too weak to control your gift.

That was what she'd said during our disastrous family meeting. But what exactly did that mean? Had my mom been unable to handle her need for anima? Had she let it overwhelm her like I had almost done?

Had she hurt someone, like I had, and been unable to forgive herself?

Something about this sounded extremely plausible, and it explained why Mom would go to such drastic measures to rid herself of her gift. But had she known what the risk would be to her life?

I had my laptop open on my legs. It felt uncomfortable to be using technology again, like I was breaking some kind of rule. She glanced at the screen and saw a window open to Blake's art blog.

She squinted at the screen. "Is that you . . . riding an ostrich?"

"Yeah."

Blake had been busy while I was away. He'd drawn more than a dozen insanely intricate panels dedicated to the extraterrestrial ostrich story he'd been inspired to create while we sat in his 4Runner at Folk Yeah! Fest. I'd forgotten all about it. That day seemed like it had happened in a past life.

Blake had made me the alien ostrich leader, a gray-haired warrior girl who rode on a silver-armored ostrich and wielded a guitar that doubled as a machine gun. The drawings were insane and wonderful, and they'd garnered more comments than any of Blake's other works to date. And, I was pleased to see, there wasn't a single troll among the commenters.

Blake had titled the series *The Gray Girl* and included a dedication: *To Kenna, my reluctant muse, my music guru, and my best friend.*

When I'd read the dedication, tears had sprung to my eyes. Blake was the best, he really was. I didn't deserve a friend like him, much less a boyfriend. Not that he *was* my boyfriend, even though last night I had practically mauled him in the woods. Now I wasn't sure we were even friends anymore, not after this morning. A lump formed in my throat at the thought.

"I can't believe I'm admitting this, but I miss your gray hair," Mom said.

I closed the laptop. "Things change," I said.

"That I know," she said softly. She twisted her hands on her lap, gazing at my empty guitar case. "I saw what's left of your guitar in the basement. Are you okay?"

I looked at my hands. Where the splinters from my busted guitar had pierced them, there was now unbroken, pristine skin. I'd taken anima after my little freak-out and had healed them. But I didn't think she was asking whether I was physically okay.

"You should have told me," I said. "About why Erin has always been so sick. About why you had us in the first place."

"Kenna . . . what good would that have done? You couldn't help what you were, or what you were doing."

"But *you* could have," I said.

"I could have done many things differently, but I didn't."

My mom lowered her eyes, and for a moment I thought she was going to cry. Instead, she took a deep breath and sighed it out.

"I knew that having you and Erin would be a risk, but a necessary risk."

"Did you even want us?" I asked. "Or were we just a means to an end?"

"I don't know how to answer that, Kenna. I was your age when I made the decision. I couldn't see far enough into the future to gauge what the consequences would be. But once I had you and Erin, I knew I wanted you even more than I wanted to be Kalyptra. I wanted to live in the real world with you, not in some forever daydream. So I made my choice, and I'm willing to live with the consequences."

I shook my head at her. "I don't buy it."

"You don't buy what?"

"That you just decided to leave one day. There's something you're not telling me." I changed track suddenly, catching her off guard. "Joanna gave me a message for you."

I told her what Joanna had said, and watched as hope and pain warred on her face.

"Who was Joanna to you back then?" I asked. "What did you and she have planned that she didn't follow through on?"

For a moment I thought my mom would refuse to answer. Her expression closed and became unreadable, and her eyes traveled the room, as though searching for a safe place to land.

After a long moment, she looked at me with such sadness that I felt it infect me like a flu, making my skin chill and my stomach churn. "There is what I thought Joanna was, and what she actually was. I thought she was my soul mate. I thought she loved me, and I knew I loved her. We made plans to leave Eclipse together, but when the time came to actually do it, she balked and refused. It was too late for me to turn back then. I was already pregnant, and she knew it. She'd gone with me to Rushing, and helped me choose my . . . my target. I thought I would have to try multiple times with several different men, but I got pregnant the very first time. Joanna . . . she didn't, but she was with me every step of the way, right up until it counted." Mom's mouth quirked in a forlorn smile. "Turns out there is a big difference between a lover and someone who loves you."

I blinked at her once, the truth hitting me harder than I'd expected. Despite the rumors that had always wandered through town, people speculating on whether or not my mom was gay, I'd never really taken the notion seriously. Though she was beautiful, my mom seemed sort of asexual to me, but now another layer had peeled back, revealing the core of the person hidden deep inside her.

"Does it bother you?" Mom asked when I didn't say anything.

I quickly shook my head. "No. I'm just . . . I'm a little . . . well, it's a lot to take in."

"I understand." She stood abruptly, crossing her arms over her chest, seeming vulnerable with this new truth out in the open. "You need a new guitar," she said, trying to change the subject. "We should go shopping in Portland this weekend. It'll help get your mind off things."

"I played your guitar when I was at Eclipse," I told her. "Joanna said you would have wanted me to have it."

"My guitar." Her gaze became distant and slightly confused, as though she were recalling a memory that made her as sad as it did happy. "Rebekah wouldn't let me take it when I left. She said she was going to burn it."

"But she didn't," I said. "Maybe she's changed. *You* did."

"Rebekah isn't made of the stuff that changes."

"Then why did she tell me I could come back to Eclipse whenever I want?"

Mom blinked at me. "She did?"

I nodded, and her hand went to her lips, her eyes moving back and forth as though she were reading invisible text floating in the air.

Then her eyes focused on me. "I know I haven't always been the kind of mother you wanted, but I'd like to change. I have been thinking a lot about this, and I decided the whole family needs a fresh start. A new house. A new city. Erin started applying to colleges, and it turns out she's eligible for all kinds of scholarships. We could go anywhere in the country. How about the East Coast?"

"The East Coast?" I said, stunned. "What about your bakery?"

"I'll expand," she said, shrugging.

But I wasn't really concerned about Mom's bakery, even though it was her pride and joy, and every time I'd ever asked her if she wanted to open more locations she'd balked, claiming she liked the idea that there was only one in the whole world. No, what I was thinking about was what was really going on here, my mom wanting to put distance between Eclipse and me.

"I know it's sudden," Mom said. "But I don't think we can stay in this house after everything that's happened."

She was right about that. I couldn't live in this house, but the East Coast was not the alternative I had in mind.

"It'll be good for you and Erin to live someplace where no one knows you," she continued. "You can start over."

That was the same thing Rebekah had said to me my first night at Eclipse. *Tomorrow you start over*—and I had. I wasn't ready to do it again. I liked who I was at Eclipse. I wanted to be that person, not the wreck of a person I'd been since I got home.

"When is all of this happening?" I asked, clenching my fists until my nails dug into the meat of my palms.

"We should start packing tomorrow," Mom said.

My lips parted and a shocked breath escaped. "Tomorrow," I repeated, wishing I'd heard her wrong. "That's too soon."

"Why wait?" she said. "We should move before summer's over so you can enroll in time for the start of your senior year."

"But what about the house? You'll have to sell and that could take months, if anyone will even buy it at all after what happened here." I had her there. I almost smiled in triumph.

Then she shook her head, and my relief turned to dread.

"I've already had offers from people who want to study what happened to the land. And I've been getting calls from news programs willing to pay very well for an exclusive interview with me. I'll call the highest bidder and tell her I changed my mind."

"But you can't tell the truth," I argued. "You'll have to lie on national television."

"It's not like I'll be under oath." She sighed. "Besides, I've been lying to you and Erin your whole lives. What does it matter if I lie to the rest of the world?"

I gritted my teeth until I felt they might shatter. "You can't do this to me," I said, tears of anger and frustration beginning to leak from the corners of my eyes. I wiped at them furiously, and then gave up and let them flow. I shouldn't hide what my mom was doing to me. She ought to know she was destroying what little hope for happiness I had left.

Mom moved to leave. "I really do think this is the best

thing for us." She didn't meet my eyes when she said it. "Welcome home, Kenna." She closed the door behind her.

I sat there for a long moment, tensed and trembling with fury, a sob perched in my throat like a cough. Mom was the one who'd abandoned me at Eclipse, who had introduced me to their way of life, and now she was willing to move the whole family to a different city just to keep me away?

Why? Who were the Kalyptra that my mom feared me becoming like them?

I needed to understand.

I opened my laptop and closed the window to Blake's blog, and then opened a new Google browser and searched: Eclipse moth, mythology.

I didn't come up with much, but there was a Wikipedia page that talked about *Calyptra* moths, a genus of vampire moths that fed on blood and tears. The Eclipse moth was mentioned briefly. The page said the Eclipse moth, if there were any evidence of its existence, would be included in the same family as *Calyptra*. The Eclipse moth was featured in certain Central and South American and Native American myths and legends, and was sometimes worshipped as a goddess. *Brujas* in Mexico referred to her only as *La Madre*.

The Mother.

The only other source of information I found was an online compendium of mythical beasts and monsters. The entry for the Eclipse moth said it lurked deep in forests, and supposedly grew to enormous size, drank human blood, and was said to bestow a "wondrous gift" upon those who worshipped it, the ability to "consume the breath of life and see beyond the veil that separates the physical world from the spiritual." It also mentioned that the Eclipse moth was elusive, but that it couldn't resist a combination of blood and fire.

I shuddered.

There was an illustration beside the paragraph with information about the Eclipse moth, depicting a moth the size of a small house hovering over a naked woman bound to a wooden stake. Her wrists were slit, streaming blood, and the moth's tongue extended toward one wound. A circle of worshippers knelt around the feeding moth, bowing in supplication.

I slammed my laptop shut, but the image stayed behind my eyes like a camera flash. The moth in the illustration was much larger than the one I had hallucinated in the forest, but still . . . a moth that grew to enormous size. Could it really be a coincidence? Maybe I'd read about the Eclipse moth at some point, and my mind had hallucinated it when I'd overdosed on midnight glory anima.

I shook my head and forced a laugh. It was silly to take anything seriously that I read on a website that looked like it had been designed by a Swedish death metal band.

I tried to wipe the memory of that illustration from my mind, but the image lingered like a song that you can't get out of your head. I needed to replace it with something else, a song I wanted to hear.

I needed to see the Kalyptra before my mom stole me away to the other side of the country, and I didn't have a lot of time left.

I crept to my bedroom door and opened it a crack to peer down the hall toward my mom's bedroom. There was no light shining from beneath her door. She must have gone to sleep.

I slipped into the hall, walked softly to Erin's room, and knocked so lightly I barely made a sound. Erin and I had never knocked on each other's doors before, but things had changed. I didn't feel comfortable walking into her room unannounced anymore, and I had a feeling she wouldn't be cool with that, either.

The light in Erin's room was off, but I heard her bed creak and a moment later she opened the door a few inches. She saw it was me and hesitated to open it farther. She simply stared at me, eyes large and expectant, and more than a tad wary.

I sighed, feeling heavy and out of place. Yes, things had definitely changed.

"I need a favor," I said, and was relieved when she opened her door wider to allow me inside.

She turned on her bedside lamp and crossed her arms over her chest. "What is it?" she asked.

I bit my lip and released it. "I have to go back."

She raised an eyebrow. "To Eclipse?"

I nodded. "Tonight. Just for a day."

"Why?" she asked, her tone defiant, but I could tell by the resigned look in her eyes that she already knew the answer.

"Mom told me about this whole moving thing. I need to say goodbye to the Kalyptra. I don't know how long it will be before I see them again."

"Then let me come with you," Erin said, dropping her arms to her sides. "I want to see where Mom came from. And . . . I want to meet our grandmother."

But she doesn't want to meet you, I almost said before biting back the words in time.

"No," I said firmly, and felt a pang of regret for my tone when Erin wilted. "I'm sorry," I told her more gently. "This is something I have to do alone."

"Then why are you telling me?" she asked.

I took a breath and let it out, bracing myself for another bout of resistance from my twin. "I need you to convince Mom not to come after me."

Erin shook her head. "What makes you think she'll listen to me? It's not like I can play the dying-wish card anymore."

I winced at the same moment she did, both of us remembering that Erin was, indeed, still dying. Or she would be without me to keep her alive.

"I'll find a way," Erin said quietly, lowering her eyes to the floor as if in defeat. "How do you plan to get there?"

I cleared my throat. "Well, that's the other thing . . ."

BEST NIGHT EVER

MY MOM OWNED TWO CARS, ONE A USED PRIUS—which was what she drove most often—and the other a beat-up Jeep Grand Cherokee that was older than I was. Mom barely drove the Jeep unless she had deliveries or was catering an event. I figured she wouldn't be doing any of that over the next few days, so she wouldn't mind if I borrowed it. At least that's what I decided to tell myself, since my mom was pretty much guaranteed to lose it when she found out I'd gone back to Eclipse.

Once I was on the road through the Cross Pine Mountains with Rushing behind me, I began to breathe easier, but I couldn't relax. I kept my eyes trained on the road, searching for the turnoff onto the rutted, overgrown path to Eclipse. It was hard to see in the daylight, which meant it would be ten times harder in the dark. I almost missed the road and had to slam on the brakes and reverse on the highway. Good thing it was after midnight and there were no other cars in sight.

The journey was even bumpier than I remembered it being, and the Jeep's check-engine light came on after I'd driven about five miles into the wilderness, and shortly after that it began to make a rattling sound. I began to think this had been a bad idea, or that I should have at least waited until first light.

I managed to reach the fence without the Jeep breaking down, but I was dismayed to find that the gate Blake had rammed open to come and retrieve me had been mended and was once again locked.

I parked and got out of the Jeep, leaving the headlights on and the engine running while I studied the gate with my hands on my hips. I could abandon the Jeep and hoof it the rest of the way to Eclipse, or I could blast through it the way Blake had done. Or I could give up and go home.

I sighed, my shoulders sagging. I didn't like any of my options.

"I knew you couldn't stay away."

The voice came from the darkness, and I almost screamed before I recognized the familiar Johnny Cash twang.

Cyrus stepped into the headlight beams, fingers hooked in his belt loops and a restrained half smile on his face. He sauntered to the gate. My heart, which had leaped into my throat when he'd spoken, now plummeted into my giddy stomach. I barely felt my feet as they moved me toward him. We stopped with the fence between us and put our hands on the top rail, our fingers almost touching. I sensed the anima singing through him, and I wanted to lay my palms over his knuckles and drink in that awareness of his vitality, that uncanny connectivity I felt with all of the Kalyptra, but most especially with Cyrus.

"It's so good to see you," I said.

"It's better to see you."

Heat traveled up my neck and my skin prickled with excitement. "What are you doing here?" I asked, and he shrugged, his smile broadening.

"Waiting for you."

"Liar," I said.

He put his right hand over his heart. "Truth."

"You've been out here since I left?"

"Off and on. Mostly on." He lowered his eyes. "The mood at Eclipse has been unusually somber. Everyone's been sulking since you went away, including Rebekah."

"Really?" I raised my eyebrows. I couldn't imagine Rebekah sulking.

"Really," he said, and lifted his gaze to mine. "But I had a feeling you couldn't stay away for long." He reached inside his shirt, pulled the key on its leather thong over his head, and handed it to me.

"Welcome back, Kenna. Welcome home."

I would have filed the night I played in front of the Folk Yeah! Fest crowd and kissed Blake for the first time in the "best night ever" category, were it not for the part where I came home to find my family massacred in an insane act of revenge. But even if the double homicide hadn't happened, I didn't think that night could compete with the night I returned to Eclipse.

The Kalyptra—all of them night owls like me—were still awake when Cyrus and I returned. They greeted me with hugs and exclamations of delight, and even a few tears. Although Rebekah didn't literally jump for joy like some of the others, I could tell she was pleased to have me back.

"I knew you couldn't stay away long," she said, echoing Cyrus's words, a satisfied smile on her lips as she wrapped me in her slender arms.

"It seems like I was gone for a month," I told her, closing my eyes and basking in her affection like I'd just stepped into the sunlight after being trapped in a dank cellar for days. But a sinking despair marred my happiness, the knowledge that tomorrow I was supposed to start packing up everything I owned so Mom could put me a safe distance from the Kalyptra.

Rebekah seemed to sense my darkening mood. She held me back and searched my face. "What's wrong?" she asked. "What's happened, sweet girl?"

I swallowed emotion thick as tar and said, "We're moving away. Like, as far as my mom can take us. She wants us to start over somewhere else. She didn't say it, but I think she just wants to get me away from Eclipse."

"No," Rebekah said simply, as though it were up to her.

"It's not like I want to go. Besides, I graduate in a year. Then I'll be an adult, and I can go wherever I want."

Rebekah shook her head and said again, "No. Anya is not taking you away from me. I won't allow it."

"She's my mom. There's not really anything you can do to stop her."

Rebekah smiled, and a wicked glint entered her eye. "I'll think of something. In the meantime, we'll make the most of every moment."

While Stig and Rory stoked the bonfire, Rebekah disappeared into Eclipse House and returned with a culling jar again wrapped in a scarf, so I couldn't see the shape of the container. But I asked no questions, simply culled when it was my turn and felt myself turn to fire and light and joy and life. I was electricity and sunrise, the stars and the moon tearing across the sky. A supernova exploding in beautiful chaos that was somehow harmonious.

And yet I was still me, only I was me to the power of greatness and glory. All that had happened in the last twenty-four hours—hurting Blake, being rejected by my twin, finding out that her condition was my doing, receiving the news that my family was moving—vaporized like so much water exposed to a blast of nuclear energy. The sad, hopeless, pathetic parts of me disappeared, and the good parts were amplified to magnificence.

When the music began, it hit me like a sonic boom and swelled through the night in liquid jewel waves of gold and silver, sapphire and emerald, amethyst and ruby and pearl, melting together to turn the heavens to a great, undulating opal.

Sunday brought me my guitar, and I joined their circle and played so hard my fingers should have bled. The Kalyptra danced around us in a whirling, revolving ring. There was a manic quality to this anima high, a need to move, to create, to touch and feel and exist and be the center of everything. It made me feel like anything was possible. I could run a thousand miles. Swim an ocean. Live forever.

It was a familiar feeling, but at the moment I couldn't recall why I knew it. So I didn't try.

Instead, I played and I sang with the Kalyptra. I joined my voice to theirs for the first time and I was harmonious with them. This was what I'd been missing at home, where the anima didn't satisfy and the hunger inside me for something more never abated. Maybe it wasn't the anima that was different at home, it was everything else.

But now I was at Eclipse, with my people, where I belonged.

We joined hands, and sang as we danced, switching partners, weaving through arches of arms, swaying among trailing fingers.

A hand found mine and squeezed. I felt something pressed into it and looked up to see it was Joanna who had taken my hand. She released it quickly and spun away, but I found myself clutching a piece of folded paper. I slid it into my pocket without reading it.

I will not let Joanna ruin my perfect night, I thought. *My best night ever.*

And almost the instant I thought this, a strangled bleat of terror cut through the night.

The music and dancing stopped, and we turned toward the source of the hideous sound. It had come from the field, halfway between the animal enclosure and the bonfire. Several pairs of eyes glowed in the darkness a hundred yards away.

The keening went on and on, and then I was running. Running toward those glowing eyes and that terrible cry of pain. I remembered what Cyrus had told me my first day at Eclipse, about how Bully was such a troublemaker, how he kept finding ways to escape and pillage the gardens at night. And how it wasn't safe to wander away from Eclipse alone because there were predators in the woods. Wolves and coyotes and mountain lions and bears.

The glowing eyes scattered when I was within twenty feet of them. I could see their shape by that point, a pack of doglike animals, too small to be wolves. Coyotes, then. They had to be. But even if they'd been wolves, I would have charged into the middle of them because I had a terrible feeling I knew who had made that animal squall of pain.

And I was right.

I fell to my knees beside the small, twisted body of the animal the coyotes had attacked. I let out a moan.

It was Bully. It was my wild, troublemaking little goat.

The leather collar around his neck had done a little to

protect him from the coyotes' teeth, but they had ripped him open in a dozen other places and he was bleeding out, his blood black in the night. His dark eyes wobbled, searching my face as though begging me to help him.

And I could, I realized. I could save him just like I had saved Erin. All I needed was the anima of some other creature. Another goat. A horse or a sheep. Something potent that I could channel into him.

"Hold on, little guy," I said, taking a moment to stroke the uninjured place between his eyes to comfort him. I wished there were more anima inside me now. If there were, I could simply infuse him, but the emotional shock of what had happened seemed to have sprung a leak in me, and the last of the anima that had filled me for the previous hour came rushing out like air from a punctured tire.

Resolved, I stood, ready to cull one of the other animals to save my pet. It wasn't fair to the animal whose life I would take, but I had to do something. I couldn't let Bully die.

Then I saw Rebekah and the rest of the Kalyptra coming toward me through the field, carrying lanterns, their expressions somber, as though they were part of a funeral march. Rebekah held a jar in the shape of a goat's head in both hands in front of her, and when I saw it, relief swept through me.

I wouldn't have to cull one of the other animals to save Bully. Rebekah would use one of her culling jars to save him. She would take care of him as she'd taken care of me after my bad trip in the forest.

Her eyes—all of the Kalyptra's eyes—were ink black as

they formed a ring around Bully's mangled body. Rebekah, at their center, knelt in the place where I'd knelt a moment before.

She opened the lid of the jar and began to chant in a low voice, in a language I didn't understand, but which I thought might be Latin.

I was confused. The cloud of light that normally accompanied the opening of a culling jar didn't emerge, and neither did Rebekah's vena. Instead, Rebekah dipped her finger into Bully's blood and spread it around the rim of the jar, still chanting the same phrase over and over again, her eyes black as obsidian. And then I did see the light, the anima, only it wasn't coming from the jar.

It came from Bully, oozing from his mouth and nostrils, from his bloodied wounds like smoke from the windows of a burning building. Only this cloud moved with purpose. It snaked and funneled through the air, straight into Rebekah's jar.

Before I registered what was truly happening, it was too late. Bully's life slipped from his body into the jar, and Rebekah closed the lid.

For a long moment, I was too stunned to react. I simply watched as the ring around Rebekah disbanded and the Kalyptra headed back to the house. Finally, I regained enough presence of mind to do something.

I rushed at Rebekah and snatched the jar from her. She turned to me, her black eyes wide with surprise at my audacity.

"What are you doing?" she asked coolly.

"I'm putting his anima back and healing him," I shouted at her.

She shook her head. "But why?"

"Because he's mine! He's my pet!" I realized I was crying, my cheeks soaked in tears and my chest hitching.

"Oh, sweet girl," she said, shaking her head. "We don't have pets here. It's not our way."

She held out her hands for me to give her back the jar. When I didn't, her mouth turned down in a scowl of disapproval. "Do you want to be Kalyptra?"

"Y-yes," I said, my voice barely a whisper.

"Then you have to respect our practices. Not some of them. *All* of them. I'm sorry you grew attached to that little goat, Kenna, but his anima feeds us, and that is a worthy sacrifice for any creature."

"But I could have saved his life," I said weakly.

"At what cost?" Rebekah asked. "Why should another of the animals give its life to save this goat? Do you really think that's fair?"

I lowered my chin to my chest and shook my head.

"Then give me the jar, Kenna."

All that lives must die, I heard Erin say inside my head. *All that lives must die, passing through nature to eternity.*

I placed the jar in Rebekah's waiting hands.

And for the second time in recent history, my perfect happiness was cut short, and what would have been the best night of my life was marred by death.

I sank down next to Bully's body in the field and sobbed. I didn't know how long I'd been out there, but eventually Cyrus came to me and touched my shoulder.

"I should have listened to you," I said, my voice hoarse from crying. "You told me not to name him, and I broke the rules. It won't happen again."

Cyrus held his hand out to me and helped me to my feet. Only then did I see Stig and Yuri waiting nearby with shovels. Illia and Rory, Hitomi and Sunday and Diego were there, too. Their eyes had returned to normal, and I realized how terrifying they had looked with their black eyes. How inhuman. *Eclipsed* eyes, that was how the Kalyptra referred to them, but they resembled insect eyes. Moth eyes.

"We'll bury him together," Cyrus said.

We dug a hole right there in the field and buried Bully and made a blanket of flowers on his grave. I cried and the girls hugged me and told me it would be okay, that all of them had been through this at one time or another.

"Let's go to the dreaming tent," Hitomi suggested. "We'll take anima and get your mind off of this."

But I shook my head. I didn't want to bury my grief for Bully. He deserved better than that. It struck me then how dangerous anima was with its ability to put away all dark and negative thoughts. Sometimes life called for such thoughts, and while I'd been at Eclipse I had swept mine into a safe and locked it.

I started walking back to the house alone. "I just want to sleep," I said.

When I got back to my room, I climbed into bed and stared at the ceiling. I tried to close my eyes, but every time I did I saw Bully's mangled body, Rebekah's finger dipping into his blood. I lay there, unable to sleep for a long time as I wondered why everything good in my life eventually turned bad.

THE LAKE

I WASN'T SURE IF I SLEPT. AT SOME POINT IN THE NIGHT I closed my eyes, and when I opened them again the sun's first rays had broken over the horizon. I was immediately aware of hunger, bone deep and urgent and not up for negotiation. My entire body felt like a mouth waiting to be fed, a stomach grinding with vacancy. Whatever anima Rebekah had given us last night, it had been potent. Maybe too potent, since it had awakened the kind of torturous emptiness I hadn't felt since my first days at Eclipse.

Last night I hadn't wanted to take more anima to drive away my grief for Bully. Now that sorrow was a raw wound on my heart, and it was the only thing I wanted to do. To escape the anguish of my thoughts, the dark, insistent magnet pulling me down into depression . . . that was what I needed.

I dressed in the jeans, T-shirt, and sweater I'd worn the previous night, and headed out to Cyrus's private wagon. It had been a gift from Rebekah, he had told me once, though when I asked him why she gave it to him, why he of all the Kalyptra lived outside of Eclipse House, he merely grinned and said, "Because I'm her favorite. Or at least I was until you came along." That had made me blush with pride. Then I thought of my mom, and how she was, undoubtedly, Rebekah's favorite at one time. Still, that hadn't stopped Rebekah from turning her back on her only daughter completely when she defied Rebekah's will. I'd thought Rebekah's love for me seemed unconditional, but there was definitely one condition: that I follow her rules down to the letter.

I sniffed and wiped at my eyes, fighting back tears as I knocked on Cyrus's door. I figured he'd already be awake, but it took him several minutes to finally answer.

He wore jeans, but no shirt, and his shaggy hair was a silky, sleep-tousled mess. His caramel-colored skin practically glowed in the early light of the sun, and his eyes were iridescent and dazzling.

"Morning," he said, grinning sleepily and rubbing his eyes like a little boy waking on Christmas morning. He stepped back, opening the door wider.

I hesitated. "I should probably just go. My mom is going to freak out when she finds out I'm gone. Actually, she probably already knows. She's an early riser."

"If she's already going to be angry with you, you might as well make your time here worth it," Cyrus reasoned.

He made a logical point, and the thought of going home and starting to pack up my stuff made my heart feel like giving up. Despite what had happened last night, I still loved Eclipse and the Kalyptra. I'd made a mistake getting attached to Bully, but it was a mistake I wouldn't make twice. I wanted to be worthy of the Kalyptra, and of Rebekah's affection.

I stepped into the wagon and gazed around. There wasn't much to the small living space, but I could see now why Cyrus had decided to make this his place instead of the house. It was incredibly cozy, with intricate woodworking on the ceiling panels and cupboards. The polished plank floor was covered in colorful rugs and the bed at the back was an inviting jumble of quilts and blankets. It smelled like Cyrus, like leather and sandalwood and spices.

Cyrus closed the door, and what had been a cozy space suddenly became scarily intimate.

"What do you think?" he asked from behind me.

I was afraid to turn around; he was standing that close. The heat reached out from his body to mine. I eyed the tangle of his blankets and thoughts of him and me wrapped together in his bed flashed through my mind.

"It's nice," I said, keeping my back to him and leaning against the long counter jammed with candles, copper pots, and ceramic dishes. "Very, um . . . private."

Cyrus moved toward me and put a hand on my hip. Where he touched me, it burned. I began to feel out of breath, like I used to when an asthma attack started, only this was both scary and exciting.

Had I felt this way with Blake, too? Was my attraction to

him as powerful as it was to Cyrus? Yes. No. Yes. Maybe? My mind was too foggy to recall.

My eyes darted around, searching for an escape even though I wasn't sure I wanted one. There was a small, round table up against one wall. On it sat a basket that contained a variety of objects: a packet of guitar strings, a wallet that didn't look at all like something Cyrus would carry—or even need to carry—a Leatherman tool with the initials A.T.P. engraved on the outside. Was that some relic from Cyrus's former life? Was Cyrus his real name? Or had he simply bought the Leatherman from a secondhand store or a pawn shop?

My gaze moved upward and landed on a piece of art hanging on the wall over a small, round table. It was some kind of cutout in the shape of an Eclipse moth. Instinctively, I reached for it and took it down from the nail on which it hung. There was a string attached to the back. It was a mask, I realized. Where the black moons on the Eclipse moth's wings should have been, there were holes for eyes to look through.

I remembered Sunday's hidden paintings, depicting people wearing moth masks, and I shuddered.

"What's wrong?" Cyrus asked close to my ear.

I held the mask up to my face and looked through the eyeholes. It didn't mean anything, I told myself. It was just a mask. So why did it leave me feeling unnerved?

I removed the mask from my face and hung it back on the wall. "Nothing," I said, turning to face him. "Nothing is wrong."

"Then spend the day with me," Cyrus said, his voice a

rumble that called to mind impending disasters, earthquakes and landslides. His neck was so close to my eyes I could see his pulse ticking away, feel his energy, his anima, a subtle vibration. His right hand stayed on my hip, and his left rose to my chest, where he flattened it above my heart, which was thudding hard and fast.

He smiled at me. "Your heart's racing."

Then, suddenly, he lowered his hands and stepped back. I braced myself against the counter, not trusting my legs. Last night I had buried my pet, and now I was simmering under Cyrus's touch. But I had to stop thinking of Bully as mine. He was just an animal. He was just an—

"Spend the day with me," Cyrus said again.

My chest was still heaving as I responded with, "What did you have in mind?"

"How much farther?" I stopped hiking long enough to guzzle water from the canteen Cyrus had brought. When he'd suggested a walk in the forest, I'd almost balked, remembering the last time I'd been in the woods around Eclipse, when I'd seen—no, *hallucinated*—the moth creature. The illustration I'd found online of the massive moth feeding on its bound victim floated to the surface of my brain, but I did my best to drown it.

I'd been expecting a leisurely stroll, but the path Cyrus chose was more of a climb. We culled anima from various sources along the way, flowers and plants and even a few insects, and the voice of my grief for Bully became a distant echo. I breathed easier and my heart stopped aching. Still, none of the anima we took came close to satisfying the craving in me for more of what we'd taken last night.

"We're almost there," Cyrus told me. "There's something I want to show you. I promise it's worth the trek."

I nodded and tried to concentrate on not twisting an ankle or getting jabbed in the eye by a branch. The mossy trees were so thick they allowed no light, only cool, dank shadows, which made it hard to see whether I was about to step onto unstable earth. I was so focused on the ground in front of my feet that I didn't notice when the forest suddenly cleared.

I heard the drone of rushing water, and felt sunlight warm my cheeks and shoulders. I raised my eyes and gasped. We stood on a rock outcropping overlooking a hidden lake. A river poured over steps of rock leading down from the mountain, feeding the lake, its water clean and clear enough to see all the way to the bottom. I spotted fish darting over the rocks, swimming their haphazard, zigzag path. At the head of the lake, a short waterfall dove thirty feet to churn the otherwise calm surface. Massive trees grew so densely around us that they seemed like a natural barrier, a wall to guard a place too perfect to be disturbed.

The anima I'd taken during the hike had dissipated, but even with my natural, unenhanced vision, this was one of the most breathtaking places I'd ever seen.

"Behold, my lady," Cyrus said, holding his arms out wide. "Your own private lake."

I moved to the edge of the rock outcropping, which had been painted with a design of interlocking moth wings. I peered over the edge and experienced a wonderful sort of vertigo, a dizzying urge to let myself fall into the blue. Erratic birdsong burst from the trees, calls and answers. And there was that forest white noise, the sound that is not a sound, but is the woods themselves living and breathing like one tremendous, connected organism.

I turned back around to Cyrus, a smile growing wide as wings on my face.

He started to unbutton his shirt. A glow spread across my skin and I felt that sense of vertigo again, like I was going to fall, and the fall was inevitable. I wanted to stop fighting. To let go and feel myself plummet toward something new. A whole new life. A fresh start.

But starting over meant leaving some things behind. Blake's face swam into my mind, his warm eyes and his boyish smile. His sweetness and sensitivity. The way he made me feel like maybe I could live in the real world as long as I could do it with him by my side. But what was best for Blake? Was I good for him? If I was honest with myself, the answer was no. I had hurt Blake so much already. If I let things go any further with Cyrus, there would be no going back. Was that what I wanted? To make a choice that would end the war going on in my heart? To force myself to let Blake go?

I turned my back on Cyrus, breath short, heartbeat a kettledrum booming against my ribs.

I wasn't ready to let go. Not yet. Not when I was still torn between people I loved.

"Kenna." Cyrus spoke my name into my ear. His body was close behind mine. His oven-warm chest against my back. One of his hands settled on my left hip. The other swept my hair aside, baring my neck. I felt his hot breath against that sensitive expanse of skin, and my breath caught. Then his lips touched, and my stomach thrilled, a geyser of excitement erupting to fill me. The hand that was on my hip pulled my body more firmly against his, and I felt every curve and knot of his taut muscles against my own tensed back. His mouth trailed wet, warm, exploring. My skin charged with sensation.

Don't let go, I warned myself as I weakened. *Don't let go.*

Cyrus kissed his way toward my ear, and when his teeth caught my earlobe I gasped, my body a reactor melting down, losing control. Losing the will to resist. His face nuzzled the side of my face. His hands spread like starfish on my belly. I felt the forest observing me. The birds had gone silent.

I turned in Cyrus's arms. His eyes scoured me, torrid, his face slack with desire. I had never been so longed for, not by Blake or anyone. It made me feel like an animal, a beast made to act on every natural urge.

Cyrus's face fell slowly toward mine, his eyes drooping closed, his lips parted, and mine mimicked his. His fingers clenched on my back, digging into my flesh until it was almost painful. His hipbones cradled mine. His mouth was a fraction of a centimeter from mine when a sudden panicked rustling from the woods split our attention. We both whirled toward the noise and saw a flock of birds explode into the air. Something heavy shook the boughs of the trees and then went still.

I realized I was clutching Cyrus's arm like a damsel in a silent film. "What the hell was that?"

"Probably just a bird," he said, but his eyes were hard, staring up at the now-silent leaves. Was it my imagination, or did he seem almost as uneasy as I was?

I pried my fingers from Cyrus's arm and turned to him. "The night I took midnight glory . . . what I saw . . ." I bit my lip, eyes still searching the treetops for signs of movement. My heart began to slow, and I shook my head, embarrassed. "Never mind. It's just, I saw this picture on the Internet, and—"

"Internet?" Cyrus blinked at me curiously.

"A computer network thingy. I don't really know how to explain it. It's, like, where you go to find anything you ever need. Anyway, there was a drawing and some information about the Eclipse moth, and it kind of freaked me out."

Cyrus's brows drew together. "What did it say?"

"Nothing," I said quickly, waving my hand as though to clear my words from the air. "It's not important. Just forget I said anything."

"No." Cyrus took hold of my wrist, his grip a little tighter than was comfortable. "Tell me."

"Okay, okay. It said the Eclipse moth was some kind of fairy tale goddess that lives on blood and grows to enormous sizes. And that, um—" My words cut off, but what I was about to say played through my mind: *And the Eclipse moth granted powers to those who worshipped it.*

"And that's all I remember," I said, smiling a smile I wished didn't feel so forced.

Cyrus and I swam in the lake until our fingers and toes were numb and our teeth were chattering from the icy mountain runoff. The tension between us didn't dissolve, but he didn't try to kiss me again, probably sensing that my mood had changed since that disturbance in the trees. I tried to shake my anxiety, but my eyes returned again and again to the spot where that flock of birds had burst from the leaves so suddenly, clearly startled by something. But there were a thousand things in the forest that could startle a flock of birds, including Cyrus and me.

I wished I could stop thinking of what I'd read about the Eclipse moth, but I'd never had much success at *not* obsessing. I tried to focus my attention on the beautiful man in the water with me, his hair and skin glistening wet and his teeth so white and his contrasting body so brown and flexed.

I wanted him. That much I could no longer hide from myself. The question was, could I have him when my heart was still divided?

I loved Blake. I knew Blake. I still wanted Blake.

I couldn't be with both of them any more than I could live both with my family and at Eclipse. Like Rebekah said, I could not live in two worlds. I had to choose.

Teeth chattering, I was about to climb out of the lake when Cyrus grabbed my wrist and reeled me in against his chest. "Are you hungry?"

"Starved," I told him. "What did you bring?"

"A frying pan." He winked at me, let go of my wrist, and dove underwater. He was under for more than a minute, and when he broke the surface he had, clutched in both hands, wriggling and squirming, a good-sized trout, its scales silver and spotted. It looked slippery, and Cyrus could barely keep hold of it.

My eyebrows went up. "Of course you can catch fish with your bare hands," I said. "That's totally normal."

Cyrus grinned. "My normal could be your normal. It just takes practice."

The fish lashed its tail, fighting for freedom. I couldn't help but sympathize with the trout.

Cyrus made a small fire on the stone outcropping that overlooked the lake and panfried the trout with lemon and herbs he'd brought in his pack. We ate the fish with our fingers while the fire dried us.

I ran my hands over the moth wings that had been painted onto the rocks. The pigment had faded from weather wear, so the depictions appeared ancient.

"Who painted these?" I asked. "Was it Sunday?"

He nodded.

"When was that?"

He shrugged. "Long time ago."

"How long?"

"Oh, I don't know. Years and years. You know time doesn't mean much to us."

Cyrus chose that moment to go down to the water to wash out his frying pan. He remained shirtless, and I noticed for the first time a series of pale scars crisscrossing his back. I sucked in a breath. I'd seen scars like that before, but only in movies. Usually movies about slavery, or children with abusive parents.

I remembered what Cyrus had told me about his mother, that she wasn't the kind any kid hopes for. I got the feeling that was an extreme understatement.

Cyrus must have felt my gaze, because he glanced back at me and caught me staring. He frowned, and I turned my eyes away, feeling as though I'd been caught going through someone else's things. I knew Blake inside and out. The boy claimed to be an open book, not a single secret to speak of. I could guess what he was going to say before he said it. Maybe it was the fact that I knew next to nothing about Cyrus that made him so attractive to me. It was exciting, but the mystery phase couldn't last forever. Eventually, you had to find out who people really were.

Cyrus began to pack up. The day was waning, but I didn't want to go yet. I put a few more sticks on the fire. Cyrus saw and smiled, pleased. He sat back down with the fire between us.

"If I'd planned better we could have stayed the night out here," he said.

His suggestion made my stomach wriggle pleasantly.

Cyrus pulled his shirt on and then took a wineskin from his pack and offered it to me. I took a drink, felt the wine pool warm in my belly, and passed the skin back to Cyrus. He swigged, and wiped his lips with the back of his hand.

"I saw you looking at my scars," he said.

I glanced away. "You didn't get them at Eclipse, did you?"

He barked a laugh. "No, those were courtesy of my mother. She was quite the disciplinarian. Spare the rod, spoil the child. That kind of woman. I ran away from home when I was thirteen." He lowered his gaze, his voice softening. "I never talk about my life before Eclipse. Barely think about it, for that matter. It's funny how you can learn to block out what you don't want to think about."

I thought about that Leatherman tool in Cyrus's wagon, and the initials engraved on it.

"I've never been particularly good at that," I muttered, twisting a long lock of hair around my fingers. Regular doses of anima seemed to make my hair grow faster. When I'd first arrived, my hair had barely reached past my shoulders. Now it hung halfway to my waist.

"Why didn't anima heal your scars?" I asked.

"I got them before I became Kalyptra," he said. "Anima can do a lot of things, but it can't take away your scars."

"And . . . how did you become Kalyptra?" I asked, trying to keep my tone casual with an edge of disinterest.

"Ahhh, I know what you're up to," Cyrus said, not fooled for a second. "Rebekah told me about your deal. There are no secrets between your grandmother and me."

"Why is that?"

"Why is what?"

"Why are there no secrets between you and Rebekah? Are you saying there are secrets between Rebekah and the other Kalyptra?"

Cyrus's face closed for a moment, became unreadable. Then he shook his shaggy hair and his mouth curved in a tight smile. "Everyone has a secret or two, Kenna. Rebekah trusts me because I've proven myself to be trustworthy. That's all."

"Fine," I said, dissatisfied with his seamless answer. I pulled my knees in so I could rest my chin on them and sulked in silence, hoping that if I pouted long enough Cyrus would give in and tell me something.

"Why do you need to know so badly?" he asked, staring into the dying flames of our intimate little fire. "Is there someone you want to make Kalyptra?"

I almost said no, but only because I'd never considered what Cyrus was telling me. Once I did, the idea bloomed in my mind like fireworks.

There *was* someone.

"My twin sister, Erin," I said. "She's sick. She's always been sick, ever since she was born." I turned my face away so he couldn't see the tears glazing my eyes. "And it's my fault."

Cyrus shook his head, brows drawn in concern. "It's your mother's fault, not yours. She made the choice for you."

"Doesn't make me feel a whole lot better." I picked up a

stick of firewood and peeled off a splinter. "Did my mom . . . do something when she was Kalyptra? Something bad?"

Cyrus hesitated. "She never told you?"

"Maybe I haven't been entirely clear about this, but the only thing my mom ever told me was to not be Kalyptra."

Seeing the grave expression on Cyrus's face, I swallowed hard, bracing myself for what he was going to tell me.

"What?" I asked. "What is it?"

"Your mom killed someone, Kenna."

I swallowed hard, and for a moment my ears rang as though someone had blasted them with noise. A part of me had suspected something like this, but having it confirmed changed everything.

"Tell me what happened," I said.

Cyrus's eyes slid from mine. "Anya was the youngest of all of us when she became Kalyptra. I don't know if that's why she lacked self-control, or if that was just the way she was back then. She was . . . well, she was downright gluttonous. No matter how much anima she took, she always wanted more. Rebekah couldn't control her. Joanna, who was her best friend, couldn't convince her to try to curb her appetite. She was on a constant rampage.

"One day she went walking in the woods, culling life along the way. Her eyes were fully eclipsed when she came across a hiker. She told us she was too filled with anima to think straight. She saw him and decided he would tell other people about her eyes if he got the chance. She knew that could get the rest of us into trouble, get people asking questions. But I think the truth is that she just wanted to know what human anima was like, and there was no one around to stop her from finding out. So she culled him."

He paused and raked his fingers through his hair, agitated. "She was tortured afterward," he said. "She realized she was out of control and decided not to take anima anymore. But catharsis, after a lifetime of taking anima whenever she wanted, was too much for her. She couldn't live with what she'd done, and she couldn't live without anima, so she found another way to live."

As he spoke, the air seemed to vacate the space around me until I felt like I was suffocating. We were the same. All this time, my mom had understood exactly what I was going through, because she had been through it, too. Only instead of locking herself up and waiting for catharsis to fade, she'd made a choice that nearly got her killed, that resulted in one sick child and one killer.

I was quiet for so long that the fire went out and we fell into dusk inside the shadows of the trees.

"Are you okay?" Cyrus asked.

I turned my eyes back to him. "I don't think I can forgive her," I said, though I doubted Cyrus would understand why. I climbed slowly to my feet, and Cyrus stood, too, as though worried I might be about to do something crazy.

And maybe I was.

"I can't go home," I said. "But I can't stay here, either. Not without Erin. You have to tell me how to make her Kalyptra."

"Kenna," Cyrus said reasonably, holding up his hands in a *whoa* gesture, "even if Rebekah would agree to that, does your sister even want to be Kalyptra?"

Just last night she had asked me if she could accompany me to Eclipse, but I thought about her reaction to seeing me cull for the first time, her repulsion, and I knew the answer to Cyrus's question would be no. But I'd only culled the deer to heal her. She could be Kalyptra and never take anything more substantial than a blade of grass if she didn't want to. And then she could be healthy and strong forever, independent of me. I didn't know if she would ever agree to it, but maybe that didn't matter.

I was her sister. Her twin. I always had her best interests in mind, and in this instance I knew what was best for her.

"She wants to live," I told Cyrus. "This might be the only way."

He kept shaking his head. "I don't know."

"At least tell me if it's possible."

Reluctantly, he nodded. "Rebekah knows how to do it. The question is, will she agree to it?"

"Maybe she will if you help me convince her."

"I'm not sure *I'm* convinced."

I knew it was manipulative, but I couldn't help myself. Once I got an idea into my head, once I began to obsess, I was like a stone falling from a great height, picking up speed as I went.

I took a step, and that was it. We were kissing.

It was nothing like my first kiss with Blake. There was no

sweetness to the heat and hunger of our mouths. No sweetness at all. There was only need. I wanted Cyrus. I had already admitted that to myself. But now I needed him even more than I wanted him.

There was nothing sweet about that.

YES

*S*HE HAS TO SAY YES. *S*HE HAS TO. *S*HE HAS TO.
This thought rode a merry-go-round in my head as I paced the length of my room in Eclipse House. The kiss with Cyrus still burned on my lips like a pleasant brand, but its memory was overshadowed by my impatience to know Rebekah's answer. When we got back from the lake, Cyrus excused himself immediately to speak with Rebekah on the matter of making my sister one of us, while I holed up in my room to obsess privately.

She has to say yes. She has to say yes. Erin is her granddaughter, too.

The question was, on the off chance that Rebekah did agree to this crazy idea, how would I convince Erin to take the plunge and leave behind everything she knew for a whole new way of living? And what about the rest of the Kalyptra? Would they accept her if Rebekah told them to? With the exception of Joanna, they had accepted me quickly enough.

Joanna.

I reached into my jeans pocket, remembering the scrap of paper Joanna had pressed into my hand the previous night. A part of me wanted to tear it up and toss it into the fire in my little stove, but curiosity got the better of me. There was nothing Joanna could do or say to scare me away from Eclipse. Nothing.

I held the paper up and read the three words she'd written: *IN THE GUITAR*

And then I remembered what she told me the night Blake came to Eclipse to take me home, that there was something hidden inside my mom's guitar that she had expected me to find.

My mom's guitar, which I'd begun to think of simply as mine, was where I'd left it, tucked safely beneath my bed. I brought it out and held it on my lap as I reached under the strings and into the sound hole, feeling around until my fingers caught the edge of something that had been stuck to the inside of the body. I pried it free, and pulled out a folded square of paper about the size of a slice of bread.

No wonder the guitar had always sounded a little off to me, no matter how often I tuned it.

I unfolded the paper carefully. It was yellowed and brittle, but I managed to open it and lay it flat on my lap without tearing it.

It was a topographical map, showing the mountains and the valley in which Eclipse was situated. I'd never been good at reading maps, but this one had been marked up, which

made it a lot easier. Eclipse was indicated with a crude drawing of a house with a circle drawn around it. A trail that
stretched through the orchard and into the wooded foothills
had been outlined. At the end of the trail was a large, red X
and a note written in black ink: THIS IS WHO WE ARE

Chills ran up my spine, as prickly as spider legs.

At the sound of approaching footsteps, I quickly refolded
the map and jammed it back inside my mom's guitar. But I
didn't have time to hide the guitar before Cyrus opened the
door. I was still sitting on my bed with the guitar on my lap,
an innocent expression plastered on my face.

I stood and set the guitar on the bed, my lips going hot
again at the memory of kissing Cyrus. As soon as my mouth
had touched his, I'd known it was the wrong thing to do, that
it was too soon for us. There was still so much I didn't know
about him, and so much he didn't know about me. But at that
point it was too late. I'd been so distraught over the things
Cyrus had told me about my mom, and my determination to
make Erin Kalyptra, that I hadn't been thinking clearly.

If Blake knew what I'd done, that would be it. He would
never forgive me.

But if I wanted to become a permanent resident of Eclipse,
I had to let him go. The thought made me ache inside, like
some essential part of me was dying. Or maybe that was the
ache for more anima. I'd taken plenty today on my hike with
Cyrus, but none of it came close to satisfying my craving for
more of what Rebekah had given us last night. And I'd been
too distracted since we left the lake to cull anything more.

Now the hunger opened wide in me, a sinkhole of desire. Was this how my mom had felt all of the time? Was this what had led to her killing a person to experience the life inside him? At least when I had killed Jason Dunn, I'd known why I was doing it. Or had I? Had what he'd done to Clint Eastwood and her kittens only been an excuse?

I tried to ignore the widening void and focus on Cyrus. His expression seemed deliberately blank.

"Well?" I said, growing impatient when he didn't speak. "What did she say?"

"She said yes." Rebekah glided into the room behind Cyrus, barefoot as always, her feet barely seeming to touch the ground. She was stunning in a blue dress the color of a summer sky, fitted to the waist and then flaring out. The sleeves and hem were trimmed with silver beads that made a sound like falling rain when she moved. Her eyes went from me to the guitar on my bed and back to me, but if she recognized the guitar as my mom's she didn't show it.

"Are you serious?" I hadn't wanted to admit it to myself until now, but I'd been sure Rebekah would refuse my request.

"If the only way to keep you here is to make your sister Kalyptra, then yes," Rebekah said. "But you have to know, Kenna, that our gift comes with a price. An . . . exchange is required. A sacrifice, if you will." She smiled. "But after what Cyrus told me, I think it's one you'll be willing to make."

I looked at her askance, uncertainty creeping in. "What price?"

Rebekah stepped up to me and touched my cheek. "Nothing you haven't paid before."

Her palm felt charged, and as I looked into her eyes I thought it strange that her pupils were so large. But then, it was dim in the room; only the glow from the stove lit the interior. Still, it was like she had no irises at all, only perfect circles of darkness surrounded by white, like the wing of an Eclipse moth.

Then, a feeling like a spark popped on my cheek where Rebekah had touched me, and I felt a wave of effervescence, like my blood had been carbonated. I forgot about her possibly eclipsed eyes, about my kiss with Cyrus, about the map hidden inside my mom's guitar, even about Erin becoming Kalyptra.

There was only me, and I was more than me. I was everything, and I was part of everything in existence, an expanding cloud of being.

For the moment my hunger was sated, and I was full.

The night sped forward in an exhilarating blur of anima, enfolding me in color and sensation. Music crashed upon us in sonic waves that sank through our skin and vibrated our veins like guitar strings. Our bodies became electric as we danced, braiding our arms, fingers entwined like lace, weaving and unweaving. Joining and searching and finding and holding.

I had never been so happy. So alive. So me, and so not me.

Things had never felt so right. Things had never *been* this right. Finally I was where I belonged, and soon Erin would be, too, and it would be perfect. I was going to make her Kalyptra. She was going to live a long, happy, glorious life. Much longer than she'd ever thought possible, maybe even forever. Both of us eternal. The goodbye I couldn't say to her in the hospital would be wiped from the slate. I would never have to say goodbye. All I had to do was convince her to join me.

Join us.

this is who we are

I didn't want them to, but as the night wore on and my anima high dwindled, the words Joanna had scrawled on the map crept into my ears and repeated themselves again and again, demanding that I listen.

I caught Joanna's black pearl eyes on me, small and watchful as ever, and I read the question in them: *Did you find it?*

My mood darkened. What did she want me to do? Sneak off and follow the trail she'd drawn to the red X?

this is who we are

Could I really ask Erin to become Kalyptra without attempting to find out who they really were?

No, I decided. I could not.

X Marks the Spot

I DIDN'T SLEEP. I SAT IN MY ROOM, A SMALL FIRE BURNING in my stove. I studied the map and tried to ignore the cavernous feeling that had set in once my anima high had worn off and I'd become my mundane self again. Was I imagining it, or were my cravings getting worse?

I thought back to the night's hazy events, an uneasy feeling heavy as lead in my stomach.

I had been filled with anima tonight, and it had been the anima of something potent, but I didn't remember culling anything. What I did remember were Rebekah's bloated black pupils, that delicious shock when she touched my cheek, and then . . . sublime abandon.

Rebekah had given me anima, but she hadn't asked my permission. Looking back, I realized it wasn't the first time she'd done this. Rebekah was always touching me, stroking my hair, taking my hand, touching my cheeks, and on numerous occasions I'd felt that same surge of energy enter me, only it had been subtler those other times. Too subtle for me to realize what she was doing.

But why dose me with anima when I was perfectly happy to take it for myself as often as possible? Was she worried that I wouldn't take enough, and that I would become dangerous again? Not dangerous to the other Kalyptra, but to the land or the livestock?

That had to be it. Later, I would ask her, and I was pretty sure that would be the reason. She was my grandmother. She was looking out for me, taking care of me.

There was a lantern in my room, and a book of matches for me to keep the fire lit. I folded the map and stuffed it in my back pocket, along with the book of matches, and then I crept from Eclipse House, the lantern swinging from my hand. I hurried across the yard toward the orchard. Once I was hidden from view by trees, I released a pent-up breath and lit the lantern. I didn't like this, didn't like sneaking around behind the Kalyptra's backs. But there had to be a reason Joanna was so secretive. Whatever she wanted me to know, it must be something the rest of the Kalyptra, or at least Rebekah, did not want me to know.

But every family had secrets, didn't they? Mine certainly did, so who was I to judge?

Following the trail on the map, I kept up a brisk pace, both to stay warm and to ensure I'd be able to reach the red X and make it back to Eclipse before anyone woke up.

It was unnerving, walking through the woods at this time

of morning, which, as far as light was concerned, was still night. The lantern provided only enough of a glow for me to see a few feet in front of me, so every rustle of leaves or snap of twigs or yip of a coyote made me walk a little faster until I was practically running. Still, the sun was coming up by the time I reached the clearing.

I slowed to a halt, peering around for a moment before entering the circle of trees that surrounded a small, grassy meadow, set against a craggy expanse of rock face. Inside the clearing, all of the forest sounds seemed to cease, and I felt as if I'd gone spontaneously deaf.

I was reasonably sure I had arrived at the place the red X indicated, but I didn't know how to process what I was seeing because I'd never before seen anything like it with my own eyes.

In the center of the meadow was a rustic altar made from interwoven branches, and in front of the altar was a round, stone pedestal, surrounded by the remains of charred firewood. The whole thing reminded me of something that might have been handy during a pagan ceremony or a ritual sacrifice.

Rebekah's words echoed back to me:

An exchange is required. A sacrifice, if you will.

Was this the place where my sacrifice would be made? What was it that Rebekah would ask me to sacrifice?

I rubbed my arms as my skin prickled.

Upon closer inspection, I saw the wood of the altar was elaborately carved with moths and moons, the same as the door to Rebekah's room back at Eclipse House. Next, I inspected the stone pedestal. It had been fashioned into a perfect full moon, and had been charred as black as the ring on an Eclipse moth's wing. I touched the surface. It was cold enough to make me shiver. Something made me shiver, anyway.

this is who we are

I wanted to leave the clearing and go back to Eclipse. If Joanna thought I was going to be scared away by this place, she was wrong. I already knew the Kalyptra had some strange, mystical beliefs and practices, that our gift derived from something old and archaic. So what? There was nothing wrong with a little ritual in life. What were Easter and Christmas and Thanksgiving and Halloween if not holidays of ritual? There were plenty of pagans and Wiccans still out there in the world, worshipping their ancient gods and goddesses of nature, and I wasn't afraid of them. And the Kalyptra . . . their worship, their magic and ritual actually worked, so it made even more sense for them to be involved in something as abnormal as this.

The whole thing made me want to throw my hands up into the air, turn right around, and hurry back to Eclipse before anyone realized I was gone. This was just a meadow where the Kalyptra performed some kind of ceremony they hadn't told me about yet, nothing more.

Except . . .

Except there was an Eclipse moth painted on the rock face, similar to the ones painted on the rocks at the lake, only this was much bigger, wings spread six feet high and wide. Only where the thorax of the moth should be, there was a long, narrow opening in the rock.

It was the entrance to a cave.

I had only been inside a cave one time in my life. When Erin and I were nine, Mom took us on an impromptu road trip to San Francisco. That was where we'd been headed, anyway. Erin started feeling too sick before we'd even crossed the border into California, so we had to turn back. The highlight of the truncated trip had been visiting the Oregon Caves National Monument. I went on the tour alone while my mom and Erin waited in the car. Inside the cave, it had been cool and surprisingly dry, and so quiet and calming it made my heartbeat slow like I might slip into a trance. At one point, the tour guide told our group to turn off our headlamps so we could experience what absolute darkness felt like. I switched off my lamp along with the others, and we were plunged into air as black as ink. For a moment I'd felt utterly at peace. Then a random thought—"What if this is what death feels like?"—ended my peace and began a panic-induced asthma attack at the idea that my sister might disappear into such darkness. Such nothing.

Such death.

Our guide had to cut the tour short and take us back to the entrance.

I didn't like caves anymore, and I didn't want to go inside

this one. I listened at the entrance for several minutes, hoping I would hear some sound—a bear grunting, a mountain lion hissing, the maraca of a rattlesnake—that could send me running back to Eclipse none the wiser about what lay inside that cave.

But there was only silence.

I held up my lantern, took a breath, and crouched to enter the cave.

Once I was inside, the cave widened out quickly. I was grateful, since I was not about to crawl and worm my way through some underground cavern system. But it appeared that I wouldn't have to do more than duck to make my way through the tunnel. I couldn't quite see the end of it, so I didn't know how far I had to go. Instead of looking straight ahead, I kept my eyes on the ground in front of my feet so I didn't step into a hole and twist my ankle.

I had been moving steadily forward for what seemed like an hour but was probably more like ten minutes when I raised the lantern to check whether I was getting close to the end.

I should have kept my eyes down. I took a step forward and the surface beneath me disappeared.

I didn't even have time to scream before I clattered to the ground among what felt like a collection of oddly shaped sticks and stones. A lightning flash of pain tore through my arm and I felt the bone in my wrist—the same wrist Erin had broken—snap with a sound like a tree branch breaking.

I heard my lantern shatter at the same moment I landed at the bottom of the pit, and then there was absolute darkness. Darkness and terrible, pulsing pain. But just before my lantern went out, I saw all I needed to see.

Bones. A carpet of charred, human remains—the skeletons of countless people—filled the bottom of the pit into which I'd plummeted.

Clutching my broken wrist, my teeth gritted against hot stabs of agony, I scrambled toward the wall, trying to find a place to stand that wasn't ankle-deep in scorched skeletons.

this is who we are

My fingers scrabbled at the wall of the pit, but it was nearly vertical, and too smooth for my fingers to find purchase, even if I had the use of both my arms.

I was trapped down here. Trapped with the blackened remains of God knew how many victims.

My panicking mind rewound to the conversation I'd had with Rebekah, in which I'd asked her if she'd ever taken human anima, and she'd answered so shamelessly: yes.

It hadn't occurred to me to ask whether she'd taken the anima of more than one person.

this is who we are

In the darkness, I let out a scream of anguish. I didn't expect it to do me any good.

But a voice I knew came from above me, a voice nearly as anguished as my own.

"Kenna . . . you shouldn't have come here."

DARKNESS

"CYRUS? IS THAT YOU?" I ASKED EVEN THOUGH I KNEW IT was him. If he had a lantern or any source of light, he didn't use it, so the darkness remained impenetrable.

He didn't respond to my question, and panic threatened to turn my mind into a cyclone of destruction. I took a breath and let it out, fighting to retain a semblance of calm. It was the only way I would get out of this alive.

Because the Kalyptra were killers.

this is who we are

I thought about the anima Rebekah had been feeding me from her culling jars, how insatiable my hunger for more, and more, and more had become, and now I understood why. She'd been giving me human anima. For how long I didn't know, but standing in a pit surrounded by human remains, I was pretty damn sure that was what she'd been doing, and that this had been going on for a long time.

I thought of what Cyrus had told me about my own mom's insatiable hunger for anima, how it had driven her to do anything to get rid of it, and I wondered what had really been going on. Had Rebekah been dosing her—all of the Kalyptra—with increasingly potent forms of anima? Had they not realized what was happening until it was too late? Until they were too addicted to ever stop, and they could never leave Eclipse, and they would be her children, under her control, forever?

Maybe they weren't all like Rebekah, and maybe they were victims, but I knew my mom would not have brought me to Eclipse if she'd had any idea what her mother was up to.

"I think I broke my wrist when I fell down here," I said in a whimper to Cyrus when he didn't respond. "Can you help me get out?"

Still no answer.

"How did you find me?" Now my voice was shrill. I was on the verge of losing it. If he didn't say something soon, I would start to scream again. I wouldn't be able to help myself.

"I couldn't sleep," he said finally, his tone deadpan and hollow. "I was at my window and saw you sneaking through the yard."

"I wasn't sneaking," I lied. He couldn't know why I'd come here, or that I'd seen what was down here. "I couldn't sleep either. I wanted to go for a walk."

"A walk in the woods in the dark? A walk inside a cave?"

He had me there. "I like caves. I was just curious what was inside."

He laughed, but there was no more humor in the sound than there was in a sob. "You like caves, huh? Well, I'm guessing you didn't find this one to your taste."

"Cyrus, are you going to help me get out of here or not? I'm in a lot of pain. I need anima to heal my wrist."

"Of course," he said. "But first I want you to tell me the truth. What did you see down there?"

"See? I didn't see anything. My lantern broke and my wrist broke and my mind is going to break if you don't get me out of here!"

"You swear on your mother's life you're telling me the truth?"

I hesitated, even though I'd never put much stock in swearing on anything. "Yes, I swear. Now for God's sake, please help me."

"All right." I heard a scraping sound, and then an orange flame burst to life in the darkness, searing my eyes before Cyrus lit his lantern, illuminating the pit and its jumbled collection of charred bones. Illuminating the truth of what the Kalyptra were.

Cyrus met my eyes, and I saw the truth in them, that he didn't believe my lies. He had known even before he lit his lantern that I already knew what was hidden in the tarry darkness of this cave.

I clung to the side of the pit and stared up at Cyrus's face, a face I had kissed less than twenty-four hours ago. A face I had found irresistible enough to make me betray a guy I loved.

"Why?" I asked him. Begged him, tears of frustration and agony and rage filling my eyes, blurring my vision.

"You would have found out eventually," he said, his voice somehow cold and affectionate at the same time. He reminded me of Rebekah, both loving and removed. "Besides, you were lying. That was obvious."

My body shook. Cold sweat slicked my back and my brow, and my teeth chattered. I wondered if I was going into shock.

"What are you going to do to me?"

He hunkered down by the side of the pit. "That kind of depends on you."

He stroked his chin for a moment and then rose to his feet, staring down at me with equal parts pity and sorrow. Then he turned and walked away.

"Cyrus!" I screamed after him. "Cyrus! Cyrus, come back!"

But he didn't return, and the farther he moved down the cave, the darker it became in the pit, until darkness was all there was.

In the pit, time crawled forward with a snapped spine and two broken legs. Seconds were minutes. Minutes were interminable. Hours were eons.

For a while I was in shock. I went numb, even to the throb of my broken wrist. I stopped feeling fear or panic or disgust at the press of knobby bone joints against my ankles when I tried to move. There was only a zombie-ish numbness in my limbs, a slowing of my heartbeat until it seemed I would slip into death, and death would be like I once feared—an absence of all light, all being. It would be nothing.

For a while I was dead. I was nothing.

But the scraping, insistent need for anima brought me back, reminded me that I was still alive, despite the hollowness in my chest cavity, like my heart had been removed. There was nothing living inside the pit from which to cull the anima that could have healed my wrist and sealed up the awful emptiness that was spreading through me.

Hours passed, or maybe it was days. It was impossible to tell. I didn't hunger for food or water. Anima was the only thing that could save me from the torment of dying cells and withering organs and the fluttering roar of wings in my ears. I imagined moths inside my head, beating against the walls of my skull, trying to worm through my earholes and escape.

A fever turned my temperature up until sweat poured off me, soaking my clothes. The fever shifted to chills, and I lay on the ground, curled into a ball to warm myself. I shivered so hard I made the bones in the pit rattle like they were waking up, coming to life.

Next came the sensation I was being eaten alive by army ants, pinching off bits of me and whittling me down. Soon I would look like my fellow residents of the pit. I raked at my skin with my fingernails until I was raw and bleeding.

When I slept, which I hardly dared to do, nightmares

waited for me, harrowing dreamscapes in which I witnessed my mom and Erin being slaughtered, not only by Thomas Dunn, but by Jason as well. I tried to stop them from killing the people I loved, but they turned on me and tore me open with knives, and instead of blood, wriggling gray worms spurted from my wounds, worms that metamorphosed within seconds into white moths with round, black eyes on their wings, and the moths converged around me, probing me with the needle-thin ribbons of their tongues, penetrating the skin and sucking at my blood. When I tried to run from the moths, I slammed against an invisible wall, and I turned around and around until I understood that I was trapped inside a glass jar with a thousand madly fluttering moths. I was in one of Jason's killing jars, and I was never getting out, because this was truly where I belonged. Not at Eclipse, but in the jar.

"I wish it didn't have to be this way," a voice spoke inside the nightmare, barely audible above the roar of moth wings. "I know you're suffering right now, but it will be over soon."

The voice was Rebekah's, and it wrenched me from one nightmare into another.

I opened my eyes. There was light now, and after my long spell of darkness it was like acid in my eyes.

"Kenna?" my grandmother said from above me. "Are you listening to me?"

"Y-y-yes." My teeth chattered so hard I could barely speak. My mind felt slow and stupid, and the joints of my jaw ached as though they'd rusted like ancient machinery. I blinked up at Rebekah, and saw her kneeling beside the edge of the pit, a candle held in her two hands, the light turning her blond hair to shimmering gold. After so long in the dark, she was the most beautiful thing I'd ever seen. The most beautiful thing that ever was.

"H-how long . . . h-how long have I b-been down here?" I rasped. My throat and tongue were as dry and rough as sandpaper. I'd sweated and cried out nearly every ounce of moisture in my body.

"Three days," Rebekah said, her brows drawn in sympathy. "I am sorry about that, but you know what they say about curiosity. I would have told you everything in time."

"Once I was ad-ad-addicted to human a-anima," I said. "Once y-you had me u-under c-c-control so I could never . . . never leave you."

"Leave me?" she asked innocently. "Why would you ever do that?"

I realized then that my grandmother was, quite possibly, insane. Not padded room and straitjacket insane, but megalomaniacal, narcissistic, cult leader, self-delusional insane.

"You k-k-kill people," I said.

"Cull, not kill," she clarified. "Remember, there's a difference. Think of those lives that sustain us as sacrifices to superior beings. We aren't greedy. We cull only a few times each year, and we store the anima so we can make it last as long as possible. You see, once you take human anima, you'll never be satisfied with any other kind."

"That's not t-true," I said. "You could stop. I culled a person, and I l-lived without it for years."

318

"You call what you were doing before you came to Eclipse living?" Rebekah shook her head. "Don't be naïve, Kenna. You're smarter than that. I've been giving you human anima since you first came here. You think you would have been satisfied with the anima of flowers and plants after how much you culled?"

Tears filled my eyes and spilled over my lids. Maybe I had willfully deceived myself, or maybe I was just stupid. Either way, I couldn't change it now. All I could do was try to fix what I had done.

"You were supposed to help me," I said, making my voice steady, fighting not to break down completely, to succumb to the misery that threatened to dissolve me into a sobbing puddle. "Why did you do this to me?"

Rebekah blinked in surprise, as though this should have been obvious from the start. "Because you're my granddaughter, and you belong here with me. I love you, Kenna. I loved you the moment I laid eyes on you and saw my face in yours, and I knew I had to do whatever it took to keep you at Eclipse with your true family. I'm sure I'll love your sister, too, once she's one of us."

"No! Rebekah, no, I changed my mind!" I clawed at the wall of the pit, sending explosions of pain through my wrist and up my arm and not caring one bit.

"But *I* haven't," Rebekah said. "You were right. She's my family, my blood, and she deserves a chance at what you have. It's only fair."

"She won't want it!" I realized as I said it that it was true.

I'd deceived myself into thinking Erin would want to be Kalyptra, that she *needed* to be Kalyptra, but she would never choose this life. She had always been the better person. The better twin.

"It may take time, but she'll learn to accept our way of life, just as you did." Rebekah smiled down at me, radiant and queenly. "I brought a few things to help you prepare for the ceremony."

She set her candle on the ground and lowered a basket tied to a rope over the edge of the pit. When it reached the bottom, she let the rope fall.

"I must go," she said. "We have to get everything ready for your sister's transformation. It's going to be a busy day."

I peered inside the basket and saw three items. I pulled out the first. It was the green dress Illia had made for me, which matched my eyes perfectly. The next item was a white mask in the shape of an Eclipse moth's wings, black holes where the eyes would look out. The same one I'd seen on Cyrus's wall. That the people in Sunday's paintings had worn.

The third item was wrapped in a silk scarf. I lifted it out, held it in my one good hand. It seemed I could feel it pulsing like a heart ripped from a chest, radiating heat and life. The hunger in me opened wide, a ravenous canyon of a mouth waiting to be fed.

"Now don't waste that," Rebekah cautioned. "It's the last of our supply until after tonight. Get yourself healed and cleaned up, and someone will return for you at sundown."

She departed then, but left her candle burning on the ledge above.

I set the jar on the ground and unwrapped the scarf from around it, revealing its true shape.

A human skull.

I thought of the items I'd seen in Cyrus's trailer, the wallet and Leatherman with someone else's initials. What had they been? A.L.P.? I couldn't remember, but I wondered if they were the initials of the person whose anima was contained inside this jar.

I reached for the lid, and then pulled my hand back as though burned. Every cell in my body wanted what was in that jar, but how could I take the anima inside now that I knew where it had come from, and what it would do to me? There would never be a point at which enough was enough. I would want human anima forever, and I would hate myself for wanting and taking, and then I would want it all the more to bury what it made me feel. Or perhaps, eventually, I would come to think of it the way the rest of the Kalyptra did, as a necessary evil. The price of being extraordinary, of feeling things no one else could feel and seeing things no one else could see.

The entitlement of being a superior being. A god.

It took every ounce of willpower I had left, but I stood, clutching the jar. I hauled back my good arm, ready to throw it.

But I didn't.

I couldn't.

I slumped to the floor among the bones, despair wrapping me like a cocoon.

I cracked open the jar and a mist of shimmering, opalescent anima leaked out. Threads of energy emerged from the palm of my hand and reached for the anima, sucking at it and drinking it in.

I couldn't resist. I wasn't strong enough.

I removed the lid and took all it had to offer.

CTRANSFORMATION

KENNA, IT'S TIME."
Cyrus's words fell on me from above like drops of warm, summer rain. He lowered a rope ladder over the side of the pit, and I climbed out and stood before him. The anima had healed my wrist and ended the terrible catharsis that had shriveled and sickened my body. Now I was as glorious as a blazing sunset. In the dark of the cave, my skin shimmered with otherworldly light.

Cyrus looked me up and down, his eyes coming to rest on my face, which was partially hidden behind the Eclipse moth mask.

He nodded approval. He wore the same mask, and he was shirtless, his chest painted with branching white lines of vena.

"I've missed you," he said, and leaned forward to kiss me. With the anima churning through my veins, the kiss felt like being reborn. I closed my eyes and saw worlds spinning on the backs of my lids. I sank into the kiss, wrapping my arms around Cyrus's neck and breathing him in.

He broke the kiss before I was ready to let him go, then took my hand and led me from the cave.

When we were near the entrance, I heard the Kalyptra's harmonious voices singing in unison, a strange, repetitive chant I'd never heard them sing before.

Matrem appellamus vobis
Matrem appellamus vobis
Sanguine et igni
Matrem appellamus vobis

I didn't know the words—they were sung in another language that sounded like it might be Latin—but even though I didn't understand them, I picked up the tune quickly and began to hum along. I was one of them, after all. I was Kalyptra. My voice belonged with theirs.

When we reached the entrance, Cyrus kissed me once more and then ushered me through.

I emerged, reveling in the smell of forest air, of cool night on my skin. The trees were frilly giants, bowing over the meadow, and the sky was a canopy of sapphires and diamonds.

My eyes lowered to the meadow, where a bonfire blazed in a circle around the stone pedestal. Through the flames, I could see a woman lying on the stone, bound with ropes and gagged. I couldn't see her face, but she was definitely a woman.

The bonfire obscured my view of her, but I could make out the shape of her naked body and shoulder-length blond hair.

The Kalyptra were arranged in a wide ring around the fire, the women wearing long dresses that appeared almost to be robes, the men shirtless, their chests painted with the same thin white lines as Cyrus's. All of them wore masks in the shape of an Eclipse moth's wings, their eyes peering out through the dark moon circles in the middle of the white.

My grandmother was resplendent in a crimson gown with a neckline that plunged past her navel, her hair a golden cape that coiled to her hipbones. Her mask was more elaborate than the others, practically a headdress. She looked like a high priestess, an ancient goddess whose mere existence commanded devotion.

But even Rebekah faded when I saw who stood beside her under the altar.

Erin.

Instead of a mask, she wore a white blindfold over her eyes, along with a loose, white shift dress. She was frail again, her bare legs knobby and her arms pale and skeletal. The look of her must sicken Rebekah, I thought, but my sister wouldn't be like this much longer. This time when Erin emerged from her chrysalis, she would be changed forever. We would finally be identical.

Rebekah glided across the meadow toward me, her arms held out as though to embrace me. Instead, she took my hand and led me to the altar made from twisted branches, which also reminded me of vena. She gazed at me proudly, and I wanted to bask in that pride, to feel deserving of her affection and her love.

But something had changed.

I was filled with anima, heady and drunk with it, but somehow the effect was not as all-consuming as it should have been. The fatalistic thoughts and emotions that usually stayed buried when I took anima clawed toward the surface of my mind.

This is wrong, I thought. It was all terribly wrong. Erin would never want this. She would never allow an innocent woman to die so that she could live.

Matrem appellamus vobis
Matrem appellamus vobis
Sanguine et igni
Matrem appellamus vobis

All that lives must die, I chanted in my mind. *All that lives must die.*

Rebekah raised a hand to silence the Kalyptra's chorus. Then she lowered that hand to take Erin's and stood at our center, linking us in a short chain. I peered over at Erin and saw she was smiling in a dizzy way that told me she had been given anima to keep her calm. To sedate her. Had the woman on the sacrificial pedestal been given anima, too? Beneath the haze clouding my brain, I wondered who she was.

"Tonight we call upon the Mother to make this child one of us," Rebekah intoned. "We offer blood and light to the Mother. In exchange, we ask her to bestow upon my granddaughter, Erin, the gift that will transform her. That blessing that will allow her to lift the veil and see beyond the mundane. To breathe the breath of life and become what she was meant to be."

The woman on the pedestal must not have been sedated well enough. She began to struggle furiously against the ropes binding her.

Rebekah called to Cyrus, "Cut her! Let her blood call the Mother home!"

Cyrus drew a knife and reached quickly through the flames to slash at the woman's bare torso. The woman tried to jerk away from him and ended up rolling onto her side for an instant—

An instant long enough for me to see the tattoo covering her back: a moth with wings laid across her shoulders.

I sucked in a silent breath.

The woman cried out as Cyrus's knife sliced into her. He brought the blade back smeared with red, dripping blood onto the grass. Cyrus held the knife high in the air and called.

Matrem appellamus vobis
Sanguine et igni

Then I heard, from above, the sound of wings brushing the air.

I looked up and saw it.

Her.

"*Matrem!*" Rebekah said in awe, squeezing my hand and

gazing up at the descending creature. "Isn't she beautiful, Kenna? Isn't the Mother magnificent?"

"Yes," I whispered, and I meant it. With the anima in my eyes, the Mother of the Kalyptra was not monstrous. She was moonlight made into wings. The sight of her dazzled me, stunned me, made me forget for a moment why she was here. Made me forget the tattoo on the naked back of the woman who was to be sacrificed in exchange for Erin to be made Kalyptra.

But the other Kenna, the one smothered beneath a shimmering blanket of anima, knew who the woman on the pedestal was, and she fought her way to the surface.

The Mother descended into the clearing and hovered over the pedestal, assessing her bleeding victim. Her thorax was the size of a child, her black, bowl eyes as large as fists, and her wings as long as my legs. For a moment she hung in the air, as though deciding between the blood and the fire.

She chose the blood.

She alighted on the body of the sacrificial victim.

On my own mother.

My stomach turned to ice.

I glimpsed the Eclipse moth's long, white ribbon of a tongue unfurling to suck up the blood it was offered, which poured from my mother's stomach in a torrent. Its tongue plunged into the open wound and snaked under the skin.

"Mom!" I cried, tearing my hand out of Rebekah's grasp as the real me, the Kenna I'd been trying to hide from, charged forward and took control, swimming through the anima trying to drown me in exuberant joy while my mother died. I darted toward the fire and the stone pedestal.

"Kenna, no!" Rebekah grabbed at my dress, trying to pull me back, but I wrenched free of her.

I must have startled the Eclipse moth because it withdrew its tongue from my mom's wound and juddered into the air, where it hovered over the flames, its black porthole eyes staring down at us.

Cyrus stepped into my path and tried to grab me, but I darted around him. I didn't know what I was doing. I only knew I had to get to my mom. I had to save my family.

My real family.

Then I felt a searing pain on the back of my head, and I was yanked backward. Cyrus had me by the hair, and he reeled me in like he was reeling in a fish. He held the knife smeared with my mom's blood to my throat.

"Let this happen, Kenna," he hissed into my ear, sounding harsh but also pleading, as though some part of him was sorry for what was about to happen.

"Rebekah knows what's best for us," he said. "For all of us. She'll take care of you and your sister the way no one ever could. She'll be good to you the way she's been to me, and eventually you'll forget the misery that was your life before. You'll be grateful."

I watched, helpless, as the Eclipse moth touched down on my mom again and unfurled its tongue.

"Let her go," Cyrus said close to my ear. He kept one hand

fisted in my hair and the other holding the knife to my neck. "We're your people now."

A part of me wanted to do what he said, to let the Eclipse moth have my mom. But that part wasn't the real me. That part was the thing I had become.

I heard my mom's voice in my head, singing.

Sweet girl, don't cry.
Sweet girl, I hear you sigh.
I'll be here when you wake,
So you won't be afraid
to dream alone.
To dream alone.

Now I understood what those lyrics meant. My mom's lullaby was both an apology and a promise, her way of telling me she was sorry for keeping me away from the one place where I didn't have to dream alone, and a promise that she would do her best to always be there for me when it came to real life. She had failed, but that didn't mean she hadn't tried.

Tears began to stream down my cheeks, and the love for my mom that had been tainted and distorted by all of our mistakes, by our disastrous history, came rushing back into my heart. It gave me strength.

I drove my elbow into Cyrus's stomach and felt his grip on me loosen just enough for me to make a break for it. Cyrus reached for me again, but a blur of dark hair flew at him and knocked him to the ground.

Joanna.

They tumbled to the grass and Cyrus's knife was jettisoned from his hand. The Kalyptra gasped and murmured, all of them high on anima, none of them seeming able to comprehend what was happening.

This would be my only chance.

Joanna scrambled for the knife, and when she had it brandished in warning at Cyrus she raised her eyes to mine.

"The Mother, Kenna. Cull the Mother."

For a moment I was confused, thinking she meant my own mother. My mind was still fighting for clarity against the anima in my system.

Then it hit me: she was talking about the Eclipse moth.

Was it even possible? I couldn't cull another Kalyptra, but could I cull their goddess? It was the Eclipse moth's anima that had made the Kalyptra what they were, so maybe . . .

Maybe would have to be enough.

I reached both hands toward the Eclipse moth and hundreds of threads of energy extruded from my palms and whipped toward the Mother. The threads connected, but for a moment nothing happened.

Then the Mother spasmed as though hit with a bolt of lightning, and her energy poured into me and filled me. It consumed me as I consumed it. The Eclipse moth's anima made human anima seem like a sip of wine in comparison. This was the anima of a goddess, and I was taking it. Taking it all as the monstrous moth began to come apart, its wings turning to powder, its thorax shrinking and crumbling like old clay.

Around me, the Kalyptra cried out and fell to the ground, writhing in pain as though I were hurting them, too. And maybe I was. The Mother had made them. They were connected. So why was I not writhing in pain like them? Because I had taken the Mother's anima? I didn't know. My consciousness was being devoured by the anima of the Eclipse moth.

The Mother's body hit the ground and broke apart like a sculpture made of dust. Its anima spread through me. Mania took hold of my brain and I was swallowed by a singular need.

Light . . .

Light . . .

LIGHT.

Distantly, I remembered what Cyrus had told me about moth anima being forbidden, because when it was in you the compulsion to go into the light was undeniable. Everyone knew a moth couldn't resist a flame, even if it would be its doom.

I had always been a moth, unable to resist those things that could destroy me. So this would be my well-deserved end.

I turned toward the fire, knowing on some level what was about to happen but unable to resist, because I wanted this, too. Not the moth part of me, but the real me. I walked toward the fire, ready for what was to come. Fire cleanses, and I needed to be washed clean of the terrible things I'd done. This would be my sacrifice. The payment for my many sins.

I was an inch from the licking flames when a hand grabbed my arm and the owner whirled me to face her.

Rebekah's face was livid, her once beautiful features pinched in pain. Her skin appeared to be both shrinking against her skull and melting off of it. Her hair began to fall out in handfuls and her lips pulled tight against loosening teeth.

She was aging, I realized. Aging rapidly now that the divine connection to her goddess was gone.

"Do you realize what you've done?" Rebekah shrieked in my face.

The flames called to me. I tried to turn away from Rebekah, to continue my path into the fire, but she dug her fingernails into my arms.

"You've destroyed everything!" she screamed, her eyes bulging like they were about to pop. The hair rained off her scalp, leaving gray patches of skull beneath. "We'll die now. We'll wither and die, and so will you and your sister!"

"All that lives must die," I told her. "Even you."

I shook free of Rebekah, and her legs buckled backward, bones giving way and snapping like ancient wood. She fell to her knees, wailing to the sky, and I turned once more toward the flames.

"Kenna, please! Don't move!"

The voice was one I knew better than any other. It had been with me for as long as there had been a me.

I looked back again to see Erin pulling the blindfold from her eyes. The dizzy smile was no longer on her face. Her anima high had faded fast.

She walked toward me slowly, holding her hand out as though inviting me to take it.

"Remember in the hospital, Kenna, when I asked you to say goodbye to me and you couldn't do it?"

I nodded.

"I get it now," she said, tears shining in her eyes. "I can't do it either. I can't say goodbye to you, so you don't get to leave me. Do you hear me? You don't get to leave me!"

I felt wetness on my cheeks and realized I was crying.

The fire called to me. I wanted it. I wanted to be inside the light.

Still, I was crying and nodding.

"Deal," I said, my voice so hushed I wasn't sure she heard it. But that didn't matter.

I ripped the mask from my face and tossed it into the fire. I was through being the moth. It was time to be the flame.

I knelt beside my grandmother's broken, diminishing body. She was becoming the age she should be, I thought vaguely. A weak old woman. That was all she was.

She looked at me, her face a horror, eyes sunken into her skull and caved-in mouth opening and closing like that of a fish out of water.

"Please . . ." she croaked. "Please . . ."

I knew what she was asking, that I save her from the death she had avoided for so long. I nodded, and I gave her what she asked for.

What she had earned.

I put my hands on her and felt my vena emerge and connect to her body, and then the Mother's anima poured from me, and with it the compulsion to give myself to the light that would kill me.

Beneath my hands, Rebekah's body knit itself back together and she became beautiful once again. A goddess. The queen of her own small kingdom. Or maybe, merely, its Mother, albeit a tyrannical one.

When it was done, I stood, my head and my eyes finally clear. The world returned to normal, and I welcomed it. I welcomed the world as it was, and I hoped it would welcome me in return.

Erin ran to me and wrapped her arms around me. We held each other for the first time in years and watched as our grandmother walked into the fire. Rebekah cried out in exultation as flames gobbled her dress and hair first, and then began to boil her skin and cook her flesh. The sweet, smoky smell of burning meat filled the air.

Rebekah stood under her wooden altar, a woman on fire, and screamed in delight until she couldn't scream anymore. She clung to the altar and it caught, too, and went up in flames. The triumphant smile never left her face, even when her lips were gone. Even when the skin on her face was charred to black.

The Kalyptra, all of them, remained crumpled on the ground, although they were no longer writhing. They were moving sluggishly, like people who'd been in comas, but were just starting to wake. Joanna raised her head and looked at us. I wouldn't have recognized her if it weren't for those black eyes of hers. Her hair had gone completely white and her face was a nest of wrinkles.

"What's happening to them?" Erin asked, her voice tremulous.

"I think they're turning the age they would have been if they hadn't become Kalyptra."

"Anya," Joanna said, reaching a hand toward the stone pedestal.

Erin and I went to work quickly, scooping dirt onto the fire and putting out enough so that we could lift our mom's body off the pedestal and onto the cool grass. She was unconscious from smoke inhalation, and blood continued to gush from her stomach. The wound on her side was deep. It could be fatal if we didn't act quickly.

But I didn't know if I could do what needed to be done.

Joanna crawled through the grass toward us. "Use my anima," she said, her voice weak. "What's left of it . . . I want Anya to have it. I'm human now. Mortal. You can take it."

Erin's eyes went to mine, huge and terrified. "Can you still . . . ?" She didn't need to finish the question.

I shook my head, not sure what the answer was. "I don't know. I might not be Kalyptra anymore."

"T-try," Joanna rasped. "You're different from the rest of us. You didn't choose this life . . . you were born this w-way."

I looked at her uncertainly. "Are you sure?" I asked softly, hesitant to take another human life. Or another life ever. I didn't want to be Kalyptra anymore.

But maybe I didn't have a choice.

"I'm sure," Joanna said. "It's my choice."

"Thank you," I told her, and then I put my hands on her and sighed in relief when I felt my vena emerge and connect to her body. Her anima swelled through me, but I didn't let

336

myself enjoy it. I closed my eyes as she withered and then I turned to my mom.

Erin had used Cyrus's knife to cut the ropes binding our mom and remove her gag.

Mom's eyes drifted open, and when she saw us she smiled. "My girls," she said. "My babies."

My vena connected to her like some alien IV and her back arched as Joanna's anima filled her and sealed up the wound in her side.

When it was finished, she sat up, and she hugged Erin and me tight to her. We wrapped our arms around each other, and the love I felt from my family—my true family—was the best anima I'd ever known.

Around us, the Kalyptra began to climb to their feet, with the exception of Joanna, her body a withered husk. For a moment I worried the Kalyptra might pose a threat, that they might try to kill us for what we'd done. But looking around at them, I saw how frail, how diminished they were, and I knew they were no danger. Their masks had fallen from their faces, revealing aged, wrinkled skin, eyes dimmed like dying light bulbs, some filmed with cataracts.

I recognized Illia, though her lava-colored hair was now a cottony, white cloud. She wore a cloak over her dress, and she removed it and laid it over my mother's naked frame.

Her eyes turned to me, and she said, "I'm sorry. I'm so sorry."

Then she drifted away, not down the path to Eclipse, but into the forest in the opposite direction.

The other Kalyptra mimicked her, murmuring apologies and goodbyes before wandering away into the night. I cried to see what they had become, but I didn't hug any of them. I kept my arms around Erin and my mom, and I said my goodbyes.

The Kalyptra, it turned out, I could say goodbye to. My family, I could not.

Cyrus was the last to leave the clearing. His good looks had wilted with age, his chest sagging and his hair thinned to reveal a liver-spotted scalp. His hands were gnarled like claws.

He didn't apologize. Instead, he said in a husky, dry voice, "She was the only real mother I ever had. I would have done anything for her. I couldn't help myself."

I thought of the scars on his back, and I pitied him. He'd been as lost as I was, maybe more, when Rebekah had gotten ahold of him. Then I thought of my passion for him, and the kisses we'd shared, and I marveled at how easy it was to mistake desire for love. But now another veil had been lifted from my eyes.

"We all have a choice," I told him.

He nodded, and then, like the rest of the Kalyptra, he disappeared into the night.

Rebekah was dead, and the fire that had consumed her under her altar had nearly burned itself out. My mom, Erin, and I stayed to scatter dirt on the flames and douse them completely. My mom wept as she covered the remains of her mother with dirt, and I decided Rebekah was wrong.

Love is not a choice.

We love who we love, and our hearts want what they want. We can't help that. We're only human, even the Kalyptra.

I was Kalyptra still, but I was also, simply, human.

I had made so many terrible choices in my life, and I had lived for a long time filled with regret for the things I could not change. But it wasn't too late for *me* to change. It was time to move on.

To move forward.

"Let's go home," I said when the fire was out and the smoke had cleared. I knew where home was now, and it wasn't a place.

It was people.

It was love.

And love was as good as anima.

And that was life.

EPILOGUE
LIFE

ARE YOU SURE YOU'RE READY FOR THIS?" BLAKE ASKED, slowing his 4Runner and pulling to the side of the highway, where the overgrown road to Eclipse snaked through a rippling, golden sea of grass.

A month had passed since I'd last traveled that road, but then I'd been heading in the opposite direction.

Heading toward home.

"I think so," I said, biting my lip. A sense of déjà vu gripped me, and I recalled the last time Blake and I had sat idling in his car, at Folk Yeah! Fest. So much had changed since then, some things good, some bad. Some in ways that had yet to be determined.

The day after I came home from Eclipse, after I almost lost everything and everyone I loved, the festival coordinators called to let me know they had good news and bad news. The bad news was that I had not won the contest, though I'd been a close third. The good news was that one of the other bands had heard my song and wanted to acquire the rights to it for their next album.

The recording session had been that morning in Portland, and I'd been invited to listen and meet the band. The whole day had been like an out-of-body experience. I still felt high from it. Not anima high. Not lose yourself high. Just . . . up. Just good.

Blake had driven me to Portland and watched the session with me. He and I hadn't figured out the romantic part of our relationship yet, but our friendship was alive and well, and that was what mattered most to me for now. During the drive back from Portland, we talked about everything and anything with the exception of my time at Eclipse. I'd already told him all there was to tell about that, leaving out not a single detail, not even the parts about Cyrus. Blake had been understandably hurt and angry, but he also understood that my brief life with the Kalyptra had been complicated. It wasn't a black or white situation. It was very, very gray.

I looked over at Blake. Worry made a little tuck between his eyebrows. "You don't have to take me," I told him. "I can drive out with my mom another day."

Mom visited Eclipse several times a week now that she owned the land and everything on it. Despite Rebekah's claims that my mom was dead to her, she'd never cut her daughter out of her will. Maybe because she didn't want to bother with going into the world to deal with a lawyer.

After coming home, Mom and Erin and I had spent hours

341

discussing what to do about Eclipse and the land and the livestock living on it, and we finally decided to trust Detective Speakman with as much of the truth as we dared. We delivered to him a revised version of the events that had taken place at Eclipse, and let him take care of the rest. He knew there were things we'd left out of our story, but for some reason he let us get away with it, maybe because it turned out he was a fan of *The X-Files* and he understood there were some things in the world that didn't look good in a formal report. Besides, he had his hands full dealing with the bodies from the cave at Eclipse, searching for their identities, and notifying the victims' families.

I'd thought Mom would want to sell Eclipse as soon as the police turned it back over to her, that she would remove all ties to her past with the Kalyptra, but Mom surprised Erin and me when she announced she'd decided not to sell Eclipse. Mom wanted to convert it into an artists' colony. My initial response to this idea was bleak. Eclipse had such a dark past. People had been killed there. They had lost their souls to a narcissistic, misguided woman there. I thought it might be better if Mom had the place boarded up and we never set foot on that land again.

But then I thought of my own dark history, and the terrible things I'd done. There was darkness in me, but there was more light every day. I didn't want anyone to give up on me because of my past, and I couldn't give up on Eclipse for the same reason. Mom's artists' colony would create good to take the place of bad. Art and beauty and music in the place of greed and addiction and death. We would start over, re-build, do things differently this time around. Nothing lasts forever. Good is superseded by bad, and bad can be steered back toward good. The world is always in flux. Light falls to dark, and dark surrenders to light, and life moves on.

At home, color was starting to return to the woods around our house, shoots of green thrusting up through ashen ground.

Life shaking off death.

Blake reached across to me, took my hand, and wove his fingers through mine. He never hesitated to touch me any-more, and I was glad. I was tired of keeping people at arm's length, tired of holding back.

When Blake pulled up in front of Eclipse House, my mom and Erin emerged from the big front doors and came down to greet us. The two of them had been busy over the last month, going through all of the Kalyptra's belongings and deciding what to keep and what to remove. The Kalyptra themselves had not returned to the house. There had been stories on Oregon news blogs about a bizarre number of bodies—all of them belonging to elderly people—that had been found throughout Oregon, Washington, and Northern California. The bodies were dessicated, and crumbled to powder when they were touched, rendering them unidenti-fiable. I couldn't decide how to feel about that. I'd loved the Kalyptra, and I was sure they'd loved me. I missed them, but they were starting to seem like friends I'd made many years ago in another life. In a way, that's what they were.

Sometimes I dreamed about them, and those dreams were good. And some nights I dreamed the Eclipse moth was hovering over me, and I woke, wondering if there were other Eclipse moths out there in the world, and if the others would go in search of them, or if the Mother was the only one.

I decided not to worry, to just let life be good.

Erin leaped off the porch and wrapped me in a fierce hug that nearly knocked the breath out of me. I kept forgetting how strong she was now. She'd decided to let me infuse her every day with a little bit of anima to keep her healthy. She'd accepted what I was, and we'd both accepted that we could not leave each other alone in this world. Neither of us would ever be normal, and we would always need each other. We would always be together, and we could live with that.

"How was the recording session?" Erin asked. "Tell me everything."

Mom leaned against the porch and smiled down at us. There was sadness in her eyes, same as always, but it seemed, for the first time in as long as I could remember, like something that might pass, a storm that might blow over. She had cried a lot over the past month, but it was better than what she'd done before, holding her sadness inside and suffering alone. Now Erin and I were there for her. We were there for each other.

"Okay," I told Erin. "I'll give you the full report. I just . . . I have to do something first."

Alone, I headed out across the yard, toward Bully's grave. The blanket of flowers the Kalyptra and I had laid over the small mound of earth had dried up, so I picked a new armload of wildflowers to place on his grave. I kept hold of one poppy, my eyes burning with tears. The urge to cull the flower was strong, but I resisted. I fought every day to control my cravings. It wasn't easy, and it would never be, but I had found a way to master my need. There was only one thing in this world that was better than taking anima, and I had it now. I had the love and acceptance of my family and Blake, who had seen the worst in me, and still loved me. I couldn't change what I was, but I couldn't hide from it either. Anima was a fixture in my daily life, and it would be for as long as I lived. But I needed to feel my feelings, the good and the bad, instead of burying them.

So I cried over Bully's grave, and I told him I was sorry I couldn't save him, and then I dried my eyes and took a few deep breaths and headed back to the house.

Blake, my mom, and Erin sat in the porch chairs, chatting. My mom had brought out one guitar for each of us, including her old guitar and the one Stig had made for me. Along with drawing his wonderful, weird art, Blake had practiced while I was at Eclipse, and had improved quite a bit, and now that Erin's fingers were strong enough, my mom and I had started teaching her to play, too.

"Are you okay?" Erin asked softly. It was obvious I'd been crying.

I nodded and took the seat next to her, picking up my

guitar. "I am," I said, and meant it. "What are we playing?"
I asked.

"I heard a really great song this morning," Blake said, grinning, his hair falling across one eye. He began to pick out the notes of my song, and when it was time, I sang.

We all did.

ACKNOWLEDGMENTS

I'VE LONG DREAMED OF FORMING MY OWN BOHEMIAN commune and inviting all of my favorite people to live there with me. We would grow our own food and bake our own bread, and there would be goats. Many, many goats.

I don't have a real commune yet, but there is one that exists in my head, populated by the wonderful people who helped me bake this book. Someday I will show my gratitude with a commune invitation and goats. For now, words will have to do.

Thank you to my early readers and purveyors of wisdom, Jessica Brody, Sara Wilson Etienne, Gabrielle Zevin, Jamie Weiss Chilton, and Elizabeth Fama.

Thank you for the unwavering support: Julia Shahin Collard, Gretchen McNeil, Nadine Nettmann, Erin Bosworth, Laura Bjergfelt Nielsen, Melissa Bosworth, Edith Cohn, Leigh Bardugo, and Lamar Giles.

Thank you to my agent, Doug Stewart, for loving my weird work, and for being wonderful.

Thank you to my editor, Janine O'Malley, for her patience and for helping me grow as an author.

Most of all, thank you to my true commune, my family. To Ryan, Berlin, and Nero for the only thing that really matters, even more than goats . . .

Thank you for the love.